ORDINARY HEROES

David Lowther

ORDINARY HEROES

David Lowther

ORDINARY HEROES

DAVID LOWTHER

*I look around and think: Good God,
what kind of hell is this?*

Chil Rajchman

CHAPTER ONE

1945: A large country house, somewhere in Hertfordshire, England.

Just over two months earlier, folk of all ages had been dancing, drinking, laughing, street partying and making love, to celebrate the victorious end to the Second World War in Europe. True, the Japanese War was still ongoing, but ultimate and quick victory there now seemed certain. Yet to the eighteen men in a large, sunlit lounge in the impressive, requisitioned house in the English countryside, none of that mattered. In fact, some had no idea at all what was going on in the outside world, and those who did couldn't have cared less. This particular space had probably once been a drawing room which hosted parties of cigar-smoking, port-drinking, wealthy men, while their wives chatted quietly in another room. Although the staff had tried to keep it clean, the carpet had seen better days, as had the furniture. Long, gloomy brown-and-green drapes hung beside windows whose frames badly needed a lick of paint. Outside, the extensive garden was bathed in sunshine, deceptively relaxed-looking as bushes and small trees discreetly masked a formidable-looking wall. Whether the wall was to keep its residents in or curious locals out was debatable.

Lieutenant George Aaron was slumped in an armchair. He was a big man but, even so, he appeared to have been swallowed up by the chair, which had sagged as though the springs or foam rubber – or both – had collapsed. Either way, when George sat down his backside almost touched the floor. On the table beside him was a folded but unread copy of the *News Chronicle* and an untouched cup of tea, which had gone cold.

George was in his uniform trousers and a khaki shirt and braces. On his feet, he wore his army boots with the laces untied. To the casual onlooker, he might have seemed to be staring into space. In reality, he was observing closely, trying to make sense of what was going on. Everybody was in some sort of uniform – Navy or Air Force blue or, like George, Army khaki – though the service personnel were joined by smart, white-clad nurses and often not-so-

1

smart, white-coated doctors. Why? One by one, George assessed his fellow patients, for that's what they were, he decided: military men who had been severely traumatised by their experiences of the war. Like him.

One sailor sat in an upright chair and cried dry tears for long periods. An airman with a horribly disfigured face talked incessantly to no one in particular. Another airman lay on his back all day long and told the ceiling about his experiences as a Prisoner of War. Most just sat in silence, like George, who exchanged 'good mornings' with staff and some patients but otherwise said little. One or two couldn't keep their fingers or limbs still. George watched them sadly. Shaking like leaves, he found himself thinking, completely overlooking the fact that he did so at times too. He'd heard of this. Shell shock, it was called. Or stress disorder. It was no great surprise, though. One of the things he most remembered about his experiences was the incessant and deafening noise of battle – amongst other things he'd prefer *not* to think about for now.

Day by day, the odd person disappeared. Maybe, George hoped, because they had recovered and returned home. That's what he wanted too, but, deep down inside, he knew he was nowhere near ready for normal life again. Yet, determined not to let himself go, George washed and shaved each morning – a ritual to be feared, because when he looked in the mirror he saw not the handsome young man he'd once been but the face of someone deeply disturbed, with dark rings, pale skin, and dull eyes that stared back at him. Where were the creases at the side of his eyes and mouth when he laughed? Where had the old George gone?

Staring through the window, George listlessly watched two airmen playing croquet. He didn't see much point in hitting a ball through a steel hoop stuck in the ground using a wooden club, so he switched his attention to a soldier and another airman patting a plastic shuttlecock to each other with racquets. He decided that activity was even more pointless. He sighed. Perhaps he'd also see the point to everything again, one day – but not today. His sour musings were interrupted by a cheerful, 'Good morning, George,' and he turned from looking through the window to see a young soldier on crutches smiling at him as he approached.

'Hello, Jim,' George replied, wondering whether it was worse to lose a leg or the will to do anything. The will to do anything, he decided, and was about to sink back into his pointless reveries when his thoughts were brought to an abrupt halt by yet another voice – this one unknown to him.

'Lieutenant Aaron?'

George slowly turned his head to see who was addressing him by his formal rank. A middle-aged man with thinning fair hair that was swept back to reveal a shining forehead had replaced Jim, standing iron-rod-straight, hands tucked behind his back and legs akimbo. For a moment, George was reminded of his old Commanding Officer, Lieutenant Pearse, but he hadn't seen him since the battle of Primosole Bridge and couldn't fully remember what he looked like now anyway. Apart from this, he thought Lieutenant Pearse was dead. It couldn't be Lieutenant Pearse. So who was this imposter? And who did he think he was, addressing George by his army rank when he was no longer army – no longer anything, in fact?

The imposter was smiling, his blue eyes looking gently down at George. George thought he could even detect some measure of kindness in his face – not dissimilar to Lieutenant Pearse's when he was encouraging the troops on, regardless of how hopeless the situation was. George stood up, using his powerful legs to lift himself from the floor – or the seat of the armchair, which was just about the same thing. His life might be a wreck but physically he was still whole, and there was no way he was going to sit in the presence of Lieutenant Pearse – no, not Pearse, he reminded himself – but someone very like him. The young soldier stood to his full six feet, trying to look strong and fit, smoothing down his neatly trimmed black hair but unable to hide the confusion on his face.

'I'm Colin Walters, one of the staff here. I wonder if we could have a little chat in my office.' Walters was a good four inches shorter than George, and he had to reach up to offer a firm handshake. George took his hand and held it limply – not quite sure what to do. Shouldn't he be saluting? He dropped Walters' hand and shuffled his feet awkwardly instead. 'Let's go into my office and have a cup of tea,' Walters continued.

George meekly followed him out of the lounge, wondering who the hell this bloke was and what he wanted. As he wasn't Lieutenant Pearse, he could be anyone. Couldn't be a doctor, though, George thought, because he was dressed in a short-sleeved, pale blue shirt and a pair of dark slacks. If he was a doctor, surely he'd be wearing

3

a white coat? Not forces either, or he'd be in uniform. Did he know him then? Was he an old friend he couldn't remember? George's head buzzed with something he hadn't felt in a while. Curiosity.

'Please sit down, Lieutenant,' Walters said, pointing to a more stable-looking chair than the one from which George had recently risen with some difficulty in the lounge. 'Shall I address you by your rank or would you prefer George?'

'George is OK,' George muttered, and sat down and stared at his unlaced boots. He'd never noticed it before but now they reminded him of worms wriggling away so he quickly leant forward and tied them. He looked up to find Walters watching him, the same kind smile on his face, but this time tinged with something else. Approval? 'What do you want from me?' George asked, prompted by that strange look, but unable to keep a hint of aggression from his voice.

'Nothing. I'm a listener, at least I like to think I am.'

That threw him. George looked Walters in the eye. 'What do you listen to?' he asked, the curiosity he'd felt earlier growing again, like a knot in his chest.

'Things that people, people like you, tell me about themselves.'

George looked suspiciously at the man. 'Why?' he asked.

'I'll answer that in a moment. Tell me, George, why do you think you're here?'

'Because I'm fucked up,' George said angrily, looking down at the floor again, avoiding Walters' eyes but expecting some kind of rebuke for his language. 'But I don't know,' he conceded. 'I don't know anything anymore, really.'

'I do. And I know what happened to you, too,' Walters gently replied.

George gave Walters a short piercing glance. 'How do you know? You weren't there.'

'No, of course, I wasn't, but I've talked to people who were, friends and colleagues.'

'Why? You've no right! What are you trying to do?' George asked, raising his voice and clenching his fists.

'I'll answer that with another question. Do you want to stay here for the rest of your life?'

'Course not, but I'm in no state to leave. What would I do? Where could I go? I can't face my friends or my family, knowing what I'm like now.'

'Then that's the answer to your question. I want to help you to be able to leave. Look, it's nearly one and I don't want you to miss your dinner. Let's pick this up tomorrow morning. Is that alright?' Walters asked.

'You reckon you can make me feel able to leave here?' George asked, incredulous. 'You'd know how to do that?'

'I certainly hope so,' Walters said. 'So, what do you say? We'll talk properly tomorrow?

'Alright.' George studied him, then added slowly, 'I suppose so.'

In bed that night, George lay on his back, thinking about Walters. What was he after, he wondered. Why offer to help him and not one of the others? Or were some other soldiers, sailors and airmen also talking to Walters? If so, what did they say? And what would he say tomorrow? Eventually, he drifted off, but his dreams were full of questions with tantalisingly close answers, and faces from the past, near and yet just out of reach. When he awoke in the morning he tried to pull those faces close again, but couldn't. For the first time in ages, he felt like crying – or shouting, he wasn't sure which, but different. It was curious, like he'd felt when Walters had first approached him. That decided him. He ought, at least, to give Walters a hearing and find out what he had to say. He didn't think it would do much good, but he'd give it a go. That decided him about something else too. The least he could do for himself was to try to look human if he was hoping somehow to join the land of the living again via Walters.

He shaved carefully and brushed his hair. There wasn't much he could do about his eyes but he went to breakfast thinking he'd done the best he could. Maybe he would have been interested to know that if he'd asked any of his fellow patients how he looked they would have said, 'more alive'.

Walters turned up about half an hour after breakfast had finished. The man seemed tired to George, who wondered if maybe he'd had a bad night's sleep or perhaps had been overworked with listening.

'Morning, George. Sleep well?'

'Not too bad, thanks. What about you?'

'Not really. I was busy writing up notes until after midnight. By the way, please call me Colin. After all, we're equals, you know. Both Army First Lieutenants.' Colin looked around the lounge. 'Some of the men look a bit sprightly today.'

'I suppose...' George looked around him. Were they? Had he noticed? Maybe... Yes, Walters was right. 'Don't know why, though.'

'Did you vote in the General Election?' Colin asked.

'I think so. One of the nurses helped me to fill in something she called a postal vote about three weeks ago. I suppose we'll hear the results sometime.'

Colin looked George in the eyes. 'We will indeed – in fact, could that be it?'

'I don't know. Why?'

'Well, what if they've just been announced?' He watched George curiously. 'Wouldn't that change things?'

'Oh,' George said. 'I don't know – would they?'

'Are you interested to know them? It's taken three weeks to count the votes with so many servicemen still being away from home.'

'Right, I suppose it has if it was three weeks ago we voted.' George frowned, wondering how that affected the listening Walters was meant to do with him.

'Anyhow, the Labour Party won by nearly two hundred seats,' Walters continued. 'Churchill's gone.'

For the first time in almost a year, a smile broke out on George's face.

'Bloody hell, Colin! That's great news.'

'Oh? Are you a Labour man, George?'

'I am. My father's a member of the Communist Party of Great Britain, but I don't believe he thought they'd ever win an election. He probably voted Labour like me and my mum. We all believe in fair dos for everyone. I just hope the new government can achieve that.'

'What about Churchill?'

'What about him?' asked George, looking suspiciously at Colin.

'Well, he helped us to win the war, didn't he?'

'Churchill? No, mate. WE won the war! Us cannon fodder.' Colin looked surprised. 'Well, alright, maybe he helped. At the start of the war, when Churchill became Prime Minister, my mum and dad said they thought he was the right man for the job. Now the fighting's over, we need someone to do a whole lot of different tasks, mostly putting the country back on its feet. Labour's the party for that. Who's the new Prime Minister, by the way?'

'Attlee.'

George dredged his memory for what he remembered of the other politician he knew about. 'Oh, he'll be good. He's an East End MP. What about Ernie Bevin?'

'He'll probably be Foreign Secretary, and Nye Bevan is going to be in charge of the Health Service.'

'Haha!' chuckled George. 'There'll be fun and games there.'

Colin gave a little smile of satisfaction, which George spotted. George sat back and watched Walters. Then he looked around the room, watching the other men. The buzzing feeling he'd felt yesterday was still there, but it was more of an 'alive' buzzing feeling now. What was he doing here, anyway? Neither he nor Colin said a word but both knew something about George had changed.

'By the way, Colin, how did you vote?'

'Labour, of course. Let's pick up on this again tomorrow, shall we?'

'Am I cured?' George caught Colin's arm as he got up to go.

'Not yet, but I think I can say I don't just hope you will be now; you will be. But there's still a long way to go, so the sooner we get started, the better, huh?'

With that, Colin left him and George sat in the all-enveloping armchair and chewed over his chat with Colin. He smiled to himself once or twice as he thought about the General Election result, but then he switched his attention to thinking about how the new Government would cope with having to replace bomb-destroyed-and-damaged houses in Britain's cities and paying back all the money they must have borrowed to pay for the war.

After lunch, he chatted with one or two patients, most of whom agreed that the election result was the right one for the country. Everybody thought that Churchill had done a very good job as a war leader but that the old fellow needed and deserved a rest right now.

George spent the afternoon reading that day's *News Chronicle*, the first time he'd opened a paper in more than a year. He liked the paper. It seemed to match his way of thinking and one of the people closest to him, Roger Martin, had been a journalist on the

Chronicle's sister paper *The Evening Globe* in the 1930s. As the day wore on, he began to feel melancholy as he remembered those times before the war when he and his pal Joe had worked with Roger and helped him to a couple of scoops in the summer of 1939. With that came more memories, tumbling over themselves until he had to call a halt to them by going to bed depressed and fearful. His dreams that night were full of sound and thunder and a nameless dread, and this was his answer when Colin asked him how he was the next morning.

'Got a bit cheesed off when I started thinking about the good times before the war,' George said without looking at Colin. 'And then the bad ones *during* the war.'

'What brought that on?' Colin asked, looking sympathetic.

'I was reading the *News Chronicle,* which was like the daily equivalent of the evening paper my Guv worked for.'

'That would be Major Roger Martin, would it?'

George lifted his gaze from the floor and snapped, 'How do you know him?'

'I don't, really. I met him briefly.'

George gave Colin a hostile stare. 'Where did you meet him?'

'Here.'

'Here. What was he doing here? Have you been checking up on me?' George half rose, fists clenching and voice cracking with anger.

Colin made calming gestures toward him. 'No, no. He came here and asked one of the nurses if he could see you. She referred him to me, and I explained to him that you'd made it clear that you didn't want visitors. He was very disappointed. He told me who he was, gave me a slip of paper and asked if I would telephone him and let him know when you were ready for visitors.'

George looked at Colin and knew that he was telling the truth. 'I'm sorry,' he said, dropping back into his seat and feeling ashamed of his overreaction.

'That's OK, George. Anyhow, it gives us a chance to talk a bit about the past.'

A look of panic spread across George's face as he remembered snippets from his dreams of the night before. 'I'd rather not,' he exclaimed.

'No, George. I don't mean the terrible things that happened more recently to you. You'll probably never forget those, but you will get over them. I'd like us to think about the good times, the things you did with your friends and family, your adventures and what you learned from them.'

'What's the point of that, Colin?'

'Because you can collect together all these everyday memories and help yourself to look ahead, into the future, taking the good things with you. Then the bad things can be tempered by the good ones, and they'll be easier to come to terms with.'

George shrugged his shoulders and reluctantly agreed. For the next hour, they talked about football, family, friends, girls, gardening, anti-Semitism, Army Cadets, the Blitz, films, dancing and everything that made up the young soldier's childhood and adolescence. As he watched Colin, he could see Colin was listening to everything that George said because a curious smile was fixed on the listener's face. And strangely, George was beginning to feel a little better and, after Colin had left, he ate his lunch and settled down to read that day's *News Chronicle* with a smile on his face that seemed to want to stay.

'How much anti-Semitism have you come across in your life, George?' Colin asked the following morning.

'In England, not much apart from things I'll tell you about another time. In the Army, hardly any. I wasn't much bothered by the church parades which always began with a bellowed instruction "Fall out Roman Catholics and Jews". They shouted Jews in such a way that he didn't think much of the Jews but I just used to chuckle to myself and go and have a cup of coffee in the NAAFI.'

'When you were in battle, did you feel you were taking on people who hated the Jews?'

'No,' George replied. 'It was only later that I learned about the awful treatment of Jews by the Germans. Obviously, I knew about Kristallnacht because Major Martin told me. He was there, you know?'

'Yes, I remember reading an article about it in the *Evening Globe*.'

'For a while, I assumed that those atrocities were carried out by a tiny minority, rather like the Blackshirts in England. But I was wrong.'

'What about religion, George?'

'What about it?'

'Well, did you go to the synagogue?'

'Now and again. Special Jewish days and so on. But I wasn't a regular, nor were my parents. I think there were probably more Jews in the East End who didn't go to the synagogue regularly than did. A bit like Christians, really. Plenty only went to church when they were christened, married and buried, apart from maybe Christmas. Or so I'd heard people say.'

'Do you believe in God?'

'I'm not sure. I think I've maybe taken Him for granted. But I didn't scream and shout at Him for letting those people I came across last year in France exist.'

Colin let this sink in then asked George, 'You must have come across the Blackshirts in the East End?'

'Course, they were always marching about shouting 'Jews out' and all that sort of rubbish. If they came looking for a scrap my friend Joe and I used to join in even though we were only young teenagers. We were pretty handy with our boots and broom handles.'

George looked at Colin who appeared to be smiling with his eyes at George's memories. George too was looking back at those happy days but ever so slowly he was beginning to realise that it was time to move on and keep his fists and boots to himself. Perhaps, he thought, he'd never have to use his street-scrapping skills again but, if he had to, he knew he'd be ready.

'How did you think you'd perform in battle, George?'

'I did have a lot of doubt, not during training, but on the voyage out. I wondered what it would be like to kill a man, perhaps a German, like me a young man roped into the war. Maybe he had a family, a wife, and children. I talked about it a lot with my friends on the way out. One of them hadn't thought like me at all but the other could see what I was getting at.'

'Did you get over these doubts?'

'When I first went into battle I was shit scared, but as we prepared to face up to the enemy I realised everyone else was too, including those that had been through it all before, and it occurred to me that the Germans and Italians probably felt the same way. So we all just adopted an if-we-don't-kill-you-you'll-kill-us attitude. Say what you like about the Army, we were well-prepared, so we trusted in our training and our mates.'

'So do you think you came to terms with fighting the Germans?'

'I think so. I had a job to do, and I did my best to carry out my duties.' George hesitated. 'But not what came later.'

'I know that, George. And we will talk about that sometime too – because we have to.'

'No!' George got up and paced the room. 'No, I won't talk about that. I can't.'

'Between us, we somehow have to get you back on your feet ready to live the rest of your life – and facing that part of your past will enable you to move beyond it,' Colin insisted.

'No,' George repeated. His hands were curling into fists again and he could feel the sweat starting to gather on his forehead and under his arms. 'I can't go back to that.'

'But we're getting there.'

Lying in bed that night, Colin's words kept coming back to him. 'The rest of your life.' He was only twenty-two. What was he going to do with himself for the rest of his life? His father made furniture, but George didn't think he'd be much good at that. He could drive his father's van. The Army had taught him to handle all sorts of vehicles. He fell asleep thinking about that. He woke up drenched in sweat, harsh words ringing in his ears.

'Put his clothes on, take him back to his cell, and give him some food and water. If he's still alive in the morning, I'll question him then and, if he doesn't respond, we'll throw him in the oven.'

'Sedated?' asked the doctor.

'What, waste good phenol on a fucking Jew? No, sling him in as he is.'

George twisted in panic, struggling to free himself from his bonds. No, No! He'd escaped, he'd escaped – hadn't he?

At last, one arm struggled free, and he slammed his hand down hard on the ticking bomb next to him. The clock. Three o'clock. 1945, and England, not 1944 and occupied France, but finally, he accepted what he knew Colin had wanted him to acknowledge. He had to go back first before he could go forward. George sat up in bed and let the memories flow, from good, to bad, to what had led finally to here, and the end of his world as he'd known it.

CHAPTER TWO

London
September 1939 - December 1940

'When's the war going to start?' George asked his friend Joe. 'All we've had for the last week was one air raid siren, and that was a false alarm.'

Joe was George's best pal. He was the shorter of the two by a couple of inches but had a slim and wiry frame. His curly fair hair looked clean but gave the appearance of not having seen a comb that morning. His ruddy cheeks hinted at the outdoor life he enjoyed, and his blue eyes were smiling, matching his mischievous grin. His arm was in a plaster of Paris pot, covered in scrawl, which was the result of a scrap with a Nazi in Harwich docks ten days previously.

'No idea. My dad says the Prime Minister is already seeking peace, hoping it'll all be over by Christmas,' Joe said.

'Let's hope he's right. Anyway, to more important things. How did you enjoy Saturday night?' George asked.

The two of them had been on an evening out in the West End with George's new girlfriend Esther and Esther's friend Mary, a Jewish refugee from Vienna, who'd come along to make up the numbers.

'It was alright. Quite enjoyed myself. Mary was a bit shy. I can't see myself falling for her but I'm okay with making up a four now and again. What about you and Esther?'

George looked at Joe. 'What about me and Esther?'

'Well,' Joe began nervously. 'Is it serious?'

'Don't be daft.' George laughed. 'I'm sixteen and she's seventeen. There's a war which could go on for years. It's a bit early to start making plans.'

'But you do like her, don't you? I'm not saying I'm jealous but if you hadn't been around, you know.' Joe laughed.

'Esther knows what both of us did for her. As far as she's concerned, you're her closest friend, like a brother.'

'Hmph.' Joe smiled.

'Anyway, in answer to your previous question, of course, I bloody well do. She's gorgeous. I really enjoy being with her. But nights out up west is as far as it goes for now. Never mind that. How are we going to fill our time now that the Guv's gone and signed up ? We're at a bit of a loose end.'

The Guv was Roger Martin, a journalist for the *London Evening Globe*. The pair of them had helped him to get a couple of scoops involving Irish terrorists and Nazi agents in the last months before the declaration. The final confrontation with the bad men had cost Joe a broken arm. As soon as Prime Minister Chamberlain had spoken the chilling words *this country is at war with Germany,* Roger had signed up for the Army and was now training to be a soldier somewhere.

Joe shrugged his shoulders. 'No idea.'

George showed his irritation. 'We can't hang around doing nothing, waiting for the Guv to come back. I'm going to ask my dad if he needs a hand.'

George's dad owned a joiner's workshop. He made all kinds of things, from lounge and bedroom furniture to coffins. 'He's getting on a bit,' continued George. 'He probably needs a hand lugging stuff into the van and delivering it at the other end.'

'Good idea, George. I'll ask my dad if he needs any help. I'm having my cast off next week so we can start then. I can go with him in the van to the docks and help unload the stuff coming in on the boats.'

Joe's dad had a fruit and veg business. He collected stuff from the docks and delivered it to shops all over East London. Both families lived in decent flats in Shoreditch, which had been built earlier in the century and had an inside toilet, bathroom and hot water, unusual for 1939.

'Not much of a war this, is it, Joe? No bombs, no gas, no bullets.'

'And no dead people. It can carry on like this forever as far as I'm concerned,' Joe replied.

The papers were calling it *the phoney war*. In the late autumn, some families took holidays. London children who had been evacuated to the countryside to avoid becoming victims of the suspected German bombs returned to their homes. George and Joe helped their fathers, had a weekly evening out with Esther and Mary and were otherwise bored. At the start of these evenings out, Esther arrived very excited.

'Good news. My family and I have just been granted British citizenship.'

The boy's faces lit up.

'That's great,' Joe exclaimed. 'Well done.'

George was smiling as if he'd just won the pools. 'Wonderful, Esther. That must be a load off your mind?'

'Of course. We're all real English men and women now.'

Mary didn't look quite as pleased. 'I'm still waiting, but the solicitor said it won't be long now.'

George patted Mary on the back. 'I'm sure it'll be alright, Mary.'

But the phoney war didn't stay phoney. What quickly became obvious was that no one was seeking peace, and it was expected that the war would not be over soon. The government announced a *Dig for Victory* scheme and parts of Victoria Park, one of London's biggest outdoor recreation areas, were earmarked to be allotments. The two lads saw their chance to do something useful and quickly signed up for a patch of land and began digging. It was none too soon. The Germans had been concentrating on blockading food and other essential supplies by sinking merchant ships in the Atlantic with submarines and surface raiders. The *Dig for Victory* idea was vital in keeping the nation fed.

As winter moved into spring the Germans struck, invading Norway and Denmark in early April.

'Looks like it's kicking off,' George said to Joe. 'I wonder where'll be next. Probably some small defenceless country like Holland or Belgium. They won't dare attack France. They've got the biggest army in the world.'

'I hope you're right. France isn't far away. Anyway, what can we do about it?' Joe asked.

'You'll be seventeen next month. You could be called up in just over a year's time and me a few months later. We could be fighting the Jerries in not much more than a year.'

'So?'

'So we could be doing something to get ready for being soldiers.'

'Like what?' Joe asked.

'We could join the Army Cadets. Learn all about being a soldier.'

'I might not want to be a soldier. I might prefer to sign up for the Navy or Air Force.'

George laughed. 'You were seasick on that paddle steamer from Southend Pier our parents took us on before the war, and by the time you learn to fly the war'll be over. Besides, the RAF is looking for blokes from the universities and posh schools. Not East End scrappers like us. I'll find out when and where the cadets meet and we'll go along, see what it's like and decide whether to join or not.'

The local Army Cadet Force unit was housed in a drill hall a short bus ride from where the boys lived. The ACF was linked to an Infantry Battalion which had a local Territorial Army unit attached to it. George and Joe met the Lieutenant in charge in his office and explained that they wanted to join the cadets. Without going overboard, the Lieutenant welcomed them, explained that they paraded twice a week for two hours and had special training camps at weekends, usually in places like Epping Forest. Each new cadet was given full uniform: beret, tunic, shirt, trousers, belt with brasses, gaiters and boots.

'And woe betide you if you ever turn up for parade not looking immaculate. That means trousers pressed, boots polished until you can see your face in them, brasses cleaned until they shine like the summer sun, and don't forget your cap badge: belt and gaiters spotless. You'll need to buy some Blanco to clean those and Brasso or Duraglit for the brasses. Got all that?'

'Yes, sir,' the two boys said in unison.

'You'll learn to march and drill, read maps, navigate your way around strange country, live off the land and shoot.' The Lieutenant paused for a moment to let all that sink in and then looked at the youngsters and asked, 'Still want to join?'

George looked at Joe who nodded. 'Yes, sir.'

'Good. Report here at 1900 hours on Tuesday. There'll be forms to fill in and then the Quartermaster

will sort out uniforms and boots for you. After that - home - and report the following Thursday at the same time for parade, immaculately prepared. One last thing, most new recruits are younger than you. You might have to take the odd order from a fifteen-year-old Lance Corporal, but he'll show respect for your age. If you're good cadets, you'll soon climb the promotion ladder. The Cadet NCOs are mostly decent lads. See you on Tuesday.'

'Yes, sir. Thank you, sir. Good night, sir.'

'He was as straight as an arrow, that Lieutenant,' Joe said on the way home. 'I think it'll be tough, but we'll enjoy ourselves.'

'Yep. I feel the same,' George replied.

Tuesday came and George and Joe reported as ordered. They spent ages filling in forms, in triplicate of course. The Army seemed to want to know everything about them. On their way home they wondered how those who couldn't read or write would manage. George and Joe were literate but plenty they knew from their school days weren't. Uniforms and boots were carefully stowed away in kit bags which were slung over their shoulders.

Apart from helping their fathers and digging their allotments, the next couple of days were spent preparing for the Thursday night inspection so they were able to set off for their first evening at the cadets looking extra smart. The hall did look a bit gloomy, though. It was still light outside, but the blackout curtains were drawn and the only illumination came from weak light bulbs hanging from the ceiling in unattractive green metal shades. There looked to be about thirty youngsters milling around. One or two George and Joe knew from school and a few more from the neighbourhood. Smiles and nods were exchanged until a high-pitched voice screamed.

'Right, fall in you lot!'

The sound came from a skinny-looking youth who seemed to be about a similar age to George and Joe. Wearing the three stripes of a sergeant, he appeared to be the cadet in charge. The two newcomers watched the others and stood in the front of two lines, following the rest by standing with legs astride and hands behind the back.

'Atten-shun,' yelled the Sergeant. The two lines snapped their feet together, put their arms down by their sides and looked straight ahead.

'Bit slow, you two,' the Sergeant said. 'Are you new?'

'Yes, Sergeant,' Joe replied. 'We'll do our best to catch up.'

'Names?'

'Cadet Richards, Sergeant,' Joe told him.

'Cadet Aaron,' added George.

The Sergeant looked carefully at George. 'Aaron. Isn't that a Jewish name? Are you a Jew, Cadet Aaron? You look Jewish.'

'I am a Jew, Sergeant.'

'Ugh! Not much use to us then.'

George said nothing but could feel Joe stiffening up alongside him. Ten minutes drill followed, with the cadets following instructions bellowed out by the Sergeant. The friends soon picked it up, even quickly mastering the TLV of the about-turn. The Sergeant watched George like a hawk, waiting for him to slip up. When he didn't, the Sergeant walked up to George and casually trod on his foot, which didn't cause any pain but left a brown smear across the toe cap. George said nothing but, as soon as the Sergeant's back was turned, he pulled a handkerchief from his pocket and wiped the smear away. The Sergeant then ordered everybody to stand at ease while he went to fetch the Lieutenant for the parade inspection. Wandering up and down the two lines of cadets with his hands behind his back, the officer stopped occasionally to adjust a beret or to speak quietly to a cadet. George and Joe, he recognised and welcomed them, congratulating them on their turnout. After the parade was dismissed, George and Joe joined a map-reading group while the others practised weapons drill.

Well, I'm keeping busy, George thought, as he ate his tea one late April evening, but not doing much that's useful. Two nights at the cadets, growing vegetables at the allotment, Saturday night out with Esther and the rest of the time fetching and carrying. The war was going badly, and Britain appeared to have messed up an attempt to take on the Germans in Norway. His father mentioned that some people were even urging the government to strike a peace deal with Hitler but he, along with just about everyone else, was saying we should take the Nazis on and eventually beat them. This gave George a shiver of apprehension as he realised that, if the war dragged on for another year or so, he would be called up and become part of it – not just be playing at being a cadet.

Parade at the cadets was becoming more interesting though, and he sensed a stepping up in the intensity of the instruction as it became likely that many of the youngsters would have a part to play in the conflict. The Sergeant continued to bait George at every opportunity, usually with nasty comments about Jews but it appeared to have little effect as George ignored him and got on with the task at hand. This seemed to infuriate the Sergeant and one evening he stepped up his anti-Semitic campaign.

'Your marching is sloppy, Jew,' he said. 'Your feet aren't pointing in a straight line. You look like a girl. Stay behind after parade. I'll give you some extra practice.'

George stared at the pasty-faced and spotty NCO, shrugged his shoulders and replied, 'Yes, Sergeant.'

At the end of the evening, George marched up and down the hall for almost half an hour while the Sergeant barked out commands. Joe had volunteered to stay with his mate, claiming he too could do with the extra practice, but the NCO had refused.

'You two are always together. Are you queer for each other? There's no room for homos in the Army.'

A seething Joe looked at George who, with a sideways nod of his head, warned his friend not to react so he sat down and watched, boiling with anger.

As they set off to catch the bus home, Joe turned to his mate and asked him how much longer he was going to put up with these insults.

'I like the cadets,' George replied. 'If we have a go at the Sergeant we'll probably get kicked out, and then where would we be? I think we'll be soldiers one day soon and what we're learning here is going to help us when we're called up. People like him always come a cropper, I promise you.'

'Okay,' said Joe, 'but how did he ever get promoted?'

'One of the other lads told me that the Sergeant's father is a second Lieutenant in the TA. He'd be humiliated if his son was booted out.'

George was happy to leave it at that. He disliked the Sergeant and hated anti-Semitism. He'd seen enough of that with the Blackshirts before the war. But most non-Jews that he knew weren't a problem. In George's experience, they'd never said or done anything unpleasant to the Jews who were one of the most hard-working and friendly communities in the East End. When the day of reckoning with the Sergeant came, as he knew it must, the number of those supporting the Jews would be far greater than the anti-Semites.

The German armies marched into Belgium, Holland, Luxembourg and France in early May. Murderous air support backed up the ground troops and the multitude of tanks that poured westwards across the German border. The British people had never been complacent about the war but they now became consumed with

19

fear as the Nazis swept all before them. Soon the British Expeditionary Force was forced onto the beaches of Dunkirk and a monumental effort was needed to rescue them. Panic gripped the country and Churchill, the new Prime Minister, had to make a rousing speech to raise morale. George knew that any chance of his generation avoiding the war had now gone.

The Germans were now just over twenty miles from the English coast, and invasion became a probability. George and an increasingly uninterested Joe continued their Saturday nights out with the girls. At the beginning of June, when the Allied defeat in France became a certainty, George noticed a change in Esther on one of their nights out. Previously, she had been full of life, laughter and willingness to make the most of living in England. As the Germans crept closer, she changed. She became quiet and withdrawn as if something was troubling her. George noticed that she'd started biting her nails and paying less attention to her appearance too. He had little opportunity to talk to her and find out what was wrong. Mary was always there and more often than not, a reluctant Joe. On that second Saturday in June, George saw her onto her bus taking her back to Hampstead, and she was quieter and more withdrawn than ever.

'Well, see you next time,' he said awkwardly.

She turned to look at him, and he could see she was crying.

'What's the matter?' he asked.

'Nothing,' she said after a small hesitation and turned away from him to find a seat. George called softly to her, but she refused to turn around, and the bus rumbled into the distance, carrying her off, but with the nagging fear for George that he might not see her again.

George's mind was in turmoil. What had happened? Was it something he'd done? He knew he'd played down the relationship a bit in the past few weeks but that wasn't because he was losing interest in her. His worry was that he was likely to be called up to fight in the not-too-distant future and could possibly be killed. What was the purpose of getting close to Esther only for her to be heartbroken when his corpse lay in some foreign field? She was young, beautiful and would find someone else, he reasoned, and he wanted to spare her the pain that his death would bring. He wished he hadn't mentioned being called up, now, but they had to face facts, hadn't they? And he had told her he'd miss her. No, she was just worried about the war. He'd talk to her about it next Saturday. But the next Saturday came and went without hearing from either Esther or Mary, and the next, and with that Saturday nights out came to an end and George and Joe put all their energies into the fathers' businesses, their shared allotment and excelling at the cadets. At the same time, the Sergeant's bullying got worse. One night he asked George what part of the Army he wanted to join and when George calmly replied, the infantry, the NCO almost fell to the floor laughing.

'The infantry? Pull the other one! The war ain't going too well for us but if we have to rely on the likes of you, we'd have no chance of winning. You'd run away when you heard the first shot. No, you need to set your sights a little lower Cadet Aaron. Maybe a cook might suit you or an office boy or perhaps cleaning the bogs. But you'll never make a soldier, mark my words. If Hitler does invade and all we can do to resist him is send out cowards like you, we might as well hand him the keys to Buckingham Palace now.'

George said nothing. Bullies always got their just deserts, but he wasn't going to become one himself by tackling the NCO. Each night he attended parade, George was greeted with an insult, being called Jew boy or Christ killer. One night after parade the two friends were setting off home when they saw the Sergeant waiting for them outside. He had two larger youths with him.

'Here they come. Jew boy and bum boy. Off to suck each other's cocks then?'

Joe started to move forward but George put his arm out and stopped him. 'Not now, Joe. Our time will come.'

The pair of friends walked past the other three. 'Good night, Sergeant,' George said, and they strolled to their bus.

'George,' Joe almost shouted, 'we could have taken them. One punch would have put that pathetic Sergeant down and we could have dealt with the rest in the usual way.'

'I know, Joe, but I've told you, I don't want to be thrown out.'

'But there were three of them. They were going to attack us. We'd be defending ourselves.'

'Yes, you're right. I'm not a coward but I think we've got enough on without getting involved in a mini gang war with those shits.'

But their time will come, George added silently to himself…

21

CHAPTER THREE

Esther was collecting Sir John's empty breakfast plates six days after the declaration of war when he unexpectedly struck up conversation – not that he didn't often talk to her, but not usually about the war or politics.

'So, Esther. Not much of a war so far, is it?'

'It's just the kind of war I like, sir, no fighting.'

'Well said, but I'm afraid it may not stay like this for long. Winston Churchill's in the War Cabinet now and he won't stand for approaching the Germans to sign a peace treaty.'

'Why not?' asked Esther.

'There are those who think he's a war monger, likes a good fight, but I suspect he doesn't trust the Germans and probably thinks that, even if we do come to terms with Hitler, we'll end up battling it out with them anyway. I suppose I shouldn't say this but I suspect he's right. But I know I can trust you, Esther, and what I say to you won't end up in *The Times.'*

Both chuckled at this and then Esther asked, 'What's a phoney war, sir?'

'As you said earlier, Esther, a war without fighting. By the way, will you be seeing George and Joe this weekend?'

Sir John was a great admirer of George and Joe and had entertained them along with her family and Roger and Jane in the aftermath of Esther's parents' dramatic rescue from Berlin.

'Tonight. We're going for a night on the town, as the English say.'

'You'll be English yourself, Esther, as soon as your citizenship comes through, which I'm sure won't be long. What about your parents? Will you be visiting them this weekend?'

'Yes. I'm going to Cambridge tomorrow.'

'Please give them, and George and Joe, my very best wishes. Now I must go to work.'

'It's Saturday, Sir John. You don't usually go to work at the weekend.'

Sir John laughed. 'There's a war on, Esther, even one without action, apart from the Germans overrunning Poland. Plenty of work for me to do. The politicians keep us busy.'

Esther regularly followed the same routine throughout the *Phoney War,* which plodded on throughout the cold winter with only British merchant ships being sunk in the Atlantic and the odd German ship going to the bottom keeping the newspapers and radio busy. Poland was beaten and occupied, and Russia joined in on the German side and grabbed part of Poland. She worried about the several million Jews living in Poland and wondered how they would fare under the brutal Nazi regime.

Just before Christmas, Mary too became a British citizen so any worry on that count disappeared. Evenings out became more relaxed after that.

Esther and Cook regularly moaned about rationing and how it prevented them from providing Sir John with food of the high standards to which he had become accustomed. Sir John himself was happy with what he was getting and never complained. Certainly, neither woman ever considered using the growing black market. The shame and humiliation for their boss should that ever come to light was too horrifying to think about. And they had the added bonus of being promised some vegetables from George and Joe when their allotment started producing the goods.

As well as their trips to the cinema, dancing had become a regular activity for the youngsters on Saturday nights. The boys were pretty useless at first, but the girls were patient with them and they slowly improved. Although all seemed well enough when the spring of 1940 came it all changed. Germany's successful invasion of Norway and Denmark marked the end of the *Phoney War* and the attitude of the British people began to harden. Esther and Cook went shopping together in Hampstead one Wednesday morning in late April. Usually, they were greeted in a very friendly way by the lady behind the counter, but this time she was very cold towards Cook and wouldn't speak to Esther at all.

Within two weeks, the Germans had overrun the Low Countries and were threatening to do the same to France. Rumours about fifth columnists filled the newspapers and suspicion about foreigners grew amongst Britons. A bus conductor asked Esther why she wouldn't go back to Germany, and she was called a 'Nazi bitch' by a waitress in Lyons Corner House. Collaborators in Belgium and Holland were claimed by the press to have made life easy for the invading Germans. Soon the call went out for all non-Britons to be locked up until the end of the war. *The Daily Mail*, which had once supported both Hitler and Moseley and his Blackshirts, led the cry, but other papers weren't far behind. Abuse of those of a foreign origin was being reported all over Britain but fortunately not in Cambridge where a nasty comment from a pupil to Esther's brother Peter was quickly jumped on by his teacher.

Esther could see that Sir John knew she was disturbed by this uncertainty when he spoke to her after Cook had left for home. 'I can see how unhappy you are, Esther, and I know the reason why. This country took you in when the government of your own country rejected you. Now there are calls for your new country to lock you up.'

'But, Sir John, this is my country now. I love living here.'

'I understand that, Esther, and it won't help when I tell you that the finger is being pointed at some people who've been here for the whole of this century. If Italy joins Germany in the war against us, and I think it's likely they will, they'll be added to the list of undesirables.'

'But isn't it just the papers calling for us to be locked up?'

'It is at the moment, but the new Prime Minister, Churchill, is in a very weak position. The Labour and Liberal members in the House of Commons support him, but plenty in his own party don't like him; and if he doesn't do what they see as the right thing over what they call aliens, the government might fall. That is the very last thing we want.'

'What do you think will happen, Sir John?' Esther asked timidly.

'I think they'll intern people they classify as aliens, and unfortunately, that includes British citizens like yourself. I've no idea where they'll send them, possibly Canada or Australia, perhaps the Isle of Man, which was used for that purpose in the previous war. Plenty of people, particularly in the Labour and Liberal parties, are saying that locking up German and Austrian Jewish refugees will weaken the war effort, depriving us of brilliant teachers, doctors, scientists, linguists, writers and so on. I believe that this attitude will prevail, and for many internment will be only short. In the meantime, Esther, I suggest you go to Cambridge, tell your parents what I've said to you and tell them to pack a suitcase. You should do the same when you return here.'

Anxiously, Esther took Sir John's message to Cambridge. Her parents were very unsettled. Having escaped almost certain death in Germany, they thought they'd be safe in England, but now they were very nervous of being shipped halfway around the world to Canada or Australia with U-boats threatening all the way. Her brother, Peter, was very quiet about the whole business, but expressed the hope that it would all go away.

George tried to address the issue of internment hysteria by suggesting. 'I can see that you're worried about all this alien rubbish, Esther, but you're English, not German. My dad says that, if you're sent away, the government will soon realise their mistakes and you'll all be back in no time. My dad's always right.'

Esther forced a smile. 'Sir John says the same.'

'There you are. Two wise men can't be wrong. One thing you should know,' George continued quietly, 'I'll miss you a lot. But that's the war. I'll probably be called up to fight next year and I won't find it easy to leave you but it's a job we all have to do. I'll be back, though, I promise you.'

Esther had no idea how George could make such a pledge, but she loved him for it. 'I'll miss you too, George,' she replied, smiling and dropping a kiss on his cheek. But, for all his reassurances, she knew life was about to change for the many thousands of 'aliens', of which she was one – and, therefore, also for her and George. When he mentioned being called up again, and again, that decided her. Best to get it over and done with than linger over it and make it harder. This time out had to be their last – probably would be their last anyway, if she got interned, but she couldn't quite say that to George. It was too final if she actually said it. Better to let it drift and wait and see...

That night, Esther lay in bed wide awake wondering if tomorrow would be the day they came for her. Churchill had announced that all aliens would be interned even if they didn't pose a threat to Britain's security.

They didn't come for her on the day she'd been with George and Joe, or the day after that, so she did her best to get on with her work.

As she was putting away the breakfast things on the Monday morning, there was a loud knocking on the door. Sir John had already left for Whitehall so Esther answered the door and came face-to-face with a uniformed policeman.

'Esther Abrahams?' he asked.

Esther nodded timidly.

'You've to come with me. Please pack a suitcase as quickly as you can. You're being interned as an enemy alien.'

'My bag's already packed. I'll be just a minute. Please wait here.'

Esther didn't feel threatened. The policeman was just doing his job. But she did feel a strong sense of uncertainty and worry. Where would she be taken? How long would she be there? Where were her parents and brother? She grabbed her suitcase, walked downstairs, placed a note for Sir John on the hall table and followed the policeman to the waiting car. Her suitcase was loaded into the boot by the policeman, and Esther was told to sit in the front seat by the policeman who looked alert and ready to deal with any escape attempts. Turning around, she nodded to two elderly orthodox Jews, easily recognisable in their black coats even though it was a warm June morning. Both looked terrified, and the man stayed silent, while the woman muttered a quiet greeting.

The journey was very short and soon ended at Hampstead Police Station. The three internees stepped out of the car and gazed in wonder at the police station – a three-storey, red-brick building with ten windows on both ground and first floors, and seven on the second, which had small windows at the top of the frontage. They were shepherded with their luggage through the main entrance, past the reception desk where a strongly built Sergeant with fair, greying hair seemed to be in charge. Continuing along a corridor, they entered a large room at the end. Esther gazed in astonishment at the others in the room, seated around the outside. There were men and women of all ages, children from infants through to adolescents, all with a bag at their feet, about forty people in all. Some were obviously Jewish. Others might have been German and Italian since, as Sir John had predicted, Italy had entered the war on the German side. Esther found one of the few remaining seats. She scanned the faces to see if the rest of her family were there but couldn't see them. Looking around the room she spotted tall wooden windows with the curtains drawn to prevent nosy parkers peering in. Hanging from the high ceiling were white tin lights shades, each with a dim bulb. Apart from the hard wooden chairs on which they were seated, the only furniture in the room were trestle tables in the middle with nothing on them.

Despite the temperature outside, it was cold in this inhospitable room, and Esther thought the orthodox Jews might have dressed with this in mind. There was a draught as well, and the scruffy decor of the light-brown walls didn't help the miserable atmosphere. Esther's chief concern was for the rest of her family. Would they be brought here or taken elsewhere? Would she ever see them again? Where was she going? Thinking that probably everyone else in the room was asking themselves similar questions, she sat back and waited for something to happen, but she really wished her mother, father and brother were there.

Shortly after her arrival, a tall, uniformed policeman came in and stood in the middle of the room. The low murmur of chatter died down. He put his hands behind his back and briefly looked at the internees. 'I'm Inspector Robins. You've all been brought here because you're enemy aliens who may do harm to my country. Soon a charabanc will collect you and take you on the next part of your journey. I've no idea where you're going. In the meantime, tea, water and sandwiches will be available from the tables.'

With that, the Inspector turned on his heel and left the room. Conversations, much louder this time, started up as the door opened and four women came in, each carrying a tray which contained teapots, jugs of water, cups and saucers, and plates of sandwiches and biscuits. Esther remained seated while the rest rushed for their snacks and drinks. A tall, middle-aged man came up to her.

'Not eating?'

'I'm not hungry,' Esther replied.

'I'd get something while you can. It could be a while before you get another chance. I'm Michael, by the way.'

'Esther,' she said, and she stood up and shook his hand. 'You sound very English to me. Why are you here?'

'I was born in Italy and brought here when I was a baby. That's my mother and father over there,' Michael said, pointing to an old couple on the far side of the room. 'My wife and two children were born here so they've not been interned. That copper talked about my country but it's mine as much as his.'

'And mine too,' Esther said. 'I'm a British citizen but not as much as you are. I came here from Germany two years ago.'

'Crazy, isn't it?' Michael said. 'Come on, let's get some food.'

Esther suddenly felt hungry and joined Michael at the table, taking a couple of damp-looking cheese sandwiches and a glass of water. The Italian collected some food and drink for his parents and then re-joined Esther.

'Have you got family?' Michael asked.

'Mother, father and younger brother. They live in Cambridge.'

'Well, they won't be coming here but, unless we're taken to some docks, they'll most likely be taken to a large holding camp so the chances are you'll see them there.'

Esther started to relax a little. She'd been worrying about seeing her family for several days, ever since she learned about internment. Michael had made her feel a little more confident. 'How do you know so much about it all, Michael?'

'My mother and father and my sister and me were interned during the last war.'

'That makes all this even more stupid. Where were you sent to?'

'Isle of Man. Let's hope we get sent there this time, not Australia or somewhere.'

At this point, a police constable entered the room.

'Right, you lot,' he said in a disparaging tone, with a sour look on his face, 'your transport's here. Grab your cases and make your way outside.'

A cream-coloured charabanc with brown stripes along the side was waiting outside the police station. The windows were blacked out, presumably to stop the enemy aliens from seeing any secret installations during the journey. A pair of soldiers, each armed with a rifle, stood on the pavement while everyone boarded. When the vehicle was fully loaded, they climbed on board and sat together at the front, still clutching their weapons. Esther sat with Michael, but she had again become consumed with worry about the rest of her family, so she said very little. The journey was hot and uncomfortable, and a couple of children were sick. The driver pressed on regardless, under strict instructions not to stop under any circumstances, Esther reckoned.

The journey passed slowly until, after about three hours, the smell of sick was replaced by a far more pleasant odour, which

Michael exclaimed was the welcome scent of the sea. The passengers were ordered off the bus with their cases and they were told to gather on a large tarmac area inside some forbidding black iron fencing. Half a dozen armed soldiers waved them into position.

'This is Butlin's Holiday Camp, Clacton-on-Sea,' Michael informed her.

'How do you know?' Esther asked.

'I came here for a holiday with my family in 1938,' Michael explained. 'It'll be okay here, but we'll be sent somewhere else before too long.'

The soldiers pointed the crowd through a pair of light-green double doors into a vast room which was already crowded with people. Tables and chairs were stacked at the side. Cries went out amongst the internees as they recognised and moved to greet other family members.

'This is the dining room,' Michael told Esther. 'Perhaps your family is here.'

An excited Esther pushed her way through the throng and bumped into her brother Peter searching frantically for her.

'Esther,' he shouted. 'Mum and Dad are over here.'

Peter grabbed hold of his sister's hand and dragged her behind him until they reached Simon and Deborah Abrahams, standing expectantly beside their suitcases. Hugs and kisses were exchanged, and Simon said, 'Thank God we've found each other. We'll all be together now.'

Further conversation was brought to a halt when a small but powerfully built Sergeant shouted, 'Pay attention, all of you.'

'Thank you, Sergeant,' said an officer who stood back with his feet apart and his hands behind his back. 'I'm Lieutenant Burt and I'm the Camp Commander.' Esther studied the officer's face which had sharp features, including a small, prominent jaw and high cheekbones. He was wearing a peaked army hat and, from what she could see, had blond hair.

'Listen to what I say,' the Lieutenant began. 'You are all enemy aliens and you have been interned. You will remain here until such time as you are sent to a permanent residence. I've no idea where you'll be sent or how long you'll remain here. You're in the dining room and this will be open three times each day at eight in the morning, midday and six in the evening. Be on time. You'll be assigned to a chalet where there will be a sink with hot and cold running water. Each block of chalets has a building attached to it with showers and toilets. These are open twenty-four hours a day. The swimming pool is closed, as are the crazy golf course and putting green. The ballroom will be open from six until ten each evening for dancing to music provided by gramophone and drinks served from the bar. Priests, rabbis and other spiritual leaders should meet me tomorrow morning at ten hundred hours in my office to arrange for weekly worship. One other thing: anyone attempting to escape will be sent to the Army Prison at Colchester where they will be imprisoned for the remainder of the war. My men will now show you to your chalets. Come forward when your name is called.'

The Abrahams family and all the other internees had not recovered from the speed at which they'd been rounded up.

Esther could see that her mother was very unhappy although both her father and brother looked more stoic about the whole unpleasant business.

'I'm sure it won't be for long,' Esther said, looking at her mother who had a worried look on her face.

Deborah Abrahams turned to her daughter, shrugged her shoulders and let out a long sigh. 'But we don't know how long we'll be here or where we go next and how long we'll be there.'

'It won't be long before you're back in Cambridge and I'm in Hampstead,' Esther assured her. 'Both Sir John and George's dad both said that.'

'Let's hope you're right.'

'Here's our chalet,' Esther announced. 'It's been freshly painted and it's nice and clean,' she added, as they opened the door. 'And there's bunk beds.'

Esther and Peter took the top bunks and their parents slept on the lower. The weather was still warm. One of the soldiers had told Simon that France had fallen to the Nazis, who were now preparing to invade Britain. Esther heard this from her father, but his confidence in Mr Churchill helped her to believe that the worst was unlikely to happen and that her new country would prevail. She often thought of George and Joe, especially George, and wondered how they were doing. They wouldn't have a clue where she was, but by now they would have worked out why she had disappeared. She didn't know where her friend Mary was either but hoped she'd turn up at their next destination.

The long, sunny days helped their detention feel tolerable. They went to the ballroom in the evenings where she chatted with Peter while her parents danced. Michael sometimes joined the youngsters in the evening, and Esther enjoyed dancing with her Anglo-Italian friend. Another German Jew, nineteen-year-old Jonathan Gerber, organised keep fit sessions and, a little later, football which Peter joined in with and enjoyed.

All too soon they were told they would be moving on the next day but, of course, their destination was kept a closely guarded secret. To everyone's dismay, their transport this time was in a number of Army lorries with the light blocked out by hessian sacking. Luckily, there were plenty of holes in the sacking so Michael was able to keep them posted on where they were, out of earshot of the two armed soldiers who were positioned watchfully on the bench at the back of the lorry.

'This is Birmingham,' Michael told her as they passed through a big city then, later, 'we're near Manchester.'

'How do you know all this?' Esther asked.

'Used to be a travelling salesman before the war. Drove all over England.'

They'd set off early. It had been a very long day, and everyone was tired. There'd been a couple of refreshment and toilet breaks, and it was almost dark when the lorry stopped, and they were told to get out.

'Where are we now?' Esther asked Michael.

'I guess we're somewhere near Liverpool so that means either the docks or Walton Jail.'

Esther could see her mother was very tired, and she shared a look of concern with her father. They all climbed out of the truck and were greeted with the sight of new buildings in the gloom. The area was floodlit and it seemed that they had been dumped at an incomplete housing estate with some completed but many unfinished buildings. The roads hadn't been made up and were full of ruts and potholes. An enormous khaki tent stood at the end of the road where they assembled. Some of the buildings were terraced houses, others semi-detached, and there were numerous blocks of flats.

Esther's family were taken to one of the blocks and shown to a flat on the first floor where the only items in the room were four straw-filled mattresses. There was a bathroom and toilet but no hot water. The electricity was working, but only a single bare bulb lit the bedroom, with another in both the hall outside and the bathroom.

Wearily, they stumbled to the dining tent where they were served a tepid stew of something passing as meat, potatoes and bread followed by rice pudding and tea. Then they were told to return to their accommodation. The Abrahams family lay down on their mattresses and tried to sleep, though this proved difficult with rain hammering down outside and Deborah developing a rasping cough. This went on for several days and her illness slowly grew worse as the damp conditions, dreadful accommodation and lousy food gradually took their toll on her health. Esther even heard some of the older men saying that conditions were even worse than in the German concentration camps where they'd been briefly imprisoned after Kristallnacht. The soldiers couldn't have cared less, or that's the impression they gave, although it was obvious that they'd be happier elsewhere, doing some actual fighting instead of wet-nursing a crowd of harmless aliens.

What added to the vile atmosphere at the housing estate was that, unlike at Butlins, there were plenty of non-Jewish Germans and Austrians amongst the internees. Most of these were harmless but some started to insult the Jews. A small group of them told Esther that Hitler would soon wrap the war up and then get down to the business of getting rid of all Jews as he'd promised. The non-Nazi, non-Jewish Germans were much more amenable, but their association with the Jewish internees soon made them a target of the unofficial Gestapo. One, in particular, started to receive almost hourly threats. He was a blond German sailor who'd palled up with Jonathan Gerber and helped him to organise more football. He was told if he didn't stop associating with Jews he'd suffer. Peter, who had rejoined Jonathan's activities, came to the flat one afternoon and reported that four Nazis had attacked the blond sailor, but Jonathan had stepped in and the two of them had beaten up the Nazis so badly they were now on their way to hospital in an ambulance.

It was a moment of light relief for Esther, but it didn't help her get over her concern for her mother's health. She was not the only one suffering. Others were also ill. As it became wetter and colder an air of helplessness hung over the estate, which Michael had found out was called Huyton. Some kind of relief was at hand when they were told to prepare to leave the next morning, but Esther had become increasingly worried about an elderly Jewish couple who carried a look of utter misery on their faces all day long.

'We were persecuted in Poland, then expelled by the government and sent to Germany,' the old man told her. 'The same thing happened there. I was beaten by the Brownshirts on Kristallnacht and now the same thing is happening in England. I'm not sure we can stand much more.'

'We're leaving tomorrow. Where we're going can't be as bad as this place, and so many people have told me that we'll be home before very long.'

The man gave Esther a weak smile. 'Thank you, dear. We'll try to hang on.' But his and his wife's faces were covered in despair. Despite Esther's efforts, it was too late for them, and they hanged themselves in the night rather than face more discomfort, indifference, and hate. Esther watched her parents' reactions with fear as they listened to the terrible news the next day. What would the future bring for all of them, she wondered.

CHAPTER FOUR

Isle of Man
July - December 1940

'There you go,' Michael said, 'Liverpool Docks. We're going on a voyage. I wonder where we'll end up?'

'Not Australia or Canada, I hope,' Esther said. 'It's thousands of miles away. It'll take weeks, and I bet we'll never see England again.' And maybe I'll never see George again, she thought sadly.

The lorry continued to trundle its way through the busy port of Liverpool, where ships of all sizes awaited attention. Men were everywhere unloading precious food and other materials. It was a warm day, and sweat was pouring off them. Pulling up after a further five minutes, the lorry was unloaded of luggage and internees, and they stood expectantly on the quayside.

They pulled up near a sign that said *The Isle of Man Steam Packet Company*. 'Ah, that's a relief!' Michael said, with a smile on his face. 'Just three hours to get there, and it looks like it'll be a smooth crossing.'

Esther looked at her mother and noticed a tiny bit of colour returning to her cheeks, but she still looked very tired. She turned and gave her daughter a half-smile.

'I'm feeling better already. Anything will improve my health after that disgusting place we've just been to.'

The passengers carried their luggage on board. A crew member stood on the deck, helping the elderly and frail onto the deck from the steps. 'We were at Dunkirk, you know,' the sailor proudly told each of the internees.

It was mid-afternoon when they reached Douglas, the main port of the Isle of Man. The bright sunshine beat down on Douglas Bay, and, in other circumstances, the island would have looked like a mini paradise. The passengers disembarked and gathered in a large room where they waited for about ten minutes until an officer and an NCO, who was clutching a large bundle of papers, appeared. He called for attention and then stunned the internees when he told them

35

that they would be split up. Men and older teenage boys were to go to Hutchinson Camp in Douglas, women and older daughters to Port Erin, and mothers and infants to Port St Mary. There was a brief period of angry dissent but the officer brought the room back to order when he told them that the accommodation would be far better than they'd experienced so far and that the first of a series of family reunions was planned for the end of the following month. The men would walk to their camp, which wasn't far, they were promised, and women and infants would travel by train to their destinations. The officers warned them again that they shouldn't try to escape, and, after taking a roll call, the two groups set off, with the men heading along the seafront of Douglas Bay.

Esther could see her mother was devastated. Her eyes were swollen from silently crying. Esther wrapped her arms around her mother in a reassuring way and helped her to pick up her suitcase. Esther thought that Deborah probably hadn't been split up from her husband in over twenty years of marriage. Esther reminded her that she would take care of her, and she told her mother that she was sure that her father would do the same with Peter. Another weak smile greeted this, and they set off for the station after a lengthy and emotional family farewell. Armed soldiers accompanied the party. Deborah stared at the beautiful crescent-shaped Douglas Bay, which looked lovely bathed in sunshine. 'Just the place for a holiday,' she grinned ruefully.

Esther was relieved to see her mother was looking slightly better and chatted with her as they walked to the station. On the way, they passed a delightful little marina full of small boats, many with gaily coloured sails. They reached the station, another red-bricked building which looked like a smaller version of the Hampstead Police Station. Passing through the booking hall, they walked on to the platform where, getting up steam and waiting for them, was the smallest passenger train that any of them had seen.

'Looks like one of those children's rides you find in the Black Forest,' one internee remarked.   'Well, hardly,' another replied, 'but it's very small.'

It was a bit cramped in the carriages, but there was room for cases in the racks above the seats. The train puffed its way out of the station, and soon the only view from the windows was fields – where cows stood basking in the sunshine and chewing the grass – farm buildings and tiny hamlets. 'This is all rather nice,' Deborah said, and then fell asleep. Esther sat back too and watched the countryside roll by, anxiously wondering what life held for them all next.

'Port St Mary, Port St Mary,' a voice shouted, and the women and infants collected their luggage and climbed down from the train.

'Where are we?' Deborah asked, waking suddenly with a look of alarm spreading across her face.

'It's alright, Mother. We've just dropped some people off. Ours is the next stop,' Esther reassured her.

The rest of the group left the train at Port Erin, where soldiers escorted them to a church hall. The roll was called again, and the ladies were allocated their billets. Small groups were taken to each of the many guest houses that were to be their homes for an unspecified number of weeks. Port Erin was a fine seaside resort with a large number of three-storey houses facing the sea. By the time Esther and her mother reached their digs, the group was down to five, all of whom were allocated to the same building. In addition to Esther and her mother, there were two rather flash-looking, late teen or early twenties girls, and a tall, handsome woman who looked to be in her forties. At the top of the steps waiting to greet them was a thin, steel-grey-haired woman who was probably in her sixties. She introduced herself as their landlady, Mrs Murphy, and welcomed them. They were shown into an immaculately clean lounge where Mrs Murphy told them they would be allocated to their rooms and would have time to unpack before high tea at five-thirty. After the meal, they were told that Dame Joanna Cruikshank, the Camp Commandant, would come to speak to them.

Esther was puzzled by Mrs Murphy's accent which wasn't at all like how they spoke in the South of England. Must be some kind of regional accent, like we had in Germany, she thought. However, their room was spotless, and had a hand wash basin with soap and towels, and twin beds. Outside the room was a bathroom to be shared with those in the other two rooms on this floor.

Esther enjoyed the high tea, bubble and squeak, followed by apple pie and custard and a cup of tea. Very tasty. Perhaps she was getting used to the English diet. Mrs Murphy didn't appear to have any problems with rationing. Maybe they didn't have it on the Isle of Man or the landlady was just very good at making use of what she could get hold of. Her mother picked at the first course and left about half of it but managed the sweet and seemed to enjoy the tea. But she still looked exhausted and Esther hoped that a week or two in the sunshine would make a difference. Esther mused that she didn't want to be here, but if she couldn't be in London with George, Joe, Mary, Sir John and Cook, she'd have to make the best of a bad job here . Besides the warm weather, decent lodgings and nutritious food might help her mother to regain her health. That was more important than anything else.

Dame Joanna Cruikshank, Commandant of the Camp, arrived at about seven o'clock and spoke to the newcomers in the sitting room. Esther thought she looked about sixty, had short, curly grey hair and spoke with the voice of authority without appearing to be a bully. Dame Joanna went through the dos and don'ts, especially getting involved with the soldiers, after welcoming everyone. She expressed sympathy with them for being dragged from their homes, and said she hoped it wouldn't be for too long, although she could make no promises at this stage. The Commandant encouraged everyone to get into the fresh air as often as possible, particularly while the weather was so fine. She recommended swimming but warned against getting too far out. There was a library, post office, bars and various shops, all of which they were encouraged to use. Any questions or problems should first be addressed to Mrs Murphy, who would pass them on if she thought it appropriate. Dame Joanna seemed to be a kind person, but also one who would stand no nonsense. She reminded them that the camp was surrounded with barbed wire and under no circumstances should anyone try to climb over, through or under it. To finish on a positive note, she promised that the reunion with the menfolk would take place as soon as possible.

Esther and her mother remained in the sitting room after the Commandant had left. The two younger women went for a walk. The tall woman who had come over on the boat with her family introduced herself as Ruth Gerber. Immediately, the penny dropped as Esther realised this was almost certainly the mother of her brother's hero, the football and fitness coach, Jonathan. They chatted for a couple of hours until it became apparent that Deborah was falling asleep so she excused herself and took her mother to bed.

In the night, Esther was kept awake for a short while thinking about her mother's illness, Sir John, her father and brother and

George and Joe. Deborah had fallen into a deep sleep and Esther soon joined her. She was woken up soon after seven by her mother's cough, which seemed to have worsened overnight. It had improved by the time they went down for breakfast. The two women spent the morning wandering around Port Erin, looking at the shops and visiting the library where Esther borrowed an Agatha Christie novel to read. In the afternoon, they sat on the beach and enjoyed the sunshine.

Deborah's cough worsened again during the night, and Esther got up twice to give her a sip of water. After breakfast the two of them sat in the sitting room.

'It would be a lovely place for a holiday, wouldn't it, Esther?' Deborah said.

'But it's not a holiday,' her daughter replied. 'We're being held here against our will. It could be worse, I know, but I'd rather be free and in England.'

'Yes, you're right, dear, but I feel I've been through so much I'm happy just to sit down and rest. Your father being thrown out of his job back in Germany, the Gestapo following us around Berlin, the fear I felt when we were escaping from the Nazis and then the internment and living in that terrible building site all feels too much. Totally drained is how I feel. And I miss your father and Peter.'

'Well, that's one thing that'll cheer you up. We're going to Douglas next week for a reunion with the men.'

'Really? That is good news. How did you find out about that?'

'Ruth told me. She heard it from Mrs Murphy who was told by Dame Joanna. All the details will be sent any time now.'

'At last, I've got something to look forward to. You go out, Esther. I'll just sit here and doze.'

Esther spent the day walking around the village, glancing in the shops before settling down to read her book on the beach. At lunchtime, she'd checked on her mother and found her fast asleep in the sitting room. The two young women who had arrived with them at Mrs Murphy's came and sat with Esther on the beach.

'Hi,' the dark-haired one said, 'I'm Maria, and this is my friend, Constance,' nodding towards her blonde companion.

'Hello, I'm Esther. I live in London and before that Berlin.'

'We're both from Vienna, but we've lived in London since 1938. We got out of Austria after the Nazis started getting at the Jews,'

Constance said, 'and then we got fixed up with jobs as maids in Mayfair.'

'Mayfair. Isn't that rather posh?' asked Esther.

'Very posh,' said Maria. 'What about you?'

'Oh, I'm the same as you, but I live in a posh house in Hampstead.'

The three of them laughed.

'We were doing rather well in Mayfair, then the police came and locked us up on the Isle of Man because we're enemies of the state,' Maria explained.

More laughter.

'Esther,' Constance began. 'Have you looked at the soldiers? Most of them are rather plain, but one or two are even quite dishy, but all of them need a bit of relief from tension now and again.'

Esther blushed. She knew where this was going. 'Bit dangerous, isn't it? If you get caught they'll lock you up in jail.'

'True, and it's difficult because of the long days. We have to sneak out after dark for our fun and then there's only time for a quickie; you know, a hand job. Still, they seem to like it, and they always give us a bit of money,' Constance continued. 'You should give it a try. You're good-looking. There'd be a queue for you,' and the two Viennese girls burst into a fit of giggles.

Esther wasn't sure what to say. The girls were very friendly and and it was fun talking about something other than the war and internment , but she was shaken that the girls had suggested she might give it a try. 'Not for me, I'm afraid.' She replied hastily. 'I'm too busy looking after my mother. She's not well. My younger brother and father are in Douglas too. Anyway, I've sort of got a boyfriend.'

'Sort of. What does that mean?' Maria asked.

'We were getting on well until the war came along. I think he's afraid he'll get killed in the fighting and leave me feeling unhappy, so we've backed off for the time being.'

'Listen, Esther. He's probably back in London helping himself to plenty of girls,' Maria suggested.

'No, he isn't,' Esther replied with confidence.

'How do you know that?' asked Constance.

'Because he's like me, a romantic.'

The three of them burst out laughing. Esther had enjoyed the afternoon and the company of the girls, despite their after-dark activities.

On her way back to Mrs Murphy's, Esther was thrilled to bump into Mary. They hugged and laughed. 'How long have you been here?' Esther asked.

'Arrived yesterday. You?'

'Three days. I'm in that house over there,' Esther said, pointing at Mrs Murphy's.

'I'm up the other end of the bay, about ten minutes' walk away.'

'What was it like when you were rounded up?'

'Awful! I got taken to Clapham Police Station and then to Kempton Park Racecourse. I had to sleep in a horse box.'

'With the horses?' Esther joked.

'Don't be silly.'

'Did you get fed straw for breakfast?'

'No. The food was worse than that.'

Together they laughed again until Esther told Mary about her mother's ill health and how she had to get back to look after her.

A look of concern flashed across Mary's face, but she quickly let it pass, and they arranged to meet again the following day. She thought briefly about introducing Mary to Maria and Constance but then dismissed the idea, knowing that Mary might be offended by their activities.

Back at Mrs Murphy's, the news was out. The reunion would take place in three days' time. Suddenly the hair salon in Port Erin was fully booked, but plenty of the internees had hairdressing skills, and they stepped into the breach. The shops sold out of dresses, lipstick and other forms of make-up, and shoes were scrubbed spotless. The big day came, and a gaggle of excited women clambered on the little train and headed to Douglas. Horses and carriages waited for them when they reached Douglas Station, and everyone enjoyed the journey along Douglas Bay promenade to the Derby Castle ballroom at the far end.

Esther hugged her father and mother, and Simon hugged his wife, but he didn't need to be told that there was something wrong with her. Deborah dismissed his worries and told everyone to enjoy themselves, which they proceeded to do. Esther danced with Michael, her father, and her brother, who introduced her to Jonathan

Gerber. Jonathan was very complimentary about Peter's football ability. Esther reported this to her father, who immediately said enthusiastically , 'Perhaps he'll play for England.'

'Well, I certainly won't be playing for Germany,' Peter laughed.

As the evening drew to a close, a slow waltz was played, and Deborah was persuaded to leave her seat and dance with her husband. Mary danced with Jonathan, Esther with Michael and Peter, who seemed to be growing every day, was snatched up by Maria, after being told by his sister, with a smirk, to watch out for her.

Another reunion was promised soon, and the women set off for the return journey. By the time they reached Mrs Murphy's, Deborah was totally exhausted and went straight to bed. She began coughing at about three o'clock, and this lasted until breakfast.

'She needs a doctor,' Mrs Murphy told Esther. 'That's one thing we're not short of. I'll go down and ask Dame Joanna to organise it. You stay here, Esther, and look after your mother.'

Esther was beginning to fear the worst. This cough was not just a passing illness. It was more serious than that. Dr Rebecca Hartstein, a successful and popular practitioner from Hamburg – until Hitler had passed laws preventing her from treating non-Jewish patients – arrived very quickly, accompanied by Dame Joanna. She cleared the room and examined Deborah. Ten minutes later, she emerged from the lounge and told Esther, Dame Joanna and Mrs Murphy that the patient was most probably suffering from pneumonia. Her blood pressure was too high, and she should be taken to hospital immediately. Dame Joanna sent another aide to order an ambulance to take Esther's mother to the nearest hospital in Douglas. Mrs Murphy produced a small suitcase and suggested to Esther that she should fill it with some things for her mother. By the time the ambulance arrived, Esther was packed and ready to go. She included one or two bits and pieces for herself since she intended to travel with her mother and stay with her until she had recovered. Dame Joanna wished her well and said she'd already telephoned Hutchinson Camp so that the rest of her family would be at the hospital when she arrived. Esther thanked her and stepped into the back of the ambulance with her mother.

Deborah was fully conscious but having difficulty breathing. Her chest rose and fell erratically. She grasped Esther's hand and smiled at her.

'Who would have thought that I'd have a miracle escape from the Gestapo and end up like this on the Isle of Man?'

Esther chuckled, then put on a serious face.

'Hush, Mama. You need to rest. We'll soon be at the hospital where they'll make you better. Father and Peter will probably be there, so we'll all be together again much sooner than we expected.'

'I would rather be fit and well at Port Erin, looking forward to our release.'

Her mother dropped into a shallow sleep, but her breathing was still heavy. Esther held her hand until they reached the hospital when the ambulance doors opened, and porters and nurses swung into action. Deborah was wheeled away and, as Esther jumped out, her father and Peter appeared. She ran towards them and all three embraced with tears pouring down Peter and Esther's faces. A rather rotund nurse with a kindly face appeared.

'Please come with me. I've a room set aside for you where you can wait while the doctor examines Mrs Abrahams. I'll see you get a cup of tea and a lemonade for the young man.'

Simon Abrahams thanked her then glanced outside the door where an armed soldier stood at attention.

'That's to stop us making a run for it,' Simon chuckled ruefully.

Tea and lemonade arrived, and they spent the anxious waiting time exchanging further details of each other's camps.

The three of them sipped their drinks and chatted about nothing in particular, then lapsed into a period of silence while waiting for news. After about thirty minutes, a short young man with straight black hair parted on his left side walked in. He was wearing a white coat and had a grave expression on his face. He introduced himself as Doctor Burton and then sat down opposite the family.

'Mrs Abrahams is very ill. She is suffering from pneumonia. I have treated her with drugs and given her a sedative. She is sleeping now. I think she may also have had a small stroke. As you have seen for yourselves, her breathing is not at all right. She is, I believe, a German Jew and you have been interned here. Is that correct?'

My father answered.

'We've been in England almost a year, that's to say, Deborah and I. The children came earlier on the Kindertransport. Deborah and I escaped from the Gestapo just before the outbreak of the war. We were arrested in Cambridge during the alien round-up earlier in the summer.'

'Where did they take you?' the doctor asked.

'First, we went to Butlin's Holiday Camp in Clacton-on-Sea. That was fine. Then we were transferred to a building site with a few more or less finished flats and houses near Liverpool. That was horrible. The roads were full of holes, the buildings damp, we had to sleep on mattresses on the floor, the food was disgusting, and it rained for most of the time. Then we came here several days ago. This -is so much better.'

Doctor Burton remained silent for a moment, then looked gravely at the three of them.

'That probably kicked off her illness. The stress of the past year, coupled with the unhealthy conditions in Liverpool, have caused her health to deteriorate rapidly. It is also possible, of course, that the stress of living in Germany over the past few years could have given her blood pressure problems which may have led to a small stroke or two. These could have easily gone undetected, particularly with the poor health care for Jewish people in Nazi Germany. How old is she?'

'Forty-five,' Simon replied.

'That's no great age,' said the doctor. 'I will do all I can, but I can't promise anything. I suggest you try to get some rest. The nurses will look after you and bring you whatever food and drink you may need. She'll sleep all night. I expect you'll want to see her in the morning. I'll get someone to tell you when she is up to receiving visitors. Good night.'

'Thank you, doctor,' Simon said, slumping in his chair. He looked utterly beaten, and Esther went to join him, putting her arm around him. Strange to be the one comforting her father when she was used to him comforting her.

The three of them sat for a while in complete silence. Esther felt tears welling up in her eyes. Peter was completely white, and Esther could see he was doing his best to avoid crying. Their father looked at them.

'All we can do is hope for a quick recovery. I'm glad the doctor was honest with us. Let's try to get some sleep.'

That was easier said than done, but it was at least better than those awful conditions at Huyton. A small sofa just about accommodated Peter at full stretch, and he was soon asleep. Esther and Simon each took a comfortable armchair, and she must have nodded off because the next thing she knew it was morning and the sun was streaming through the window. Peter was still fast asleep, but Simon was sitting in his chair bolt upright, staring into space. He saw that Esther was awake and gave her a weak smile.

'Good morning, Esther. You seem to have slept well.'

'I did. What about you?'

'I was awake for most of the night, remembering. You know your mother has had a good life. Better than many of our friends who were murdered by the Nazis or locked up in those camps like Sachsenhausen and Dachau. And, whatever happens to her, she had you and Peter and those who risked their lives to save us. We have been very lucky to have known such good people.'

'Oh, Dad…' Esther began tearfully, but was interrupted by a nurse who appeared to tell the three of them that they could see Deborah as she was now awake and had managed a small breakfast. Doctor Burton had been with her all night but had now left for a short rest.

There were about thirty beds in the large, high-ceilinged ward. Most were occupied by women who didn't seem too ill. Deborah was close to the door, lying on her back but propped up with pillows. She looked terrible, like a ghost with sunken cheeks. She had been washed but her hair was a mess, so Esther brushed it to make it look a bit better. Deborah smiled at her daughter.

'Thank you, Esther. Now I feel fit to be received by your young man, George.'

Esther suppressed a little giggle that somehow turned into a sense of guilt that swept through her. So wrapped up had she been with her own problems these past weeks, she'd hardly thought about George or his friend Joe, her saviours. Vowing to write to him as soon as her mother's hospital stay ended, Esther turned her attention to her sick mother. Her breathing was growing heavier. Doctor Burton appeared and shook his head.

'I just can't get a grip on the infection. That so-called wonder drug penicillin might do the trick, but it's not being mass-produced in any quantity, and priority for it is given to wounded military personnel who might be made fit enough to return to the action. And that especially applies to pilots. Quite right too! It's uncomfortable saying this to you but you seem the type of people who'd understand. In fact, I don't believe we've got a single dose of penicillin on the island. But I'm not giving up and neither should you.'

'Thank you, Doctor,' Simon said. 'I'm sure you'll do your best.'

For the rest of the day and for the week that followed, Simon and Esther took turns sitting at Deborah's bedside. Peter was usually with one of them. Doctor Burton was never far away, and he and the nurses did everything they could to keep Deborah alive. Sometimes she was able to talk quite coherently for short spells. At others, she lapsed into unconsciousness with only her ever-worsening breathing giving any sign of life.

'There's nothing more I can do. I'm so terribly sorry,' Doctor Burton said quietly one day, looking at the three of them with moist eyes. 'I'm so terribly sorry.'

Simon bowed his head and then reached out to grasp the doctor's hand. 'Thank you, Doctor. You've done all that could have been done.'

Doctor Burton nodded. 'I only wish…' He sighed. 'She'll be leaving us soon. Perhaps you should say your goodbyes.'

Esther leant forward, kissing her mother's cheek as the tears streamed down her cheeks. Peter buried his head in Deborah's breasts as he had done all those years ago as a child. Then they stood to make way for their father.

'I'll stay with your mother now,' Simon said. 'You and Peter sit in the room where we were last night.'

Esther and Peter gave Deborah one last look and left the ward. Her mouth was wide open as her life slowly ebbed away. Thirty minutes later, Simon rejoined his son and daughter. His face was etched with sadness. He nodded sorrowfully and then sat down with his children to grieve.

CHAPTER FIVE

The next parade was eventful. The Sergeant spat out his most devastating insult yet.

'I know I shouldn't be saying this, Cadet Aaron, but if Hitler did win the war, it might not be such a bad thing. He's always said he's nothing against the English but just wants to get rid of Jews, Pikeys and queers. We'd have a few of those concentration camps over here, and you'd get in on two counts. What about you, Richards? Are you a Pikey? Be good if you were. You could keep Jew boy here warm as you both wait for your execution.'

George and Joe stayed silent, but this angered the Sergeant so much that he conducted the drill with more shouting and screaming than usual, so much so that his voice eventually gave out and turned into a high-pitched shriek like a seriously out-of-tune choir boy. The parade tried not to laugh but one young boy couldn't control himself and burst into a fit of giggles. When the Sergeant finally recovered, he punished the boy by ordering him to remain behind after parade and scrub the toilets with a toothbrush.

The Lieutenant called George and Joe into his office when they arrived for the next parade. 'I'm sure you'll be sorry to hear that the Sergeant has gone down with diphtheria, and he'll be out of action for many months,' he said, with more than a hint of sarcasm. 'Corporal Hudson will be promoted to Sergeant and you two will each get a couple of stripes and be promoted to Corporal. I know Corporal Hudson is younger than the both of you, but he is next in line and is a capable Cadet. He'll look for support from you and I hope you'll give it freely.'

'Of course, we will, sir,' George said.

'Yes, sir,' Joe added enthusiastically. Both of the new Corporals saluted the officer, thanked him and turned to leave, but the Lieutenant stopped them.

'I'm aware of the bullying you've been subjected to, Corporal Aaron. There wasn't a lot I could do about it then, with his father being an officer in the TA. But he's gone now and you two showed remarkable restraint. Well done.'

'So you see. It's all worked out. Perhaps he'll never come back,' George said on the way home that night.

'He might even snuff it,' Joe added, grinning. They looked at each other.

'Well, something nasty, at least, maybe not actually snuff it...' George replied. Joe nodded, and they continued home.

George took advantage of the fine weather and the light evenings in the summer of 1940 to make sure that the allotment was producing what his and Joe's family needed to keep them eating healthily. Rationing was now in full swing, and this was helping to keep the nation going with the threat of invasion ever-present. Shortages of food, fuel and other raw materials were creating a very real problem. Joe was often there to do his bit but was spending more time helping his father, as he was needed to push handcarts laden with food to customers, and they often had to collect from suppliers in the same way because of the shortage of petrol. Merchant shipping carrying supplies across the Atlantic continued to be sent to the bottom of the ocean by the German Navy. Things were getting desperate but Britons, spurred on by Prime Minister Churchill, rose to the occasion

The two Corporals flourished at the Cadets and, working with Sergeant Hudson, demonstrated effective leadership skills. Epping Forest was the setting for a tough weekend camp where the young men learned to apply their map-reading skills to a night-time exercise in the heavily wooded area. They learned to live off the land and to load, fire, strip and clean Lee Enfield .303 rifles. George was enjoying himself, but he often thought that this was not the real thing, and it would be much different in the heat of the battle.

All the talk that summer was of invasion. As a preliminary move, the German Air Force – the Luftwaffe – first began to attack shipping in the Channel and then, soon after George's seventeenth birthday in August, airfields in South East England. A fierce conflict in the skies followed, which soon became known as the *Battle of Britain*. Men and machines were lost, more so to the Luftwaffe than to the RAF. Knowing that they had to gain mastery of the skies to make the invasion possible, the Germans threw everything into the conflict but, by early September, it became clear they were going to lose. Frustrated by this lack of success, they drastically changed their tactics.

George and Joe were working hard at their allotment on September 7th. As they dug, they talked about the war and wondered if the Guv had seen any action yet. Suddenly the sky was full of planes, German bombers it looked like, and some distance away in the docks area, the terrifying sounds of loud explosions could be heard.

'It's a bloody air raid!' George shouted above the sound of the warning siren and the roar of aeroplane engines. 'Let's get out of here.'

Joe needed no prompting. He'd already started to gather up the tools. George picked up the rest and together they raced to the shed, threw their spades and the rest of the stuff in, locked the door and began to run steadily towards their homes. In the distance, the bombs continued to explode but, so far, Shoreditch and Bethnal Green seemed to have escaped. As they neared their flats, the all-clear sounded, and people began to pour out from the air raid shelters and were greeted with a scene from hell in the sky over the docks. The planes had gone but they had left behind evidence of their work. The sky was red in parts, gathering its colour from the large numbers of fires burning below. Elsewhere, it was grey, with thick, ugly clouds of smoke proliferating overhead hinting that the dockland rubber factory had been hit. A vile smell accompanied the fires from the scene of the raids.

'You lads okay?' Joe's father, Charlie, shouted at them as he, George's Dad, Isaac, and their wives returned from the shelter.

'Fine,' said George. 'We were at the allotment when the raids started so we locked up and came straight here. What about you four?'

'We were tucked up in the shelter,' Charlie replied. 'It was hot, crowded, and stank of sweat but at least we all felt safe. Most people were worried that their houses might not be there when they got home but it looks like the docks were the real target.'

George and Joe went their separate ways to have their tea. It was a late tea because the raid only started around 5 o'clock. George asked his parents if they thought there'd be another raid, but, of course, they didn't know. George finished washing up the crocks shortly before 8, the wailing sign of the siren started up again. George put his army boots on, and they set off for the shelter. Joe and his family joined them and soon they were wedged in the shelter. Almost immediately, the bombs started dropping again, only this time much nearer to them. Several times the walls and door of the shelter rattled as a device exploded nearby, and some of the children in the shelter began to howl with fear. Later that September evening, the door was flung open, and an Auxiliary Fire Service Officer shouted above the din, 'We need men to help us. The shelter under the Columbia Road Market's taken a direct hit. We need volunteers to help us get people out who are trapped under the rubble.'

Charlie, Isaac and ten or so others jumped to their feet.

'That's us,' George said.

Joe joined his mate and the two of them fell in with the others and began following the AFS man. Neither father dared to stop their sons and felt a touch of pride at the way they had joined the rescue group without hesitation. Little did they know but both lads were scared to death. The raid was still in progress, but the docks were getting the bulk of the attention. As the Columbia Road Market came into view, the men and boys were startled at the site of the magnificent Victorian building which now seemed to be almost falling over. The AFS man told them that the big storage area under the market had been used as a shelter and, somehow or other, a bomb had exploded in that basement.

'It probably slipped down an air vent,' the AFS man said. 'There's hundreds down there, some dead, others badly injured, loads trapped under the rubble. The lucky ones walked out. We need to free those trapped and help the injured out. Leave the dead for the time being.' George and Joe looked at each other with fear and sadness in their eyes.

By now, the area outside the market was littered with vehicles: ambulances, fire engines and police vehicles. Dozens of stretchers covered the ground but there were still nowhere near enough to help the injured. Some would have to be carried out by the emergency services and the volunteers.

George and Joe joined their fathers as they made their way towards the basement and, as they neared the scene of devastation, they could hear groans, shouts of 'help me', crying and howling. On the floor, they could hardly make out a single thing in the total blackness, but soon rescue personnel came with torches and lit up the scene of horror. The basement ceiling had collapsed entirely, and the floor was a sea of rubble under which those who had been sheltering either lay still or writhed gently so the first impression was of a gently rolling sea.

'Here, you four,' a policeman said to the lads and their fathers, 'take this torch and work down the left-hand side. Shout "stretcher" for anyone you think needs one and help the others out who are not too badly wounded.'

Carefully moving bits of rubble, they found a woman who, apart from shock, didn't seem too bad; they lifted her up, and Joe took her to the medical teams outside. Charlie unearthed a child crushed to death, hardly recognisable as a human being, while Isaac found a terrified little boy and helped him to safety. George was the unlucky one. He moved some slabs and came across a young woman who had been literally flattened. Her face was completely destroyed. He couldn't even spot a nose. and, where the eyes once were, just a couple of sockets remained. Heaven knows what had poured out of her skull. He stood for a moment and felt himself going colder and colder every second, despite the warm summer night, and then he dropped to his knees and vomited until his stomach was empty. Even then, he dry-retched for several more minutes until the others rejoined him, but somehow he carried on with the grisly work, which lasted through the night, even after the all-clear sounded at four o'clock.

George slept in on the Sunday till after lunch. When he surfaced, he found his mother and father sitting in silence, staring into space in the living room.

'Do you want something to eat, George?' his mother asked.

'No, thank you,' he replied. 'I wouldn't mind a cup of tea, though.'

'Good idea,' his father said. 'I don't suppose any of us feel like a Sunday dinner after last night. There were a thousand people in that shelter. I've no idea how many dead, but it would have been a lot more but the efforts of you and Joe and the other volunteers.'

'Thanks, Dad. How long do you think all this bombing is going to go on?'

'Well, they're saying that it's just revenge by the Germans because they're losing the air battle with our fighters knocking them out of the sky. I reckon they'll be back tonight.'

Isaac was right. The Luftwaffe came back that night and many more afterwards. Within a week, they'd abandoned daytime attacks because they were losing too many bombers to the British Spitfires and Hurricanes, but nights were a different matter. RAF night fighters were a scarcity.

'I suppose we're all getting used to this,' George said to Joe at the allotment one afternoon. 'Helping our dads in the morning, digging in the afternoon and then sheltering in the evening, except when we're at the cadets.'

'Good job they haven't hit our hall. There'd be no more cadets if they did. I wouldn't like that much,' Joe said.

'Nor me. It's been great there since that bloody Sergeant vanished. I wonder if he'll ever come back. We'll ask the Lieutenant on Tuesday.'

It turned out that the Sergeant hadn't died but didn't fancy any more boy soldiering after he'd recovered so that chapter was closed. To the lads' great joy, Esther reappeared just before Christmas. Sir John had encouraged her to call George, and they arranged to meet in the Oxford Street Corner House. Joe didn't join them. George found Esther very quiet and withdrawn, but now, finally, he knew why she'd disappeared, and he was relieved it wasn't anything he'd done wrong. The death of her mother had clearly hit her very hard and, almost six months on, she was still coming to terms with it. George told Joe the next day who, like his friend, was deeply saddened by the news. A week or so later, Mary made it back to the mainland, and she and Esther started helping out at the WVS refreshment stand outside Liverpool Street station. They were there dishing out hot drinks and sandwiches night after night, bombs or no bombs. George and Joe sometimes went down and chatted to them in the evenings. They talked about the Isle of Man, trying to steer clear of the tragedy of Deborah's death. George still thought Esther was beautiful but, despite this, he couldn't bring himself to make any kind of commitment to her. In less than a year he'd be eighteen, and he knew that he'd be called up and sent to fight and maybe get killed. What was the point of it all? If they both survived the war, maybe they'd try again, but how could he ask her to wait for him? He was careful not to voice any of that to her now, though – just in case she got the wrong idea…

1941 brought no let up in the destruction of British cities, and George and Joe became regular volunteers in their area of the East End. Neither of them enjoyed it, but they knew the Civil Defence people needed their help and others like them. George was sitting at home one evening listening to the radio with his parents when there was a banging on the door. Isaac answered it and found an ARP warden he knew standing there, looking very worried.

'Hello, Isaac. There's a stick of high explosives taken out a line of houses in Bateman's Row. We need your lad and his mate to give us a hand. You stay here and look after the wife. It's bad out there. You might think about going to the shelter.'

George had already left the room to put on his boots and warm clothes. He dashed out to collect Joe and, minutes later, they were sprawled in the back of a van heading for Bateman's Row. Both had brown helmets and had been given torches some months ago. The van bumped and swerved its way to Bateman's Row, avoiding potholes and burnt-out vehicles. When they arrived, they leapt out of the back of the van and spotted that, apart from two or possibly three high explosive bombs, the whole street was littered with small fires from incendiaries. Quickly, George, Joe and others got to work with stirrup pumps and buckets to extinguish the flames. Vehicles of all types had arrived, including a fire engine, several ambulances and a police van with a couple of special wartime uniformed constables standing beside their vehicle. Many of the properties were still burning, with flames licking up towards the sky. Noises of men at work, buildings crumbling, shouted orders and warnings and coughing, as the thick smoke caught at the back of the rescuers' throats, dominated the terrible scene. The local ARP man was taking a roll call of residents and questioning bystanders to see who was missing. As far as he could judge, everyone was accounted for apart from the old couple in number 10, the end of a terrace. One of the neighbours, who had returned from the shelter when she thought the raid was over and had seen a pile of bricks that was once her house, said that the elderly man and woman who lived in number 10 never went to the shelter, telling their neighbours they preferred to die in their beds. The ARP man looked at number 10. It appeared still to be standing but seemed to be leaning like a drunk against the pile of rubble that had once been number 8.

'George, Joe, check out number 10 but be careful. It doesn't look too stable. The residents are an elderly man and his wife.'

The lads raced to the badly damaged house and entered carefully.

'Check down here, Joe. I'll take a butcher's upstairs.'

It was a tiny house, much smaller than the apartments the two lads lived in. George climbed the stairs cautiously, leaving Joe to have a good look around the living room and kitchen and check the toilet in the yard. George reached the top of the stairs, flashed his torch and spotted just two doors. Carefully opening the door, he looked around a small room which had probably been a second bedroom but was now a junk store with old furniture, bedding, towels, and books, all nestling alongside parts of the ceiling, which had caved in when the bomb exploded. As usual with this type of house, there wasn't a bathroom. The residents probably washed in the kitchen and used the outside khazi, George thought.

He turned his attention to the second door, which he guessed opened to the front bedroom facing the street. The beam of his torch swept the room, and he spotted an elderly lady lying on the bed covered in plaster alongside her husband. But it wasn't the sad sight of the obviously dead couple that made him turn cold. Immediately his blood began to boil as he saw a figure, armed with a knife, crouching over the woman's corpse, sawing away at her finger so he could get hold of her rings. The figure flashed his torch at George, who was shouting to Joe for help.

'Bugger me, it's that Jew boy from the Cadets,' said a voice that George clearly recognised as belonging to the Sergeant, who had obviously completely recovered from his illness. 'Give us a hand. We'll polish him off. Nobody'll miss a dead Jew.'

Out of the corner of his eye, George became aware of two others who appeared to be ransacking drawers and cupboards on the other side of the room. They approached him from his right while the Sergeant was coming straight at him, blade pointing. The Sergeant swung the knife at George's throat but missed – George had moved to the left to avoid the other two – as George let fly his right boot and caught the assailant a mighty blow between the legs. The Sergeant howled in pain and leaned forward. George grabbed his nemesis' shoulders and aimed his knee at his face, making contact with the chin. Another loud crack followed, accompanied by a scream that filled the room as the other two moved in on George, who was sending the Sergeant into unconsciousness with a powerful punch at his left ear. As the first youth grabbed George, Joe came rushing in.

'You take the other one, Joe!' George yelled. 'I'll deal with this one. The Sergeant won't be a problem. He's out of it.'

George then became engaged in a mighty struggle with the third member of the looters, who was almost as strong as he was. Joe was making short shrift of the last of the trio, who was no match for the East End scrapper and was soon thrown down the stairs. In a mixture of boxing and wrestling, the remaining two landed powerful blows. George felt a tooth come loose and a hefty blow burst his nose. An elbow to the side of his head sent George reeling as the youth reached down and grabbed his balls. George grunted but tried to ignore it as he aimed blows with one knuckle from each hand into the other man's eyes. A loud scream was accompanied by an end to George's excruciating pain as the other released his grip and squared up, but before he could land a blow, George struck him on the jaw with two rapidly delivered hooks, after which the looter sank to his knees. Despite feeling not so great himself, George grabbed him and dragged him down the stairs to join the other two.

The Sergeant was being loaded onto a stretcher when George got there. 'He's lucky to be alive,' an ambulance man said.

'It wouldn't be a great loss,' Joe was saying. 'He tried to knife George, who acted in self-defence. Anyway, he'll be in loads of pain so he'll probably wish he was dead.'

'Right,' one of the ambulance men said, staring distastefully at the Sergeant. 'Anyway, we're taking him to hospital.' The Sergeant was still on the stretcher but muttering plenty of swear words and even one or two threats.

'Shut up!' the ambulance man shouted. 'There's enough din here without looters like you adding to it.'

'I'll come with you,' one of the policemen who'd joined them said. 'We don't want him running off.'

'We know who he is,' George told him. 'He won't be difficult to find, nor will he be going anywhere, officer. He's probably got concussion, a broken nose and jaw and heaven knows what else.'

'Right.' The officer gave George the once-over. 'Ok, then. You lads give your details to Constable Harrison here, then get yourselves home. Tomorrow, come to the station and give a statement, but get that nose checked out in the meantime.'

George went to the doctor's first thing and had his nose reset while Joe was at the police station reporting on the night's events. When the two got together after lunch, Joe told his mate two of the youths would be at the Juvenile Court later today and the Sergeant would face trial as soon as he'd left hospital. 'The copper said they were too young to be hanged like the Home Secretary wants for looters, but would probably be sent to Borstal. When they're older, they'll probably be shifted to a proper prison,' Joe added.

'See,' George said for the second time. 'It all came out in the wash after all, didn't it? Told you our time would come, but I must say it wasn't how I expected it to be.'

'No,' Joe laughed. 'It was even better than we thought it would turn out. I imagined a scrap somewhere but it was awful for the people that died in the bombing.'

'Yeah.' George fell silent for a while. 'But that's war,' he added. 'And it ain't going to be the worst of it, by far, I reckon.'

CHAPTER SIX

A miserable Esther spent the next few months sad and bored. She knew her father and brother were just as unhappy in Douglas as all three mourned Deborah's death. Simon sounded inconsolable when he wrote to her, but her brother was putting on a brave face and poured his teenage energy into football, playing an important part in his team, which competed in Inter-Camp matches. All this she learned both from her father and Ruth Gerber, whose son Jonathan was the man behind the growth of football in Hutchinson Camp. The Isle of Man was a decent enough place, and many people were kind to her, but Esther wanted to be back in London with George and Joe and Sir John. She began to resent being locked up for no good reason. As autumn turned into winter, the Jewish internees began to talk of rumours that they would soon be released.

Esther had been told to report to Dame Joanna's office in Port Erion in mid-December. She sat nervously outside the Commandant's office whilst waiting to be asked to go in. Internees had started being allowed to leave more than a month previously, and Esther had been anxiously awaiting her chance. Her father and brother, as well as Mary, were also on tenterhooks, wondering when they would be released. Ruth Gerber had gone but her husband and son were still in Douglas.

'Esther, you're free to return home,' Dame Joanna began. 'There's always a lot of paperwork with these things so it's taken longer than I would have liked to process the release of you and many others. I'm sorry.'

For the first time in months, Esther felt an uplifting in her spirits. Her mother's death still weighed heavily on her and, while she was on the island, she could think of little else. Now she could look ahead. She would see George and Joe again and Sir John. Looking forward to living again in the beautiful house in Hampstead filled her with the beginnings of a return to the happiness she'd felt before the war.

'Thank you, Dame Cruikshank. Do you know when my father and brother will be allowed back in England?'

'Before Christmas, I hope and believe. There's the usual hold-ups with red tape and so on, but I will get it cleared as soon as I possibly can. The same applies to your friend, Mary. Before you leave this building, please collect a travel warrant for the ferry leaving Douglas the day after tomorrow and your train ticket to London Euston. Transport will be provided from the Docks to Lime Street Station. I've asked Mrs Murphy to let you telephone Sir John so that he can collect you from Euston. I'm dreadfully sorry about your mother, Esther. When you return to England, you'll find much that upsets you and the war will continue for some time. But it will end, and we shall win.'

'Thank you, Dame Cruikshank. You've been very kind. Goodbye.'

'Goodbye, Esther. Seek the good things in life and try to live by them. Good luck.'

Esther was shocked by the state of the mainland when she stepped from the Isle of Man ferry on a cold December morning. She'd heard about the Blitz, of course, but had no idea of the extent of the damage that the Luftwaffe had caused. Liverpool was just a heap of rubble and dust, yet people seemed to be trying to go about their daily routines. An Army lorry took her to Lime Street Station, itself looking much the worse for wear, but she had to hang around the station concourse for more than two hours before she could get on a train to London. It was late in the evening when the train crawled into Euston Station in a wrecked London. Sir John was waiting for her, and soon she was seated in the back of his chauffeur-driven Daimler Limousine.

'The journey won't be easy, my dear. Many of the streets are impassable because of destroyed buildings and burned-out vehicles of all shapes and sizes. Londoners have had it very rough, but by some miracle, they're getting through it,' Sir John told her.

'Liverpool was in a dreadful state as well,' Esther said.

'Yes, of course. It's easy for us to feel sorry for ourselves down here and forget that almost all of our cities are taking a pounding.'

Sir John seemed unperturbed by the bangs and flashes to their right as the chauffeur made his way cautiously north.

'Looks like the south of the river is getting it again tonight,' Sir John sighed. 'There can't be much there left to bomb.'

Esther felt tears coming into her eyes as the car drew up at Sir John's Hampstead home. It was, like every other house, totally blacked out yet appeared unexpectedly sinister. But it was her home, and she was so glad to be there after almost six months of an uncertain future in internment.

'Put your bags in your room, Esther, have a quick wash, then join me in the lounge. Cook has left some supper for us.'

Esther sat on her bed, feeling the familiarity of the room and the house slowly returning to her. Despite being in a country under attack from the Luftwaffe, she was glad to be back in Hampstead, and she hoped that the pain of the past few months would soon begin to heal.

'I'm so sorry about your mother, Esther. She was too young to die.'

'I think it all got too much for her. The heartbreak of watching the Nazis destroy everything that she once held dear, persecution by the Gestapo and then internment. If we'd stayed at Clacton or gone straight to the Isle of Man, she might have been all right, but that terrible unfinished housing estate at Huyton set her off and there was to be no recovery.'

'The whole business was a shambles, a ridiculous knee-jerk reaction to a pile of rumours spread by the press. One good thing is that those who never should have been interned in the first place are now being brought back, and public opinion is behind them. I think everyone recognises that we were wasting valuable war resources by keeping some of the best brains in the country locked up,' Sir John said.

'My father and brother are still there. They were at a different camp in Douglas, but I think they might be sent home to Cambridge soon.'

'Yes. I checked up on them today. They'll be back next week.'

'Thank you, Sir John.' Esther hesitated. 'Have you heard from George and Joe?'

'They called here a while ago asking after you and enquiring about my health. I hadn't seen them since that wonderful day before the war when we welcomed your mother and father to England after their escape from the Gestapo. George, in particular, was quite concerned. Anyway, there wasn't a lot to tell them, but I do have George's father's telephone number, so you're free to call him whenever you wish. I believe they've been very busy helping their fathers, looking after their allotments, attending Army Cadets and helping the Civil Defence people in the areas affected by bombing.'

'Thank you. I'll do that and then start thinking about what small part I can play in helping the war effort. May I go to bed, Sir John? I'm very tired.'

'Of course, my dear. We'll chat further tomorrow.'

Esther walked into the kitchen the following morning and joyfully exchanged embraces with Cook, who seemed as pleased to see Esther as she was to be there. Together they prepared Sir John's breakfast which he downed quickly before departing for the Foreign Office.

'We'll talk again tonight, Esther,' he said as he dashed out of the door, leaving Esther's stomach churning over in knots for the rest of the day. What had she done wrong?

'No, no, nothing wrong at all,' Sir John reassured her later that evening. 'But, Esther, you can't spend the rest of your life looking after me. You need to be thinking about the future and when the war is over.'

'Oh,' she sighed, relieved.

She'd been thinking like that herself. Even though she'd been insulted by one or two people in the pre-internment panic, she was confident, from what Sir John and Cook had told her, that those attitudes had softened, and she'd be made welcome to at least carry out some voluntary work in support of the war effort. Cook had told her about the WVS refreshment points where folk who had either been bombed out or were returning from a night in a shelter could find a hot drink and a sandwich.

'I'm not sure what I want to do, Sir John. I do need time to think. Perhaps talk things over with my father and you. In the meantime, I'm going to offer my services to the WVS.'

'Of course, you realise it'll be dangerous, but nobody in our cities is ever entirely safe. If it'll help, you can do less hours here and spend some time with the WVS in the evenings and nighttimes. But please don't overstretch yourself. Like the rest of us, you need to stay fit and healthy to get through these terrible times.'

The next day, Esther contacted the WVS, and her offer of voluntary help was quickly accepted. That gave her the confidence to tackle the next part of her future: George. When she telephoned George's flat, his mother told her he was out, but she would ask him to call back as soon as he came in. George rang back at teatime, and Esther breathlessly answered the phone

'Esther? It's George.' He sounded nervous too!

'How are you, George?' she asked hesitantly.

'Alright...Look.' He sounded even more awkward now. 'I was terribly sorry to hear about your mother. Joe and I liked her a lot...' She heard him breathe out heavily, as if he'd just run a hundred yards, and then he said, less awkwardly, 'Anyway, when did you get back?'

'Yesterday night.' Esther smiled to herself.

She could almost feel George smiling on the other end of the line.

'When can I see you?' Now Esther felt like she'd just run the one hundred yards, as her heart thumped and her head felt giddy.

'I've got a bit of a job at the WVS tea stand at Liverpool Street Station. It starts every evening at seven, from Monday to Thursday, but...' She waited, holding her breath.

'Would it be OK to call in to see you there on Wednesday?'

Now the smile was all over her face, and her head really was swimming! 'Of course, it would.'

'Oh, that's good! Where's Mary, by the way?'

'Still on the Isle of Man. My father and brother are stuck there as well, but they'll all be back by Christmas.'

'Oh, right – that's good as well, then. Oh, it's smashing to hear from you, Esther. See you on Wednesday.'

'I can't wait for that, George.'

Esther put the phone down and grinned like she hadn't for ages. There *was* something between them. She knew that now from George's reaction, but had to remind herself that George was still in his eighteenth year and would be called up in 1941. But she'd wait, she decided firmly.

It was tiring for Esther, and dodging the bombs was frightening at times, but she felt it was the least she could do after what had been done for her. These sessions became regular. Fortunately, she wasn't on duty on December 29th when a massive air raid set the City alight. George, and, after a while, Joe too, when Mary returned, dropped by regularly, and the four of them resumed their nights out. The Blitz continued throughout the winter and, in the early spring, Joe was called up. Everything changed then. Bombings tailed off in May, and George still met up with Esther, and they had coffee together; but, once again, Esther was worried about becoming too attached to George. She knew he was due to follow Joe into the Army later in the summer, but neither spoke about the future because it was so uncertain. Nevertheless, there would come a time when George was called up, and what then? The Russians were in the war now, on the British side, and folk had become a bit more optimistic about the outcome – but everybody knew there was a long way to go before the Germans were beaten.

The time Esther dreaded came when Sir John's phone rang one early evening in August.

'It's George, Sir John. May I come round and see Esther?'

Three quarters of an hour later, Sir John's doorbell rang. Esther answered it and found George standing there, with a weak smile on his face.

Esther's hands flew to her mouth. 'Oh no! You've been called up, haven't you, George?'

'I knew it would happen, but I hoped the war would be over before they got round to you. Silly of me, I know.'

'I have to go, Esther. You wouldn't want me registering as a conscientious objector, would you?'

'Of course not.' Esther took George's hand and pulled him inside as Sir John joined them in the hallway.

Sir John briefly interrupted. 'Why don't you two go into the front room. I've some work to do in my study. I'll join you for a spot of supper later.'

Esther nodded gratefully and, still hand in hand, led George to the front room, where the couple sat side by side in silence, with their arms around each other. After a while, George explained what he thought might happen.

'We'll be in England for months, training and whatnot. I'll have leave, and I'll come to see you. We can spend time together, just like the old days. I doubt I'll be going overseas until next year at the earliest.'

'Have you heard from Joe?'

'I've had a few letters, and his mum and dad keep me up to date. I've no idea where he is. We're not allowed to say because of censorship.'

It helped Esther come to terms with what was happening when George told her it would be a while before he would be going overseas. Sir John joined them for tea and sandwiches, and the evening ended when George thanked him.

'You're a brave young man, George. Look after yourself and come back to us,' Sir John said as he accompanied them to the front door, and then tactfully melted away to leave them on their own again.

George and Esther stood on the front porch.

'Please don't get killed, George, but give the Nazis all you've got,' Esther said tearfully, as they embraced.

'You've got your own war to fight, Esther. You take care of yourself too,' George replied, peering down into her face. 'And God willing, we'll both come through it unscathed. Then it'll be a different story.'

Esther nodded and watched George all the way down the road until he was just a speck in the distance. Then she went to her room, lay face down on the bed and wept.

CHAPTER SEVEN

Great Britain and the Middle East
March 1942 - August 1943

The Corporal energetically rang the handbell to signal the start of another cold winter's day.

'Right, you lazy buggers, hands off cocks and on with socks.'

'Can't you think of anything else to say?' a tired voice asked with a yawn.

'Come to think of it, maybe I'll start using my bugle again.'

A collective groan echoed around the hut.

George swung his legs out of his bed and stood up. His eyes travelled around the barracks, giving a weary smile to one or two of his friends,then he grabbed his towel and wash bag and trudged out of the door into the dark, cold winter morning. Fortunately, it was only ten yards to the ablutions hut, and he gratefully went inside and began the morning ritual which had recently been extended on alternate days by the need to shave.

Eight months I've been here, George thought. When will we see some action? He had expected to be overseas by now but the only fighting happening was in North Africa or the Far East, so he was one of many young men just kicking his heels in England. Thoroughly bored, he wasn't even sure he wanted to fight, but he knew he would have to resolve the issue somehow when the time came. Still, at least he'd become an efficient soldier. George was smart on parade, could shoot straight, read maps, live off the land, knew how to drive vehicles of several sizes and kept his nose clean. The Company Sergeant Major acknowledged this by giving him his first stripe, so he was now Lance Corporal Aaron.

Baked beans were on the breakfast menu again,followed by toast and marmalade washed down with sweet, hot tea, giving the troops a nutritious start to the day. One thing that could be said about the lads was that they were physically fit. George was in very good shape and could easily cope with the physical side of being a soldier. He ought to handle it, he reasoned, but putting the boot into

Blackshirts was a lot different to facing up to enemy troops armed with weapons. In the East End riots, nobody had expected to get killed but in war, that seemed to be the whole purpose; kill the enemy even though that person might just be an ordinary teenager like he was. George knew that he had to resolve this before he was thrust into battle, undecided.

Morning parade was next and there was a lot of shouting and stamping of feet. Afterwards,for George and a few others, it was off to the range to learn how to handle a Bren gun. As the lads were all infantrymen, they were expected to be able to manage a variety of weapons, including the Bren, standing and prone, as well as the Lee Enfield .303 rifle and a Webley revolver.

'Blimey, I'm still shaking after that lot,' said Bert Davis to a grinning George as he made his way back for lunch with George and Steven Morgan. Bert was another East End boy, shorter and much skinnier than George, but the Army had developed a tough frame on him beneath his cheeky face, topped with curly blonde hair, since he'd joined the Infantry. Steven was tall and fair-haired with blue eyes. He spoke without an accent and had been educated as a day boy at a public school in Essex. He could have tried for officer training but wasn't interested.

'Thought it was great when they switched from bullseye targets to models of German soldiers. I shot a few Jerry heads off,' Bert boasted with a smile on his face.

'As long as we can still do that when they're shooting back,' Steven said with a smirk.

That thought kept them silent until they reached the dining hall. George asked the other two if they had girlfriends.

'Not yet,' declared Bert, 'but I've got my eye on one or two in Hackney. What about you, Steven?'

'Like you, really, but anyway, now's not the right time with the war going on. Remember that rush to get married just after the declaration? Quite a few of those girls are widows now. How about you, George? Got a sweetheart?'

'Well, sort of.'

'What do you mean, sort of? Come on, tell us.'

George talked for fifteen minutes about Esther. She was Jewish as well, he told them, and had come to England with her brother on the Kindertransport while her parents had been kept in Berlin.

'She and her family were interned on the Isle of Man for almost six months, and her mother died while they were there. When she got back, she was pretty miserable after her mother's death, but we got together whenever we could. We were going on nicely when I got called up. She and her friend, Mary, are volunteers with the WVS at a refreshment stand outside Liverpool Street Station. They dish out cups of char to anybody who wants one. People made homeless by the Blitz, Civil Defence staff and so on. Can be dangerous too. 'Two sugars, please, love,' as a bomb explodes a couple of hundred yards away.'

'Poor girl. It's all a bit much, I think,' Steven said. 'We bring them over here to escape persecution in their own countries, then lock them up.'

'That's true,' George agreed. 'It was the papers that called for them to be collared, and the government had too much on its plate to start a big row, so they just arrested the lot.'

'To be fair to the government,' Steven continued, 'they soon realised their mistake and began bringing them home pretty quickly. By all accounts, the Isle of Man was teeming with scientists, teachers, professors, doctors and so on. The kids got a better education there than they would have back in England.'

'That wouldn't have been difficult,' murmured George.

Steven ignored this, and Bert let out a cynical laugh of agreement.

'So now,' Steven went on, 'they're back here helping the war effort. I suppose the Isle of Man must be empty now.'

'Not according to Sir John, her employer, who says non-Jewish Germans and so on will be kept there till the end of the war,' explained George.

'Sort of like prisoners of war,' Bert said.

'Suppose so,' agreed George.

'How strong is the relationship, Corp?' Steven asked.

'Very, I think,' George replied, 'but it feels like it's on hold at the moment, what with the war and all that.'

'Is she good-looking?' Steven enquired with a harmless smirk.

George's face lit up. 'Bloody gorgeous.'

Bert asked George what he'd been up to before the war.

'My mate, Joe, and I worked for a journalist called Roger Martin. We called him the Guv, tracking a big IRA terrorist in London. We saw the Irishman link up with a suspicious-looking German, and by following the Kraut, we came to Esther, who was being blackmailed to get info from the man who employed her, Sir John Blum. He worked in the Foreign Office. The Nazi warned her that her parents back in Berlin were for the chop if she didn't come up with the goods.'

'Sounds dangerous, George. What happened next?' Steven asked.

George recounted the parents' rescue from Berlin, organised by the Guv and his friends and how, when the German realised the game was up, he tried to flee the country but was stopped by George and Joe, using their street-scrapping skills, as he tried to board a ship in Harwich.

'Sounds like you're well in there, George, but she could've been keen on Joe as well.'

'Course she could've,' George replied, 'but she kissed me on the lips, whereas he only got one on the cheek. So I knew...'

There was some ribald laughter at that, but the conversation ended there. All three were due to have instruction on motorcycles in case any of them were needed as messengers when they were at the front. George could sense that his friends were impressed with his pre-war adventures. What they didn't know was that he was full of self-doubt about his ability to perform in battle.

Winter turned into early spring, but there was still no sign of the three friends being posted abroad. That surprised them since the war was going so badly for the Allies. The Germans were on top in North Africa, the Japanese forces held sway in the Far East, and the Axis forces were treating the Mediterranean as their own private lake. Surely, they felt, they must be needed somewhere.

There was some optimism in Britain because the Russians were hitting back at the German Armies who had invaded the previous summer, and the Americans were now in the war. Britain was no longer alone.

The three friends became skilful soldiers. They mastered all the challenges asked of them, and each was rewarded with promotion. George was given an extra stripe and became Corporal Aaron, while the other two became Lance Corporals. One thing George understood was that he could help his mates with this soldiering business after his experience with the cadets.

One evening, the three of them were sipping the revolting watered-down beer that had become all you could get during the war. Sitting around a table in the NAAFI, Steven looked nervously at George and asked him:

'Did you get any anti-Jewish stuff thrown at you in the East End? Don't answer if you don't want to.'

'A lot before the war, mostly from Moseley's Blackshirts. But it didn't bother us because the Jews and other anti-Fascists in the East End outnumbered Moseley's boys. The men in black were always marching up and down shouting rubbish like 'Jews out' and so on. They were usually outnumbered by anti-Fascists and Jews. We roughed them up a bit with our boots and fists, but nobody got killed, and the coppers usually broke it all up. That's it. I'm tired. Off to bed. PT in the morning. Want to be at my best. But I don't want to look too keen in case they make me an officer.' George laughed. 'That wouldn't do at all. I might even have to fight.'

A couple of hours of PT, then brushing up their lorry driving skills, took up most of the day. At half past five, it was back to the NAAFI for another wind-inducing tea, before settling down to more under-strength beer. Bert was on good form telling tales of the Blitz in the East End.

'Whole streets that had stood for years were just piles of rubble. People I'd known since I was a nipper were either dead or horribly injured. Fires and smoke everywhere. It was awful.'

'I was lucky,' said Steven. 'There weren't too many bombs in our part of Essex, just the odd one dropped by a tail-end Charlie running back to Holland.'

'Any of your dads in the forces?' Bert asked.

'My dad volunteered for the Navy but was turned down,' Steven told them. 'He'd had TB when he was younger. What about yours, Bert?'

'Reserved occupation, docker.'

'And mine's too old,' George added.

'Do you think we'll ever take part in this war?' asked Bert.

'Oh yes,' said Steven. 'When we joined up, we were on the back foot. Now we're on the attack, the Russians are in, the Yanks are in, and the Allies are starting to win.'

'Can't say I'm looking forward much to that,' George said, looking down at his feet.

'Why not, George?' asked Bert. 'You're built like a brick shithouse, and you're as fit as hell and brave as a lion. What's to be afraid of?'

'Someone on the other side who's the same as me,' George replied ruefully.

The other two could see the way the conversation was going and didn't like it.

'Last time I was on leave, I met some lads from Durham,' Bert told them. 'They've been in since 1939, and all they've done so far is traipse about the country transporting anti-aircraft guns and firing them at the Jerries.'

'That would suit me fine,' said George.

George soon had his wish. He and his pals and half a dozen others were transferred to Ipswich, where they lit up the sky and fired anti-aircraft shells at the Germans. Though the Blitz was officially over, the Luftwaffe still mounted periodic raids in different parts of the country. As far as they knew, none of them ever hit an enemy bomber, and most of their time was spent chatting, playing cards or keeping fit under George's direction. An officer was nominally in charge, but he only visited them now and again, and they were usually left to their own devices. They took weekend leave once every three weeks, and George usually went to see Esther. But it wasn't like the old days. Joe had been posted abroad, and George and Esther sipped coffee and drank beer, happy to be together - and yet anxious too. It was unspoken, but they were waiting for the war to end, and until then... Then he was back in camp.

There was more training and honing of skills. George, Steven and Bert speculated about whether they would soon be sent into battle. They knew something was up when the Commanding Officer turned up and stepped forward to inspect, and then address them when the square-bashing was finished. He first showered them with compliments, congratulated them on working so hard, and told them they were well on the way to being the finest infantry unit in the Army. Then he thanked them for their patience, recognising that they were desperate to get at the Nazis. Next, he promised them that it wouldn't be too long before they got their chance and, with that in mind, they would be taken to the Brecon Beacons at the weekend for a seven-day Battle School.

A loud murmur passed through the ranks. The CSM shouted for silence. Quiet returned, and the men were dismissed.

'What are the Brecon Beacons?' Bert asked.

'A range of mountains in South Wales,' Steven told him.

'Will it be cold?' wondered Bert.

'Fucking freezing,' George said with a sneaky grin.

A convoy of Army trucks left the Suffolk barracks soon after dawn the following Saturday. Most of the trucks were full of tired-looking men, though one or two contained supplies. They were told they'd be stopping en route for lunch and a pee, and the overall journey would take between six and eight hours. Steven, who knew a bit about geography, gave a sort of guided tour as the journey progressed. He pointed out Cambridge and then Coventry, which he informed them was an important manufacturing centre that had been heavily bombed during the Blitz. As they passed Ross-on-Wye and approached Wales, one or two men laughingly asked if they could get out and return to Suffolk as they'd forgotten their passports. Abergavenny, with the Sugar Loaf towering over it, looked a pretty town, but Merthyr Tydfil didn't. Its steelworks were belching out smoke which had turned the local houses orange.

It was pitch dark by the time they reached Brecon. They couldn't glimpse much of it but didn't see any damaged buildings, so the Luftwaffe must not have visited Brecon. As they headed towards the mountains, they could make out dark shapes looming above them. The trucks stopped at Dering Lines, Battle School HQ, a large tented village with several wooden huts nearby. The men were told they'd be sleeping in a barracks tonight, but after that, they'd be under canvas. Beds were allocated, and a hot meal was served in the mess hall. Then sleep.

Bright sunshine greeted them the next morning, but George forecasted rain later, although where he got that information from was anybody's guess.

After breakfast, the CSM appeared and informed them that the day's activity would be to climb Pen Y Fan – at two and a half thousand feet, the highest mountain in South Wales – in full kit. Cold sunshine saw them off but, halfway up the mountain, it clouded over, and the rain started pouring down in sheets. Some of the men shouted obscenities, but George, Steven and Bert plodded on, while the only words spoken were from George, who reminded them about his earlier weather forecast.

All three reached the peak without incident, and they set off on their return journey, passing cursing men lying by the side of the footpath, still some way short of the top. After washing and changing, they found their tent and set off for a meal. They ate and chatted for over an hour, then made their way to the NAAFI. It was nearly dark, but exhausted men were still making their way back from the mountain. Over a pint, they heard that one man had fallen and broken his leg while two others had collapsed from exhaustion.

The next day, it was time to practice survival. Instructions on how to handle their bivouacs were followed by a brief guide to the surrounding mountains using their maps. They were each given a minimum of dehydrated food and some map references and were told to report back twenty-four hours later. If they got hungry, they were told, live off the land.

George, Bert and Steven coped well and got back within an hour of one another. It had rained for twenty-four hours. After all the soldiers had reported in, two were reported missing, absent without leave. The Army showed sufficient concern by despatching the Brecon Beacons Mountain Rescue team to find them and, if necessary, rescue them. By midday, one had been located fast asleep in his bivouac, propped up against a wall. There was no news and a lot of concern for the other, but he was eventually found and arrested by the Military Police at Swansea High Street Station, on his way home. His journey was diverted to the Military Glasshouse at Shepton Mallet.

Mercifully, the next day was reserved for classroom stuff. The morning was set aside for lectures on tactics and the afternoon for battlefield First Aid training. After that followed two days of exercises. The first was during the day and involved attacking enemy positions, armed with machine guns., although blank ammunition was used, of course. The second was a night exercise and included making an improvised stretcher, silent killing using bayonets and knives, and attacking pillboxes and machine gun nests with grenades. Once again, blank ammunition was used so there were no mishaps.

The week ended with an exhaustive recap of all that they had learned. Next time, they were told, it would be for real. Their posting was announced for seven days hence but they were not told where they were going. On return to the barracks in Suffolk, they would be issued with railway travel warrants to Glasgow, where they would report at 2200 hours on Monday week. Until then, they were on leave.

George spent a good deal of time with his parents, helping his father when he needed it, and visited Joe's mother and father only to find that his best friend had already been posted abroad, but nobody knew where. George managed a few hours with Esther and Mary, who were still helping at the WVS stand at Liverpool Street. Esther told him that she was keen to do more to help the country that had rescued her from the Nazis. She'd spoken to Sir John about this, and he'd agreed that she should try something different, and so the Foreign Office diplomat had arranged for both girls to take driving lessons to give them more appeal when they went looking for a job. Both would have liked to become nurses, but neither was old enough. He wished he could have spent more time with Esther alone, but Mary always seemed to be there. Yet maybe that was a good thing – stopped them becoming too close, in case....

One night in the family flat, George spoke to his father about his uncertainties concerning the war. He made it clear that he wasn't a coward and that he believed that probably most, if not all soldiers, carried some degree of fear into battle. He just wasn't sure why he was fighting. His father listened sympathetically. He, like Joe's father, Charlie, was a member of the Communist Party of Great Britain. This shared passion had brought first the fathers, and then their sons, closer together.

'You need a reason to fight,' Isaac told him. 'In the previous war, thirty or so years ago, Britain had become involved, along with France, without motive.

'I thought at first it was just a squabble between Germany and Austria-Hungary on the one side and Russia and Serbia on the other,' Isaac began. 'Before you knew it, half the world was mobilising, and four years later, twenty million people were dead, many of them innocent citizens. I refused to fight. I couldn't think of any good reason to kill Germans in France. But my country needed something from everyone, so I joined the medical corps and drove an ambulance in France.'

'So what's different now, Dad?' George asked.

'I'll come to that in a minute. Just think of the things that you and Joe have done. Before the war, you battled the Blackshirts and took on German agents and Irish terrorists in our own country. And lately, you've contributed to having some nasty looters arrested and locked up. Ask yourself what those three things have in common.'

George looked at his father, then down at the floor. He thought for several minutes, turned to his father, looked him in the eye and said, 'We were having a crack at people who were bad and doing things that were wrong. Apart from being Jewish, what did the Blackshirts have against us? What right did the Gestapo have to kidnap a young girl who had fled her own country because she was being persecuted? And how dare the Sergeant and his mates steal valuables and money from old folk who had been killed by a bomb?'

'Exactly;they were all bad people doing bad things so, without any regard for your own safety,you took them on.'

'I understand that. So what's the difference between the previous war and now? You didn't think you should be fighting the Germans then. Why should I feel any different?'

'Look, George. In the last war, the Germans were the bad guys but without any real reason. Sure, they'd done some pretty awful things in South West Africa, but no worse than we, the British, had done in India and other parts of our Empire. This war is different. You already know how the Nazis treated the Jews on Kristallnacht from your friend, Roger. Since the war started, things have got much worse. It started in Poland, where they murdered as many Jews as they could lay their hands on when they invaded in 1939. The rest they herded into ghettos. Then, after June 1941, when they marched into the Soviet Union, the soldiers were followed by special squads whose task was to kill every Jew they found. They shot them, hanged them, locked them into barns then set fire to the buildings. Men, women and children all died at their hands.'

'How do you know all this, Dad?'

'From Communist Party meetings, which I go to with Charlie. Take it from me, George, this is really happening. There are also unconfirmed rumours that they're clearing the Polish ghettos and transporting the people who live there to camps, where they're gassed on arrival, and then their corpses are burnt.'

George was horrified and sat in complete silence.

'You're right. Most of the men you'll be fighting against are just like you and Joe, caught up in a war they neither want nor understand but their orders come from a bunch of murderers who must be stopped at all costs even if it means that many young men will have to sacrifice their own lives. I don't expect you to suddenly change into a warmonger, George, but think about what I've told you. It may help you when you face the enemy.'

This was George's last evening at home. Earlier, he had called on Joe's parents and said goodbye to them. He'd already been to Hampstead to tell Sir John and Esther that he was being posted, but he didn't know where. Sadness never threatened to overcome them. Everyone, including George himself, thought that he would return and that, when he did, the war would probably be over, and they could all resume their normal lives.

George put a brave face on as he left the flat in the East End. On the bus to the station, he wondered if he would ever see any of them again despite the fake optimism of the previous day. The early morning darkness added to his morose feelings. He listed the people in his mind that he might never see again. It was still dark when he reached Euston. The station was packed with almost everyone in uniform - soldiers going to Scotland and sailors to Liverpool. Somehow or other, in amongst the throng, he managed to find Steven and Bert, and they grabbed seats together on the crowded train. Those not in the compartments sat in the corridors or leaned against the walls in the vestibules at the end of each carriage. Heaven knows where civilian passengers would find a seat.

The train pulled out of Euston and headed north. Sitting with his mates made George feel so much better, and he realised how much love and friendship would help them all get through this bloody war.

'Ever been to Scotland?' Bert asked Steven.

'No. Furthest north I've been is the Lake District for a family holiday. It was nice there, but it rained a lot.'

'How about you, George?' Bert continued. 'You been to Scotland?'

'No. We had our holidays in Southend. But I am much travelled. Scotland will be the third country I've visited after England and Wales.'

'Well, Corp,' another voice in the compartment interrupted, 'you'll be able to add other countries to your list when we start fighting. Any idea where we are going?'

'No,' George replied. 'But if I had to narrow it down, I'd say either the Far East or North Africa.'

'Hasn't the fighting nearly finished in North Africa?' asked Steven.

'It has, so I guess if that's where we end up, it'll not be too long before we're in Europe – Greece or Italy or somewhere,' George told them.

'I hope it's Europe, not the Far East,' Bert said. 'I don't fancy Burma. Nasty place.'

'What's wrong with Burma?' one of the other soldiers asked.

'It's got five things I can't stand: heat, rain, insects, snakes and Japs.'

Everybody in the compartment laughed with Bert then silence took over till they reached Crewe.

Half the train seemed to get out. Sailors bound for Liverpool's seats were taken by other sailors returning home for a spot of leave. The train set off again and passed through Warrington, Preston and Lancaster before reaching Oxenholme, where Steven pointed out various fells which were part of the Lake District. Carlisle was next, where, for some obscure reason, the train ground to a halt.

'The train will be delayed here for an hour and a half,' came an announcement over the loudspeaker. Everybody jumped out and joined a long queue at the refreshment buffet. The sandwiches were bully beef, as usual, and the tea was hot and wet. Nobody complained. Darkness swept in, and the whole compartment, and probably the entire train, was asleep within minutes.

'Glasgow in ten minutes!' a member of the railway staff walked up and down the train shouting, wakening the slumbering soldiers.

Struggling to their feet, George, Bert and Steven got hold of their kit and walked sluggishly to a large concourse area where a Sergeant was falling them in.

'Right, lads, there's lorries outside to take you to Greenock where the next stage of your holiday will begin. Fall in on the quayside, and Lieutenant Pearse will tell you what's next.'

Outside the station it was, as one of the railway staff told them, a typical Glasgow night: black, cold, wet and with prostitutes lining the station entrance. The twenty-five-mile trip took over an hour. They lined up on the quayside in the pouring rain. Lieutenant Pearse, a young, tall, dark-haired officer, told them that the ship tied up was the *Franconia* and would take them south, but he didn't know where. 'Get below decks, men, grab a hammock, then a meal from the mess before you turn in. We'll be sailing at dawn.'

'So,' George said, 'we're going south. Will we get there before the U-boats or the Atlantic storms get us?'

'We'd hardly be going north, would we?' Bert announced. 'There's nothing north of Scotland, is there?'

'Just the Arctic Circle,' Steven informed them, 'and the war hasn't spread there yet.'

George and the other soldiers were sorting out their hammocks and storing their gear when Lieutenant Pearse's voice came over the loudspeaker system.

'Welcome to the *SS Franconia,* men. In better days, this was a passenger liner. Now it's part of a convoy of four others, converted merchant ships and liners, transporting us to our theatre of war. Three destroyers will be accompanying us to keep us safe. The main threat is from German U-boats, but, after the horrors of the past three years, they're becoming easier to detect and fewer and fewer are sinking our ships. Surface raiders shouldn't bother us at all. All the big German battleships have either been sunk or are bottled up in Norwegian fjords. I can't tell you where we're going because I don't know myself, but when I know, you'll all know. I can tell you that we'll be at sea for about two months, perhaps a little more, but we will be making a couple of stops en route. When I've finished, make your way to the mess for something to eat, then turn in. A member of the ship's crew will be telling you about conduct on board the vessel and safety procedures when we're under way. We'll be casting off at dawn. The only other thing I can tell you is that, for the first few days, you'll all, including me, be seasick, but once you get your sea legs, you'll be OK. Good night, men.'

'Right,' said George, 'let's get some grub to throw up tomorrow,' with a good humour he was far from feeling.

Whatever faced him and his mates in the months to come, George was determined to remain cheerful, at least outwardly. None of them would make inroads on the enemy if they moaned all day long.

The supper was some kind of stew, and it was hot and filling. Nobody knew what was in it, and some of the troops made unflattering suggestions. Just to make absolutely sure that their bellies were full, jam roly poly was served, followed by mugs of tea.

The *Franconia* slipped her moorings at six in the morning, and, by the time they'd edged through the North Channel between Scotland and Northern Ireland, everyone, except the sailors on board, was being violently seasick. Although it was a dull day, visibility was reasonable, but nobody was in the mood to appreciate the Isle of Man as the troop ship passed it by. Most of the men stayed below and vomited, then cleared the floor up and threw up again. Some went on deck, where they spotted the remainder of the eight-ship convoy and were ill there instead. The threat from the U-boats never entered their heads.

Down into the Irish Sea, things got no better, and one or two of the troops even said that they hoped a German torpedo would bring an end to their misery. It picked up when they sailed into the Atlantic, but now the ever-present threat from beneath the surface was occupying their minds. Passing within striking distance of the great Nazi U-boat pens at Brest, St Nazaire and La Rochelle kept everyone's minds focussed on the sea, but the southern end of the Bay of Biscay unleashed a new horror, an Atlantic storm. A fresh bout of seasickness hit them but not as extreme as before, and, by the time the convoy had passed Cape Finisterre, the troops were settling down. The weather improved and daily exercise classes began, conducted by the unit's PTI.

Lieutenant Pearse's voice came over the tannoy again just as they were climbing into their hammocks one evening.

'I told you I would give you what information I had as soon as I got it,' he announced. 'Our destination is the Port of Suez in Egypt. When we get there, we'll get fresh orders. That's it. Good night, men.'

'Great,' said Bert. 'No snakes and Japs.'

'Just scorpions, mosquitos, sand, Italians and Nazis,' Steven replied with a snigger.

Each morning, the soldiers were dragged out of their hammocks to engage in some rigorous physical training. It was a bit like school, with lots of arms raising sideways at the same time as the legs jumped apart. Then variations were introduced, such as feet and arms moving forwards and backwards, clapping above the head. Then there were at least four different kinds of press-up, half a dozen different exercises to strengthen their abdominal and back muscles, running on the spot, running around the deck and skipping. Few soldiers had problems with co-ordination since they'd been perfecting their skills for more than a year back at camp. The further south the ship sailed, the warmer it became, and they soon found the sweat pouring off them at the end of these daily sessions.

It wasn't just PT. There were lectures on battle tactics, various forms of weapons training, including recognition of Nazi and Italian equipment, and what they could expect from enemy ordinance. Naturally, there were parades and drill. Everything possible was being done to stop the troops from getting bored.

Singlets and shorts were the accepted form of dress, but Lieutenant Pearse did tip off the men that they might consider covering their arms and legs when they went into battle. When asked why by one of the men, the Lieutenant tapped his nose with a finger. The *Franconia* pulled into Freetown Harbour, Sierra Leone, a well-sheltered inlet where fresh water and supplies would be taken on board. Shore leave was forbidden.

George was leaning on a deck rail, in the steaming temperature, watching natives scurrying along the quayside, carrying bottles, flasks, boxes, packing cases, and every kind of receptacle to fetch the supplies on board.

'Part of our Empire,' Steven's voice whispered into his ear.

'What is?' asked George.

'Sierra Leone,' replied Steven. 'Those natives live to serve the British flag.'

'I gather from your tone that you're not a great fan of the Empire,' George commented.

'I'm not,' Steven said with surprising conviction. 'We're ruling their country when they should be doing it themselves. The bigger countries, especially India, want their own independence, and I'm certain they'll get it after the war.'

'But they're on our side,' George protested.

'That's fine,' Steven replied, 'but they should be fighting with us as allies, not for us as subjects.'

'Okay,' said George. 'But what's the big deal? Why do we need colonies?'

'Resources, my dear Corporal. People, as you can see, and food, minerals and precious metals, sometimes even whole colonies, can be strategically important. Take India, for example. It's a huge country with the potential to be able to recruit hundreds of thousands of fighting men. If the Japanese invaded, they'd soon be thrown back into the Burmese jungle.'

'If these minerals and metals are so important, why don't they sell them to us and spend it on their country?' George asked.

'Good question,but they're not theirs to sell. They're ours, and we take all the profits out of the sales. We return a modest amount of the profits to the country to keep them alive, but most we spend ourselves.'

'You seem to know an awful lot about this sort of thing, Steven,' George said. 'Where did you get these ideas from?'

'I'm a Communist,' he told George ' A member of the Communist Party of Great Britain.'

'So are my father and my mate Joe's father, Charlie.'

'Really. You should join.'

George looked unconvinced.

'Not just yet. I've got a lot of thinking to do.'

Bert appeared.

'What are you two talking about?' he asked.

'Politics,' Steven replied.

'Oh!' Bert said. 'Not my cup of tea. I'm here to fight, not argue. We had enough politics in the East End before the war with Moseley and his crowd. '

By the time the *Franconia* had reached Freetown, the sun was high in the sky each morning, and it was baking hot. In the harbour, there were no refreshing breezes to cool their baking bodies. Although the daily exercise programme was scaled down, even doing lesser exercises was hard work, and it wasn't all that unusual for men to keel over during a session. Sunbathing became very popular, and the pale skins of the British *tommies* were either slowly heated to a golden brown or burnt to a ripe tomato colour, depending on how much common sense each soldier displayed. Lieutenant Pearse repeated that he still didn't know the final destination of the unit, but wherever it was, it was bound to be hot. Card playing became very popular, but some time each day was set aside for battle preparation, either through tactical talks or weapons training, as the men were introduced to the bazooka, two, and three-inch mortars, as well as knives and new types of handgun.

Taking into account the length of the voyage and the potential harm done to fighting men through poor diet, the Army made sure that the food was nutritious, tasty and plentiful. The ship continued its journey south, and soon the soldiers became aware of some sniggering amongst members of the crew. Steven found out that an embarrassing ceremony was planned for the 'landlubbers' who had not crossed the equator before. Such people were known unflatteringly as *Pollywogs* and had to pay some kind of forfeit to become initiates. In peacetime, Steven was told, ceremonies were long and, especially for the uninitiated, arduous. There wasn't much time or inclination for elaborate events in wartime, but some lip service was paid to the ancient tradition, which probably dated back to the eighteenth century or even before, so King Neptune put in a brief appearance and drenched the *Pollywogs,* who were dressed in either PT kit, their underwear, women's clothes or, in a few cases, nothing at all.

The threat from U-boats receded the further south they sailed. Since beginning to edge close to the African coast, there were frequent welcoming sights of planes from the Fleet Air Arm, which were based in nearby British colonies. One early morning, there was great excitement on board as soldiers shouted and pointed at the magnificent Table Mountain. The public address system announced a forty-eight-hour leave in Cape Town. A big cheer went up, and soon George, Steven and Bert joined the others on the quayside in Cape Town harbour.

'Is this another one of our colonies?' Bert asked Steven.

'It is, but we didn't have it all our own way when we seized it.'

'Oh, what happened then?' Bert asked.

'The Dutch were here as well, and they wanted a large piece of the cake. We fought a couple of wars against them, the Boer Wars.'

'What were the wars about?' asked George.

'Diamonds,' Steven replied, 'and control of the trade routes to India.'

'Who won?' asked Bert.

'The Boers won the first war and the British the second.'

'So another complete waste of time, money and lives,' George said.

Steven looked deeply into George's eyes and recognised a fellow traveller.

'Indeed, Corporal,' he agreed. 'Shall we have a good look around, down a few drinks and grab some food? Let's forget about politics and the war for a while.'

Cape Town was a beautiful city. It was the end of the South African summer, and autumn was approaching. The temperature was perfect, and the restaurants, bars and market stalls of the harbour were very busy.

'What lingo do they speak here?' Bert asked.

Steven replied, 'The English speak English, the Dutch speak a kind of Dutch called Afrikaans, and the natives speak their own languages, like Bantu.'

'There are a lot more natives than white people,' George observed. 'But I would guess that the whites live in the best houses and eat the best food and wear the best clothing.'

'You're right, Corp. The white people treat the natives like shit.'

'How do you know, Steven?'

'We had a South African teacher at school. He hated it here, so he left and brought his family to England. The whites rule everything. There are more and more separate toilets for the natives. They're not welcome in white restaurants and shops and must sit in their own seats on buses. See those beautiful houses?' Steven asked, pointing to several white buildings in the distance. 'That's where the whites live. The natives mow their colonists' lawns, clean their houses, sometimes cook their food, then at night go home to foul-smelling huts in the townships. It's a bloody disgrace.'

Despite the bad taste left in their mouths by seeing how the white settlers treated the native South Africans, George and Steven found Cape Town a pleasant enough diversion from the endless voyage. Bert also had a good time but seemed less troubled by what he saw around him. The *Franconia* left Cape Town and sailed around the Cape of Good Hope before turning north into the Indian Ocean. The Lieutenant told them that they would be stopping over in the Port of Suez in Egypt before transferring to another destination, where they would undertake further specialist training.

Rumours were soon confirmed by Lieutenant Pearse that the Germans and Italians had been defeated in North Africa, and that those who hadn't been captured had fled across the Mediterranean, which clarified where the next action would be – Europe. Exactly where and when wasn't yet clear, but it was obvious that Allied troops would be stepping onto European soil for the first time in three years.

Disembarkation in Suez, after endless days on board *Franconia,* came as a great relief to all the men, even though they knew that it brought them closer to that day when their courage, ability and preparedness would be tested in battle against Axis troops. Mental preparation was essential to George if he was to overcome his uncertainties, so he first cast his mind back to that long conversation with his father the evening before he left for Glasgow.

A twenty-four-hour leave gave them the chance to stretch their legs and wander around Suez. They were at the entrance to the great waterway that carried the name of the town they were now strolling through and which carried large and small ships to and from the Mediterranean. Most of the buildings were flat, one or two stories, and white. The finest of them, with their domes and tall towers, were the Mosques. Suez was teeming with men, mostly robed, and women with scarves around their heads. Livestock were everywhere – cows, horses, donkeys, goats and camels. It was fascinatingly different from anything the soldiers had seen before. And it was steaming hot and smelt, they guessed, of camels. Some animals had bells on, ringing almost in unison. There was an endless hum of chatter, and, from time to time, prayers could be heard escaping from the Mosques.

All too soon, it was time to leave, and trucks took them on another hot journey, this time to the Little Bitter Lake, where their specialist training would begin. The next day, after breakfast and the early morning parade, they sat in a vast, open area and listened to the man who now introduced himself as their Commander, Major General Kirkham. The General explained to them that, irrespective of their home regiments and battalions, they now formed an important part of the 50th Northumbrian Infantry, a vital component of the Allied Eighth Army under the leadership of the famous General Montgomery, the victor of El Alamein. Major General Kirkham told them that the 50th consisted of troops from all parts of Britain and some from the Empire. Many had already been tested in battle and emerged triumphant, while, for many others, this would be their initiation into the horrors of war. The General reminded them of the thoroughness of their training and how he was confident that all would be prepared for the challenges which lay ahead. Then he delivered the sting in the tail. The assembled troops would be a vital part of the largest air, sea and land invasion in history. The men would have the honour, he told them, of being the first Allied troops to set foot on European soil since the retreat from Dunkirk.

Initially, 160,000 troops would be landed on the Axis-held island of Sicily. Further landings would bring Allied numbers up to almost half a million, supported by six hundred tanks, fourteen thousand vehicles and nearly two thousand guns. Named *Operation Husky,* the invasion would be a joint operation with American soldiers under General Patton and backed up by the air forces and navies of both Allies. The objective, the General told them, was to kill, capture or throw into the sea every single Axis soldier on Sicily, before crossing the Straits of Messina and invading the Italian mainland.

Even cynics like George were impressed by the scale of what he was now part. He decided that the best way to handle his uncertainties was to acknowledge that he had been fully prepared for what lay ahead. He was a trained and efficient killer, and the people whose lives he now sought to end, if not bad themselves, represented a vile and evil regime, which he believed was planning to murder all European Jews. He believed his father. Neither did George wish to let down the others fighting with him, especially his friends, Steven and Bert and his absent mate, Joe. He said nothing to the others and readied himself for the final preparations for *Operation Husky.*

Most of the time, rehearsals were for what was likely to happen after the landings, but they were also transported to the Gulf of Aqaba to practise landing on beaches from small landing craft.

'I can't swim,' a panicky Bert announced. 'Can you two?'

'Hackney Baths,' George said.

'My school pool,' Steven added.

'So what'll happen to me?'

'The landing craft are flat-bottomed,' George told them. 'So we'll be jumping out in shallow water, as near to the beach as possible. You'll never be out of your depth, and if you do get into a spot of bother, we'll be there to help you.'

'Thanks. I feel better now.'

The landing craft were rapid, and the waters of the Gulf of Aqaba calm, so they soon mastered a swift escape onto the beaches.

'Perfect the exit, men. Stoop low, heads down. It might seem quite straightforward now, but under fire, coming in off a choppy Med will be very different,' they were told by instructors. Each craft accommodated about three dozen men. They followed orders about their crouching positions while live rounds were fired over their heads. What astonished the men most was the sight of Royal Engineers handling much larger landing craft carrying tanks, trucks, cars, motorcycles and field guns. The craft themselves dropped the soldiers off, then did a quick about-turn and returned to collect the next batch. In the real thing, they'd be fetching them from converted merchant ships which, like the landing craft, could be under heavy fire from the enemy. The men worked hard and were efficient in landings when they returned to the Little Bitter Lake where, in the Egyptian furnace, they practised everything: firing at towed targets, shooting from prone and standing positions using both rifles and Bren guns, silent killing, digging foxholes and rehearsing repeatedly the infantryman's attack instructions – down, crawl, observe, fire. Lieutenant Pearse briefed his unit and told them what to expect once they landed in Sicily. Even though he'd never been to Sicily himself, he'd familiarised himself with the island through various pamphlets, including the famous Baedeker German Guide to Italy, which had been translated into English and included a section on Sicily. NCOs were told to share these with the men.

Then, suddenly, after more than two months of intensive training, it was all over. Gathering their gear together, the infantrymen climbed aboard their transport to Alexandria, from where they would sail to Sicily. It was blazing hot and the height of the Northern Hemisphere summer. They were all quiet and nervous and spoke little on the journey. They scrambled onto the merchant ship, which would take them first to Malta, where they would rendezvous with other craft, and then to Sicily. The landing craft were all attached in full view to the side of the vessel, a reminder of the grim task that lay ahead. Once at sea, they were briefed by a Major who told them they would be landing on D + One, July 11th, 1943. Their target beach was Avola, which would already have been secured by the Durham Light Infantry in the vanguard of the attack. The Navy would have already demolished the Axis coastal defences. By the time the RAF and the US Army Air Force had finished bombing the island, there would not be a usable airfield left for enemy planes. US, British and Commonwealth Airborne troops would be dropped inland to secure vital positions, and gliders, towed from North Africa, would support them. George and the others were told that, once the beach at Avola was totally secured, they would proceed along the coast road and seize the important ports of Syracuse and Augusta before heading north to capture Catania. American troops, landing further west, would drive the Axis northwards and trap them in a pincer movement near Messina. It would be all over in a month.

As their part of the invasion fleet slipped quietly across the Mediterranean on a calm sea, many men wrote letters home, George, Steven and Bert amongst them. George wrote to his parents and to Esther. He told her how much he missed her but repeated his promise that he would be back and that they would enjoy the good times together again. They began to talk about the battles to come but not, of course, where they would be fought. Despite his cynicism and inner doubts, which he occasionally expressed to the others, George was seen as the leader of the trio. Each of them knew that a very small number of men would take fright and let the others down. They were desperate to avoid it being them.

'How are you going to handle this, Corp?' Steven asked.

'I've been in the Army, like you blokes, for almost two years. I've practised every skill over and over again. After a lot of worry, I've decided that we should be fighting this war. I know most Germans are ordinary men like you and me. But the men at the top are bad bastards, so we have to whip their support from under them by destroying their soldiers, sailors and airmen. Then Hitler and the turds alongside him can't survive. I shall keep reminding myself that whenever I've come up against evil, I've not been afraid. Joe and I took on the Blackshirts before the war, stopped the Gestapo blackmailer from escaping back to Germany, and put paid to the blokes who were looting dead bodies. I wasn't afraid. I knew I was right. I believe I can take that same attitude into battle. And another thing. Whatever we say about the Army, they've trained us well, like a champion runner who's put in the miles and knows that, when he goes to the starting line, he's done all he can to get ready. He might not win. But he'll do the best he can.'

George could see that his friends, sitting in silence, were thinking about what he had said as their ship joined the others in the vast attack armada off Malta. Then they were off, but as they approached Sicily, a violent storm blew up. It grounded planes and made those in the vanguard sick as they approached the beach at Avola. Gliders broke loose from their towing plane. Some plunged into the sea, drowning dozens of airborne troops, while others crashed into the low bluffs at each end of Avola Beach, meaning more dead and injured. Some made it past the shoreline and headed north to seize and hold strategically important road crossings, railway and other bridges, and airfields. Many troops in the vanguard of the landing had battled the high winds and lashing rain and settled uncomfortably on the beach. The Lieutenant passed on details of the report sent back from the beach, which said that the beach had been largely undefended. The Italians, it seemed, stayed at home, having persuaded themselves that nobody would attempt a landing in such foul conditions. From afar, George and the others watched as the Navy pounded the Axis positions behind the beachheads. The noise was incredible, the flash of the huge guns terrifying, and the black smoke blotted out even the storm clouds. As they waited for their turn, the three of them chatted to a tough-looking Sergeant from the Durham Light Infantry.

'You scared, Sarge?' asked Bert.

'Always,' the Sergeant replied in a strong Geordie accent.

'You been in battle before then?' George asked.

'Belgium, France, the beaches of Dunkirk being shelled by the bleeding Luftwaffe.'

'How did you feel, you know, about the threats from the enemy?' asked Bert.

'Just like I do now, shit scared,' came the reply. 'If you're not frightened, you won't be alive tomorrow,' the Sergeant added.

CHAPTER EIGHT

London
December 1940 - Summer 1944

Mary had returned from the Isle of Man just before Christmas 1940 and resumed her duties looking after the two infant children of a wealthy financier and his wife, who lived in a big house in Kensington. Esther didn't say anything, but she felt that her friend had enjoyed spending evenings with George and Joe even though it was obvious that there would not be a romantic attachment with Joe. When first Joe, and then George, joined the Army, Esther suggested to Mary that she join her on the WVS stall. By the time the two began working together, the Blitz had ended, but there were still some air raids, though fewer than before. Despite this, people still needed something to eat and drink: night workers, Civil Defence staff and just passers-by. Mary enjoyed the work and was good at it, and they carried out their regular shifts together until the summer of 1943. George had put in an occasional appearance when home on leave, but a chat at Liverpool Street was all that happened, and then he was off again.

In August, soon after the invasion of Sicily had begun, Sir John gave Esther the devastating news that Joe had been killed in action at the tail end of the North African campaign. He didn't have any details except that George was not with him and that Joe had been posthumously decorated for gallantry. Esther received the news in stunned silence, and her face became ghostly white. 'Excuse me, Sir John,' she mumbled as she stood up and walked out of the lounge and climbed the stairs to her room, where she threw herself onto the bed and cried herself to sleep in her clothes. When she awoke in the morning, she remembered, with a start, the awful news that Sir John had given her the night before, and another wave of misery swept over her. Joe and George had been her guardian angels and had rescued her from the clutches of the Gestapo four years previously. Roger, their Guv., as they called him, had helped to bring her parents to safety from Berlin. A wave of misery overwhelmed her, but she pulled herself together, washed and dressed and made her way downstairs. Sir John was waiting for her in the kitchen and immediately, without saying a word, took her in his arms.

'It's no consolation Esther, but this kind of scene is being repeated in households throughout the country. To lose anyone is heartbreaking, but to lose one so young is really awful.'

'If it's okay with you, Sir John, I'll go to Cambridge at the weekend and tell Peter and my father. They loved Joe like a son.'

'Of course. George is fighting overseas and probably doesn't know. I've spoken to both sets of parents and offered my condolences.'

'And I'll tell Mary,' Esther continued. 'Although they weren't that close, they were good friends and enjoyed each other's company.'

Cook had been watching the tragic scene. 'I think you both need breakfast,' she said. 'Sit down, and I'll get it for you.'

Esther spent the day trying to drive the sadness out of her mind but couldn't. She carried out her duties almost mechanically and continued with her WVS work, told Mary about Joe, visited Cambridge and went to see Joe's and George's parents in the East End. She hated the war. It had killed her mother and now one of her closest friends. Her sorrow was slowly being replaced by a determination to do something more than serve snacks outside of Liverpool Street Station.

One evening she told Sir John about this and said she would like to do something a bit more useful. Mary felt the same. What she really wanted was to train to be a nurse, but she was too young for that. Sir John suggested that both girls learn to drive so they could perhaps get jobs as ambulance drivers and assistants. Esther was keen on this, although a little nervous, as she'd never been behind a steering wheel. Sir John used one of his contacts, and they began lessons one cold November morning in 1943.

At first, both girls were hopeless, but their instructor, an elderly lorry driver called Fred, who had been recommended to Sir John, was very patient and stayed calm, and whenever either of them mounted a kerb or drove into one of the many potholes littering London's streets as a consequence of the bombings, he merely quietly corrected them. Reversing was a challenge but by Christmas, they'd both mastered that too. Fred pronounced that they were now fit to be let loose on the roads, and Sir John made the necessary approaches for them to volunteer for the London Ambulance Service.

The Ambulance Service welcomed them, but they first had to undergo a further extensive period of training before they could be given the responsibility for a vehicle. Walking from a bus stop to work in the dark evening, Esther and Mary were wondering what would be in store for them that night. There had been spasmodic air raids since the Blitz, and plenty of damage had resulted. Much of their time was spent waiting, sitting, and chatting to other shift members and to each other in the common room in LAAS Station 39 in Weymouth Mews, not far from Broadcasting House and the Oxford Street shops. More than eighty people were based there, though not all at one time. Most were women. Some were drivers only, others were escorts only, while some, like Esther and Mary, were both. In their relatively short time there, they had developed a reputation for being totally reliable both in timekeeping and the way they carried out their duties. Next to the station was the Dover Castle pub, where ambulance staff relaxed before or after work. Esther and Mary were hardly regulars, but it was sometimes a pleasant place to unwind. The girls stuck to soft drinks. Alcohol could affect their performances in the ambulance, they reasoned, although another reason for being teetotal was that the beer was so heavily watered down it would have been better to save money by drinking straight from the tap.

Station 39's area of responsibility was a rectangle bound by Oxford Street in the South, Edgware Road in the West, Marylebone Road in the North and Tottenham Court Road in the East. It was a densely populated area with many of London's great shops, hotels, restaurants, museums and art galleries within its boundaries. Some of these had already been heavily damaged in the Blitz, but all were operational now, if not fully. Lyons Corner House in the extreme South East of Station 39's area was a reminder of happier days for Esther and Mary, who remembered with great fondness those West End nights out with George and Joe.

As with any Civil Defence organisation, a hierarchy existed at Station 39. In charge was the Station Officer, who wore a uniform with one pip and three stripes. She was a very competent woman whose Deputy wore a uniform with three stripes only. Each shift had a Leader (2 stripes), and there were Leading Hands with a single stripe. Esther and Mary weren't sure what they did and didn't care since they didn't aspire to any of these positions. They just wanted to do their job properly and help to save lives. Pressure didn't really exist for the LAAS staff in late 1943, but they were reminded constantly that this could change at any moment should the Germans decide to mount another bombing campaign on London. Daily training kept them on their toes, and they were never bored because they were also responsible for their own basic maintenance and checked oil, water, fuel and lights before the start of each shift. The ambulances themselves were kept in garages in Weymouth Mews. A few were purpose-built vehicles, but most were saloon cars with a large box attached. Blankets and stretchers were carried in the box together with basic first aid equipment. Training reminded them of basic skills and judgements: how to extinguish incendiaries, how to administer first aid, and whether to take an injured person to hospital or have them treated at one of the numerous first aid posts dotted around the capital. They had the tricky task of identifying the walking wounded, to decide who needed an ambulance, who required only to be transported by car or, in the case of large numbers, Green Line buses, some of which had been requisitioned for the duration of the war. The LAAS was ready, but for what?

June the thirteenth turned out to be a memorable day, for all the wrong reasons, for the London Auxiliary Ambulance Service. Until that time, Esther, Mary and all the other part-time volunteers had been kept fairly busy. The Luftwaffe had returned the previous December with a series of small-scale raids, one of which had dropped its bombs on a school in Catford and killed six teachers and thirty-eight children. From January 1944 onwards, the German flyers made a number of low-key night attacks, preceded by pathfinders who dropped flares to light the way for the bombers, many of which dropped incendiaries. Continuing until the spring, these assaults did plenty of damage and made demands on the ambulance service but were nowhere near as severe as the mayhem caused by the Blitz three years earlier.

All went quiet at the end of April. The newspapers speculated that the Germans were running out of planes or that the Luftwaffe was concentrating its efforts on the Eastern Front, where the Russians were taking big steps and driving the German Army back towards their own homeland. Or perhaps they were saving themselves for the Allied invasion of France, which everyone expected to start very soon. But the real reason was that Hitler had an alternative. East Enders were mostly sound asleep as the clock ticked towards 4.30 on the morning of Tuesday, June 13th. Early risers may have heard what they later described as a loud noise or, if they looked up, seen something with flames shooting out of its rear or even been stunned by the sudden silence followed, seconds later, by an enormous explosion. The V1 flying bomb, which soon became known as the *Doodlebug* or the *Buzz Bomb,* had arrived. That first bomb hit a railway bridge in Mile End, north of the river and firmly located in London's tragic East End. Six people were killed, nine seriously injured, and two hundred made homeless. Esther, Mary and other Weymouth Mews staff rushed to the scene even though it was well outside their area.

'What are we doing here?' Mary asked. 'It's outside our patch.'

'Evidently, it's a new type of bomb. There's crews from all over London. We need to see how dangerous it is.'

'Looks very dangerous to me. Look at all those wrecked houses. How many bombs did that, Esther?'

'Just one.'

CHAPTER NINE

Sicily July-August 1943

Less than twenty-four hours later, George sat in a landing craft, ready to land on a European beach. The sunny, warm weather had returned, but so had the Axis defenders, mostly Italians who had taken up threatening, elevated positions at either end of the beach. George crouched forward, his head between his knees as murderous enemy machine-gun fire spewed from nests above the beachhead.

The Italian air force and Luftwaffe attacked the landing craft as they approached Avola Beach. One Private in George's craft looked up to see what was happening and took a round between his eyes and slumped forward dead. George saw this as well as another craft take a direct hit and sink, well out from the shore, taking thirty-six men with it. More casualties resulted from a bullseye on one of the waiting ships. German fighters, Me 109s, used their guns to kill and injure dozens of troops desperately sheltering on the beach. Spitfires and Hurricanes quickly made the skies safe, and then attention switched to the area away from the beaches where an unending hail of fire was peppering the Durham soldiers, some of whom had been pinned down for almost twenty hours, lying on the sand. The constant rat-a-tat of the enemy machine guns instilled more fear into George, who was chewing his bottom lip and whose eyes were bulging with terror. His mates were the same, but he knew they must not let this distract from their main task of securing the beachhead or they would soon be thrown back into the sea, or dead.

George and the others scrambled out of their craft under heavy fire. The sea was a myriad of splashes as enemy rounds hit the water. There was a constant crescendo of rapid machine-gun chatter from the Italians, seemingly safely ensconced in bunkers and nests on cliffs at either end of the beach. The enemy had quite an arsenal. In addition to machine guns and rifles, there seemed to be a number of field guns dropping shells onto the beach and into the sea. A thought flashed through George's mind. This beach was probably a beautiful, sandy paradise in better times. Now it was just a pocked-marked hole-strewn killing field. Allied troops were running up the beach, friends and colleagues were dropping, some dead, some mortally wounded, and others injured, who would be patched up and live to fight another day. Three bullets pierced the helmet of a man next to George, and he was dead before he hit the ground. Next, he saw a soldier he vaguely knew take a round in the throat and quickly perish. Others were shot in the face, lost ears, or had kneecaps and ankle joints blown off as the interminably murderous fire from the enemy's machine guns continued. Flabbergasted, he looked in horror as one of his men lay screaming on the sand, desperately trying to push his innards back into his stomach. He rushed to help, but the soldier died even before he got to him, leaving George on his knees beside the dead comrade, hands wet with blood and face wet with tears, cursing this 'bloody, bloody war!' Such was the bedlam and din created by the murderous defensive fire, several times George felt as though he had been hit, but each time he checked, signs of wounding couldn't be found. Though he was terrified, George knew that if he let fear overcome him, he wouldn't be able to defend himself and would most likely be killed or badly injured.

None of the infantrymen had time to admire the beach. Now it was a mass of men and equipment with machine gun fire punctuating the frantic efforts to bring tanks, field guns, armoured cars, food, tents and ammunition to safe storage. George had to make sure he concentrated on the tasks in hand and not be distracted by the jaw-dropping spectacle of a dozen or so huge landing craft delivering as many as a dozen tanks, several trucks, armoured cars and men to the battle zone. He and his comrades worked frantically to bring order to the chaos, egged on by a very demanding Beach Master. Sappers had made safe the mines, destroyed various other obstacles, including tank traps and dismantled the barbed wire. But the beautiful sand was soft, great for holiday sunbathing but useless to transport tanks, trucks and other vehicles. Many of the tanks had what appeared to be wooden and metal fencing strapped to their front above the guns. These were quickly rolled out, providing a firm pathway which allowed the huge vehicles to proceed smoothly up the beach.

George spotted Steven and Bert lying in the sand, close to tears and holding their breath until the endless crescendo of fire stopped. But it didn't. The deafening noise from the enemy ordinance, Allied ships' guns blasting away at the interior of the island, the British soldiers shooting from their positions and, first from Axis planes, and later Spitfires and Hurricanes, combined to create an endless, deafening sound which George thought might damage his eardrums.

'All right, lads?' George shouted above the din.

'Bloody hell. I never thought it'd be like this,' Bert yelled back. 'This bloody noise!'

'And the body parts, the corpses and the blood,' added Steven. 'Christ! This is like hell on earth!'

The troops on the beach had to keep their wits about them as machine gun fire threatened throughout their landings and the establishment of the beachhead. The Italians seemed only to have two machine guns, which meant there was a brief respite as empty magazines were changed. The Italians also fired mortars onto the beach, and there was evidence of a number of soldiers firing traditional rifles at the Infantry. George and the others flung themselves onto their stomachs from time to time and fired towards the cliffs but without much hope of actually hitting anyone. Resistance to the invaders, strong at first, soon petered out, and, unfortunately for the Italians, the cliffs were difficult to defend. Although these were at either end – pretty high at the northern part – the central area was relatively flat, and just behind the sand, there was a heavily wooded area. While George and the others were lying flat on the beach trying to avoid being killed, the Durhams were taking advantage of the weak topography of the beach for the defenders by moving through the woods to approach and kill or capture them from behind and to the side of the enemy positions. Before long, there was a welcome sight of about three dozen Italian soldiers being marched towards the sea accompanied by those of the Durham Light Infantry who had silenced their guns. Several landing craft appeared, and the Italians were loaded on before being transferred to one of the waiting ships, which would take them to Prisoner of War camps in North Africa.

'Good riddance to bad rubbish,' Bert shouted as the sheepish-looking enemy soldiers shuffled by.

George and Steven gave a half-hearted laugh, but all the troops were exhausted. Their mouths were as dry as a bone as they gratefully and greedily gulped down water. They'd been shelled, fired on from the air and land and spent most of the day fetching, lifting, carrying and dodging bullets. The Durham Light Infantry were even worse off. They'd landed twenty-four hours earlier in appalling weather and then had to get rid of the Italian defenders. One battalion of that regiment was stood down while the other prepared to move north. George and the others had been so busy that they hadn't had time to feel afraid once the action became really intense and had scarcely spoken a word at all while being totally occupied by their essential jobs. They'd hardly fired a killing shot, but at least their constant rifle and Bren gunfire had kept the defenders fully occupied. Their training was serving them well. As they settled down for the night, they tried to recall their feelings as they crouched in the landing craft approaching Avola Beach as tracer fire created a crescendo of noise as it struck the craft. Or when they lay prone on the beach as the never-ending machine gunfire from land and air sent thousands of tiny handfuls of sand flying about in the air, with many landing on their uniforms and their helmets. But they could remember little about it. Totally focused on what lay ahead, George and the other soldiers fell into a deep sleep knowing that they had helped to secure a foothold on enemy territory for the first time since 1940.

Lieutenant Pearse briefed them the following morning. It was baking hot, even shortly after nine. He congratulated them on helping to secure the beachhead.

'The Americans are making slow progress on the Eastern side of the island, but the going is tough.'

'No wonder,' a voice shouted,' they're fighting Germans whereas we only had to face up to Italians.'

There was loud, prolonged booing which soon died down, and then the same voice shouted, 'But they're only Americans.' Laughter and cheers.

Pearse tried to conceal a smile but failed. 'All right. Settle down. The idea is for us to take the ports of Syracuse, Augusta and Catania, then link up with the Americans, force the Italians to surrender and kick the Nazis into the sea.'

'Sounds simple, sir,' a Sergeant shouted.

'It won't be,' Pearse replied. 'But, if you're all at your best, we'll flatten the bastards.'

A loud cheer went up.

'We're setting off at eleven hundred hours. There's not much transport so you'll have to walk.'

A loud moan went up, but Pearse's motivation was working.

The troops prepared to leave. Certain items were taken by the limited amount of transport available, weapons like grenades, mortars, and bazookas alongside tents, cooking equipment, food, medical supplies and the like. George and the other members of the company carried their own rifles, with bayonets fixed, personal clothing and bivouac sheets. George had a .45 calibre Webley pistol with ammunition and a commando knife. Field guns were part of the procession that left Avola beach, and there were four Sherman tanks as well as lorries transporting essential supplies. For an hour, they walked in silence. George, Bert and Steven wore long trousers, but plenty of other soldiers wore shorts. Steven had warned them about insect bites, especially mosquitoes, and suggested that they kept their legs covered.

'I'm sweating like a pig,' Bert exclaimed suddenly, breaking the silence.

'You smell like one, too,' George replied.

'I can feel moisture running down the front and back of my torso, and my underpants are ringing wet,' Steven announced.

'You know,' George suggested, 'that could be a useful battle tactic. When the Jerries smell us approaching, they'll be horrified by the stench and beat a hasty retreat.'

'Germans sweat as well, Corporal,' Steven said. 'One thing I am pleased about is that I chose to wear trousers instead of shorts. It keeps the number of these mosquito bites down even if it won't keep the Jerries off me.'

Then came some good news.

'Syracuse is ours,' a Sergeant told them. 'We'll billet there and then push on to Augusta tomorrow.'

'They seem to like us,' Bert said as the men slogged their way wearily into Syracuse. Cheering and waving and displaying the Italian tricolour, the inhabitants plied the troops with oranges, olives and wine. Their relief in greeting the Allies was almost as great as hearing that their own army was in retreat. The Mayor of Syracuse addressed the Allied troops, welcomed them to Sicily and urged them to boot the Germans and Italian Fascists into the sea so that they could have their island back.

'And hand it back to the Mafia,' Steven smirked.

Before they kipped down for the night, the Sergeant told them that Augusta was in Allied hands as
well.

'Will we ever see action?' wondered Steven aloud.

'We've seen plenty on that bloody beach,' Bert complained.

'You're right. I wouldn't want to spend too many days pinned down like that,' George said. 'You remember I was always going on about what a waste war is and how we shouldn't be fighting. Then I explained to you why my dad told me it was important to resist Hitler?'

'What of it?' Bert asked.

'Well, he's my dad, and I took what he said to be the truth. So I got on with it, even though we seemed to be stuck in Suffolk forever. Now I know why we were held back for so long. We did so much training we behaved like robots on that beach. All that stuff back home seemed pretty boring at times, but I'm glad I did it. It meant I didn't have to think at all.'

'Anyhow, Bert, in answer to your question,' George went on, 'I'm sure we'll see plenty of action. And, from what some of the Durham lads told me, it'll be a lot tougher scrapping with the Germans.'

Despite the cloying night heat and the incessant noise of insects, they soon fell into a deep sleep, disturbed only by more guard duty. As they slumbered, a disaster was unfolding forty miles to the north of them.

Lieutenant Pearse briefed them in the morning.

'A platoon of elite Allied paratroops, the Red Berets, has attacked the bridge over the Gornalunga River at Primosole, a little to the south of Catania. Drop and landing zones for the supporting gliders were missed. The Germans, recognising the strategic importance of the bridge, had flown in members of the elite First Parachute Division from France. We're on our way to relieve our men.'

By the time George's unit trudged into Augusta, where they received another enthusiastic welcome from the population, the full extent of the catastrophe was coming to light. The Red Berets had seized the bridge, but the Germans had counter-attacked and retaken the north side, blocking the route to Catania, while the Red Berets hung on to the south end. The pressure on the Allies was mounting.

The Germans were heavily armoured and well dug in. Shifting them wasn't going to be easy. Failure to capture the bridge would throw the whole of the Allied timetable for seizing Sicily into confusion. Lieutenant Pearse provided an update first thing the next morning.

'The Red Berets are hanging on to the south end of the Primosole Bridge for grim life. The very best of the German troops are attacking them. These Germans have fought with great distinction and courage in Poland, the Low Countries, France, Russia, North Africa, and heaven knows where else. At the moment, they outnumber our boys. An eighty-eight mm field gun, one of the deadliest and most effective pieces of ordnance in the German armoury, has been fetched to the bridge from the troops on the Catania plain. We need to relieve the paras who, not to put too fine a point on it, are knackered. They've seen plenty of action already. You are fresh troops, more or less untried in battle, but you've been well trained, worked very hard, and I know you'll not let the side down. Another battalion of Durhams, not the one in the vanguard of storming Avola Beach, is behind us, and heading north as we speak. They should be in good shape too. Our job is to get to the bridge as quickly as possible, link up with the DLI, throw the bloody Germans off the north side of the bridge and send them packing. The bridge is not rigged to blow up as soon as we step on it. It was, but the Red Berets dismantled the charges before the krauts had a chance to press the plunger. While we're sitting here, thinking about attacking a small group of tough Germans at the bridge, one of history's greatest battles is taking place in Russia. Over one and a half million men and ten thousand tanks are facing each other along an enormous front. And because we're here in Sicily, Hitler has had to divert troops from Russia to face the Allies. That's how important this campaign is. We have to take Sicily, and that bloody bridge is holding us up.'

George listened to Pearse, and he knew that he, and the other troops, had to win this battle. It wouldn't be like the beach landing, he thought, with bullets and bombs striking all over the shop. Anybody killed or injured there was unlucky. This, George reminded himself, would be fighting man-to-man to death with the enemy. A shiver of apprehension passed through him. Pearse was right. They were all well trained to carry out this mission successfully, but for George at least, the doubts remained.

A race against time for George's fellow soldiers faced them. Not only would securing the bridge open up the route to Messina and trap the Germans in the north-east corner of Sicily, but, even more important, at that moment, it seemed, they'd be helping to save the lives of those hanging on to the bridge. Blue sky was above them, with not a cloud to be seen, no wind to cool them from the blazing sun, flies and mosquitoes in their thousands to trouble them, dysentery, tiredness after the previous day's march from Syracuse; none of these were excuses not to put every ounce of energy into getting to the Primosole Bridge in double-quick time, though.

'You afraid, Corporal?' Steven asked George as they marched along.

'Of course, a bit, quite a bit, I suppose. It helps to know that being a soldier in 1943 means helping to stop Hitler from taking over the world. I'm a Jew and he hates Jews, so I hate him. He's a bully, and I fuckin' hate bullies. He's had laws passed that prevent Jews from getting decent jobs, sometimes any job at all, going to cafés, cinemas, dance halls, swimming pools, from marrying whom they please, sitting in parks where they want to, and just living in their own homes. Some get sent to camps - who knows what happens to them there. The Nazis call themselves the National Socialist German Workers' Party, but they're neither socialist nor do they support the workers. No trade unions, no freedom of speech and no freedom of the press. Everything he does threatens our way of life. He wins, and we lose in a very big way. He's a total bastard. That's what motivates me.'

Steven and Bert looked at George in astonishment. They'd never heard him talk like this, although they knew he held certain strong views.

'Most Germans aren't like Hitler,' George continued. 'They didn't vote for him because he doesn't allow free elections. They're fighting because they love their country, and losing frightens them, just like us. It's not personal. Their job, and ours, is to kill the enemy before they kill us. And when we do kill them, we won't be thinking that's someone's husband, son, brother, father, lover. There'll be time for that after the war. None of us want to die. I love my parents, my mate Joe, and maybe I've got a girlfriend in Esther. But I won't be thinking of them when we get to the bridge. I'll be thinking, if we don't kill you, you'll kill us.'

'Do you think war is a good thing?' Steven asked.

'No,' George replied. 'Men, women and children get killed, towns and villages get destroyed, synagogues, churches and mosques get reduced to rubble. Places of work, factories, shops, offices, all get razed to the ground. Most wars are fought by ordinary men and women who are just following orders. Fighting happens because men, mostly older men, think it's a good idea. Let's grab land from the natives, let's steal their crops and their valuable minerals. The white man back in his comfy home gets rich, and the natives stay poor. Then some other country comes along and says we'd like a bit of that, so they declare war on them. The result of the previous war was twenty million dead, with another twenty-one million casualties. And what was it all for? Most of the world became poorer, and here we are again with another sodding conflict. Most wars are utterly pointless, the playthings of politicians. But this one's different. This bloke Hitler is a very bad person. We have to stop him.'

Silence followed. Only the crunching of the soldiers' boots and the incessant chirping of the crickets disturbed the peace apart, that is, from the men's curses as they swatted away the ever- present insects. Eight miles from the bridge, they pitched camp for the night. Pushing on when they were tired would have made no sense at all. Better to wait until the morning when they were refreshed, but recovery from the route march was easier said than done. Guns thundered in the distance, and flashes lit the darkening sky, reminding them that their compatriots were fighting for their lives just a short distance away. 'Hold on until morning, lads,' the troops said to themselves, thinking of the Red Berets as they slid into an uneasy sleep.

An early start was the order of the day, and, as they came within a couple of miles of the bridge, the din of battle became apparent, the noise of exploding shells and the rat-a-tat of machine gunfire. Smoke blotted out the early morning sun. The nearer they came, the noisier it became, the denser the smoke and the more throat-catching the stench. All of the troops had smelt gunfire before but nothing like this. Breathing almost became a problem. The Germans were incessantly attacking the Allies with machine guns and mortars as well as shells from the deadly eighty-eight mm field gun. Allied return fire came from Bren guns, rifles and mortars. George and the others crawled into position on their stomachs and shouted to make themselves heard.

'If the lads don't get over the bridge, we've had it,' George suggested. 'Presumably those three tanks,' George continued, pointing at the stationary vehicles in the middle of the bridge, 'are dead.'

'Quite right, Corporal,' Pearse said as he joined them. 'Probably the wretched eighty-eight got them. And there's two machine gun nests on their side which are causing havoc. We could be held up here for days. Get rid of the nests and the eighty-eight, and we could fight our way across the bridge.'

'By "we", sir, who do you mean?' asked George above the endless racket.

'The 50th, of course. It will still be a tough fight, but superiority in numbers should eventually see us through.' As Pearse finished speaking, a mortar shell exploded nearby, covering Steven in shrapnel, none of which seemed to penetrate his skin.

'Glad I didn't wear shorts,' he said again, letting out a huge sigh of relief. Another member of the company peeped over the edge of the slope leading down to the river and took one in the eye from a sniper. He was still alive but clearly only for a short time. Another round clipped the edge of Pearse's helmet. 'Saw that one, sir,' George shouted. 'Orange muzzle flash in the window of the top floor of the farmhouse.' Steven checked there was one in the spout, then turned his attention to the farmhouse. Within milliseconds of a second flash, Steven fired and watched as a German soldier toppled out of the window.

'Good shot, Morgan,' Pearse bawled, 'but there'll be others.' Steven nodded and cast his eye on not one but two farm buildings.

'Where are the paras, sir?' George asked.

'Gone back to Augusta. They're exhausted, and they've done their bit.'

Pearse took a close look at the German positions. They were well settled in on the north side of the bridge. Apart from the two buildings, there was an orchard, a vineyard and some stone walls behind which was a sunken track. The bridge itself, an impressive box steel structure, was miraculously intact.

'That bridge isn't going to be taken by some Boys Own paper heroics. Once the machine guns and eighty-eight are out of the way, it'll be a hell of a slog. Fancy knocking them out, Corporal?'

'No,' said George, 'but I'll give it a try. These two can come with me.' He pointed at Bert and Steven.

'And me,' added Pearse. 'We'll have to wait till dark.'

'How deep is the river, sir?' Steven asked.

'No idea,' Pearse replied, 'but shallow. OK for troops but no good for vehicles. The riverbed is soft and sandy.'

'What's that German tank doing in the middle of the bridge, sir?'

Pearse laughed. 'Resting in peace. The Paras got it with a bazooka. Why do you ask?'

'Thought it might provide cover,' Bert said.

'It would, as far as the middle of the bridge, but then where? No, we'll have to go via the river and approach from the side,' Pearse said.

A machine gun nest was located on either side of the road leading from the bridge north towards Catania. George and Steven were to pair, and Pearse would lead Bert to attack the nest on the seaward side of the road, with the other two focusing on the landward side. The rest of the 50th were getting some rest, having been told that the German machine guns and the field gun would be out of the picture soon so they should be prepared to attack the Germans at dawn. The four men grabbed some sleep, then awoke and prepared themselves for the mission. All four were to carry their rifles with bayonets fixed. Each had a Webley forty-five handgun. Additionally, George and Pearse carried vicious but highly effective commando knives. Both Bert and Steven had a satchel full of grenades and were armed with bazookas. A bombardment from the artillery behind them to distract the enemy was expressly forbidden by Pearse, who reminded them that lives had already been lost to friendly fire. So the night passed with sporadic firing from both sides and occasional mortar attacks from the Germans. Pearse's company remained intact with only that one early casualty. Stalemate ruled on both sides of the river as the four men made their way silently across it and up the shallow slope on the other side. About fifty yards separated them, but they could see each other moving stealthily in the dark. Before they set off, Pearse had spoken to them in a low voice.

'This is only a small mission, gentlemen, but it could lead to a rout of enemy forces. However, it's dangerous. Focus on one thing only, doing your job.'

George's heart was hammering in his chest, but he steeled himself to ignore it and focus on what he had to do.

Two German guards, looking sinister and threatening in their helmets, which resembled upside-down buckets, were lying in wait at the north end of the bridge. The moon was shining, and the cloudless night gave the guards the appearance of still shadows. They were doing their best to conceal themselves in some bushes adjacent to the road. George and Steven were on their hands and knees, crawling silently past the Germans. Other than insect noises, the night was silent, so the two lads had to move as quietly as they could across the wrecked fields, once the source of crops to feed hundreds of Sicilians, without attracting the guards' attention. This wasn't the time to examine the wreckage surrounding them. Killing Germans was all that mattered. Clear the krauts off the island, and the peasants could start to transform the killing fields back into pastures. Nor did Steven and George bother with the filth that had gathered on their uniforms from their stealthy approach across the soil and stones of the once green meadow. Undetected, they lay down on their stomachs just ten yards from the closer of the guards, with the other a road's width further away. Steven had already proved his worth as a sniper, and he now squinted along the barrel of his rifle with his right eye closed and his left lining up the sight of the weapon. He was sweating, but nothing was going to detract him from his job. He squeezed the trigger, and the bang and recoil of the rifle was followed less than a second later by the first of the guards falling sideways. George watched Steven, who slid back the bolt, ejected the shell, pushed another round into the spout and took out the second guard, who had no idea where it had come from. Both guards were dead or at least out of action. The German machine gunners now unleashed their murderous fire towards the bulk of the Allied soldiers who were trying to sleep. They were well dug in and unharmed, but the Germans were distracted long enough to miss George and Steven and the Lieutenant and Bert as they moved towards the German positions. The noise of firing masked the ping of hand grenades as George threw two into the nest, which was surrounded by sandbags. Two big explosions were followed by screams as the German machine gunners took the full force of the grenades. George gasped wide-eyed as the gunner had his head blown off by the blast while the second, smaller bomb rolled under the soldier feeding the ammunition belt into the weapon, and he lost both legs. Neither of them took much notice of two similar explosions from the other enemy nest. George had no time to think about the fate of the two enemy soldiers or he'd soon be joining them, maimed or dead. The third German was so stunned he didn't even spot George jump into their position and cut his throat. Steven quickly joined him, and their only disappointment was that the destroyed machine gun was now useless. George spotted the first dead German whose head was still in his helmet though no longer attached to the rest of his body.

'Blimey, Steven, his helmet strap must have been tied extra tight.' He looked at his hands and battle dress top, both saturated in blood.

Then the German machine gun, with which Pearse and Bert had been keeping the Germans occupied, fell silent. George looked at Steven, a look of concern on his face.

'Keep them occupied with your rifle. I'm going to crawl over and find out what's happened to the other two.' It was still dark, but dawn wasn't too far away. Unseen, George crawled from his position to the other nest, disturbing only insects on the way. He found Bert slumped lifeless on the ground, and a wave of sadness enveloped him. Maybe hundreds of his fellow troops had died already on that blood-soaked island, but he and Bert had been together for more than eighteen months, along with Steven, and all three were great friends and comrades. He snapped out of it as he spotted the Lieutenant sitting up against some sandbags. He was bleeding from his shoulder.

'Davis dead?' Pearse asked.

'Looks like it, sir,' George said mournfully. 'What about you?'

'Took a round from a sniper, but I reckon it's gone straight through.'

'Do you reckon you can manage that machine gun?'

'For a short while.'

'That's all we need.'

'What are you going to do?'

'Crawl back to Lance Corporal Morgan and tell him to get back here, and we'll attack the eighty-eight with the bazookas. I need you to distract them with the machine gun while I do it.'

'Watch out for the sniper,' Pearse warned him. 'He killed Davis.'

'He's no longer a problem,' George explained. 'Lance Corporal Morgan got him, but too late to save Bert.'

Then George set off. Time for remembering Bert would come later. For now, he had to keep his wits about him, or he would soon be dead too. The tiniest rim of sunlight was peeping over the horizon, and he knew he had to be quick. The intermittent rattle of the machine gun started up, and the Germans responded with rifle fire. He'd never crawled so fast in his life and scared the pants off Steven as he threw himself into the nest.

'Shit, George!' Steven cried. 'You frightened the life out of me. What's happened with Bert and the Lieutenant?'

'Bert's dead,' he said quietly, 'and the Lieutenant's badly wounded.'

'Aw, shit!' Steven's face crumpled briefly with regret before he added, 'How bad?'

'He thinks the round went straight through him and came out the other side,' George replied.

'And what happened to Bert?' Steven asked nervously.

'He's fucking dead. That's all there is to it,' George exclaimed, then got himself back under control. 'Sorry, Steven. If we don't get our arses together, we'll be joining him.'

'That's OK, George. I feel the same. So, let's do it. What did you have in mind?'

Weighed down with ordinance, they crawled back to where the Lieutenant had by now stopped firing. Praying he wasn't dead, the two infantrymen doubled their efforts to reach relative safety. Steven re-armed the machine gun while George got the bazookas ready. Lieutenant Pearse had passed out but was still breathing. Behind them, the pair could hear the squeak of tanks moving forward, and they feared for the men in them unless they could destroy the eighty-eight mm field gun. His stomach went horribly weak as he imagined what it would be like to be hit by one of those menacing guns. The clatter of boots told them that Allied troops were on their way as well.

'They're sitting ducks for that field gun. It'll be like a turkey shoot,' Steven said, a hint of alarm in his voice.

'You're right,' replied George. 'But, at the moment, they're concentrating on us. Keep firing.'

'We're almost out of ammo,' Steven warned him.

'Get your bazooka ready.'

'Right, Corp.'

Pearse was moaning in the corner of the mini-fortification, but the bleeding had stopped, and he appeared to have come round.

George took over the machine gun while Steven lay down and took aim with the bazooka.

'One of your specials, please, Steven,' he encouraged as he emptied the machine gun and then grabbed the second bazooka. They heard a squeaking noise behind them. 'That's one of our Shermans on the bridge. We've got to knock that gun out before they realise the threat. Good job they're thick, these Nazis. Spending their shells on us instead of stopping our tanks.'

'Too late,' cried Steven. 'They're recalibrating the gun to take out the tank.' Sweating profusely, Steven took aim and hit the eighty-eight full-on. 'Bullseye,' he shouted, but his voice was drowned out by George letting fly a second shell which reduced the field gun to a pile of smoking rubble.

Dawn was lifting as the 50th Infantry poured across the bridge. Large numbers of very tough German soldiers were preparing to drive the Allies back. Fire was arcing across the lightening sky, and shells from mortars were landing, exploding and sending clouds of dust into the air as the Allies pressed on. George and Steven were lying back, exhausted, and in silence on the sandbags in the German machine gun nest. Sadness for Bert and maybe the Lieutenant threatened to overwhelm them even though they knew they'd done well.

'Well done, bonny lad,' a Sergeant in the DLI said as he leapt into the nest alongside George and Steven. The north easterner immediately spotted Pearse and bellowed 'Medic!' and signalled to the advancing Allied troops. Two soldiers appeared.

'Get this lad back to our lines for medical treatment at once.'

'Yes, Sarge.' Pearse was still conscious but ashen faced. The top left-and side of his battledress was covered in blood. He muttered something as the two soldiers lifted him out and carried him back towards the south side of the bridge, dodging shells and bullets. George and Steven watched sadly. They'd got on well with Pearse and thought him a good officer. Little did they know then but they would never see him again.

'Is your friend here dead?' the Durham Sergeant asked. George nodded. 'We'll get his body sorted out when we've finished off these krauts. Wait here until the bulk of our lads arrive, and then make your way back to rejoin your own company. I think you've earned a spot of R and R.'

Patiently, George and Steven waited for the bulk of the 50th. to arrive. It wasn't long before they were heading back to the south side of the bridge. Neither spoke. They felt Bert's death weigh heavily on them and were worried about the Lieutenant. They ate, slept fitfully and then joined the march north. George thought about Bert, who'd become such a close friend. Never again would he stroll through the streets of Hackney, and those two girls he'd fancied would never know what they'd missed. 'This bloody war,' he muttered to himself as he fought to prevent his sadness from overwhelming him.

'Tough nuts to crack, these Jerries,' Steven said to him as they hounded the retreating Germans who never seemed to give up. Routine soldiering suited them fine. No more heroics: just kill or be killed. Eventually, after a long and demanding campaign, Sicily's second largest city, Catania, fell to the Allies on August 5th. The welcome the Allies received there was even more enthusiastic than at the other ports, even though the numbers of cheering Sicilians had dwindled considerably. Non-combatants had fled to the safety of the hills, either because of fear of retribution from the Fascist police or to avoid being caught in the action. Rumour was that the hated Mussolini had resigned and had been arrested. The Germans were trapped up ahead and were preparing to evacuate their troops to the Italian mainland. What the lads could see had once been a beautiful city. Catania was now a heap of smoking rubble, having been repeatedly bombed by the Allied Air Forces. The inhabitants had no time for the Germans, Mussolini, Fascism or, indeed, the war. Well, for them at least, it seemed to be all over. To the west, the Americans were herding the Germans north eastwards towards Messina. Still facing some tough resistance in the shadow of Mount Etna, Patton's men were toughening up. Entering the war two and a half years after it had started, US troops had been caught napping by the Afrika Corps in Tunis. They'd learned their lesson and were now becoming a formidable fighting force.

The 50th Northumbrian camped outside Messina, one of the largest cities in Sicily. At over 100 degrees Fahrenheit, the tropical temperature had drained the last drop of energy from the men, who had been either marching or fighting for more than a month since landing on the beach at Avola. Fleeing across the two-mile-wide Straights of Messina, the Germans had cut their losses. The skies were quiet as the Luftwaffe, too, had left the scene. *Operation Husky* was a victory but had come at a high price with the death toll of the Allies more than four thousand, and another fifteen thousand either wounded or captured. German and Italian prisoners amounted to more than one hundred thousand, with almost ten thousand killed.

George and Simon weren't aware of these figures, but they knew that casualties were high and included their friend Bert Davis, whose body they had buried on the battlefield of Primosole Bridge. The officers were responsible for letting Bert's family know of the fate of their son, but George made it clear that, when he got the chance, he would personally tell them of Bert's bravery.

'Any news of the Lieutenant?' Steven asked.

'No,' George replied. 'I don't think his life is in danger, but I will check with the Medical Officer before too long.'

'So, how do you feel about war now, George?'

'Fucking awful. Someone I knew and liked was killed. Another was badly wounded. Every man probably lost a friend. And they all had families who had a husband, a father or a son taken away from them. The noise was unbearable, and the stench of smoke and death made us cough and retch. All those buildings destroyed, and people's homes. Farmers' fields left fit for nothing but burying the dead. Think of all of the innocent women and children killed by our bombers. Not sure I could go through that again. See that German I got with the first grenade? His mouth was wide open in surprise, even though it was on his head inside his helmet, and his headless body was still five feet away. He looked to be about our age. I hope he wasn't married, and I'd left his children without a father. What about you?'

They were sitting on the ground. Steven was playing with the dirt in between his knees. He was silent for a minute. 'The way I look at it was that we survived, and they died. I'm grateful for that, but I feel awful about Bert. I really didn't think much during the fighting, and I'm grateful to the Army for training us so well that I could cope, and you, too. And remember when you told me about what your father said to you? The Germans in charge of this war are bad bastards, and the only way to stop them is to kill their soldiers and beat their armies.' Steven paused. 'So what's next, do you think?'

George looked wearily at his friend.

'Rest, then Italy and more shooting, flames, smoke, noise and death.'

'We should write letters home while we've got the chance,' Steven suggested.

'Yes,' George replied, 'but there's not much we'll be able to tell them about the war. The censor will be working overtime with his pen. But we can tell them we're still in one piece.'

'The CO wants to see you immediately,' a tall Corporal told George and Steven after breakfast the following morning. 'Follow me, please.'

They'd been sitting on the wall of a church near their billets when their summons came. One of the villas in Messina now housed the Allied Forces' admin building, and it was outside a grand-looking pair of double doors that the two friends found themselves with the Corporal. They'd no idea why they were there, but it must have been important if Major-General Kirkham himself had sent for them. There were that many top brass about that they nearly wore their arms out saluting as they followed the tall Corporal through the building. After a very short wait, they were ushered into an enormous office which must have been an expansive sitting room in happier times. The General was standing behind a large desk about the size of two table tennis tables. The two friends marched forward, stopped, stood rigidly to attention and saluted, which was promptly returned.

'At ease,' the General instructed them. 'I'm sorry there are so few chairs, but I won't keep you long. I wanted to thank you personally for the part you played in securing Primosole Bridge. I'm told you were brave, decisive and very effective. You will all be mentioned in dispatches. Decorations may follow. You are a credit to your regiment, to the Eighth Army and to your country.' The General stepped forward and shook each man's hand firmly.

'Congratulations. I'm very sorry that Lance Corporal Davis died in the fighting. He, too, will be mentioned in dispatches and may receive a posthumous decoration. Your regiment's CO has written to his parents and told them of their son's death and his courage. Lieutenant Pearse is recovering from his wounds in Malta. He was really quite fortunate. The bullet passed through his shoulder and came out the other side. After a period of rehabilitation, he will rejoin his battalion on the Italian mainland, which is our next stop, in pursuit of the Germans. He has been promoted to Captain. You two will be going to Italy, and I'm pleased to confirm you've both been promoted. Corporal Aaron, you are promoted to Sergeant, and Lance Corporal Morgan, you now become a Corporal. Both of you have earned fourteen days' leave, so when we've finished here, get yourselves over to Biscari Airfield and hop on a transport back to England. There's plenty of trucks and cars going that way. Thank you, men. Congratulations once again. I'm proud to serve in the same army as you. Dismissed.' The lads came to attention, said their thanks, saluted and then marched out. While they were gathering up their gear, Steven looked at the new Sergeant. 'We did all right, we three. I'm really sorry about Bert.'

George looked at his friend and whispered, 'Yeah. Me too. It's just the bloody war.'

They bummed a lift to the airfield and jumped on an ageing Bristol Blenheim. After a refuelling stop in Gibraltar, they were flown to an airfield near Oxford. More lift-cadging saw them take different trains from Oxford Station. Before they left, the warmest of handshakes were exchanged.

George had telephoned his parents to let them know of his arrival. At two in the morning, there was an emotional reunion. The three of them hadn't been together for six months. George told them what he could about his war so far and the likelihood of a decoration. He was now a Sergeant, he told them. But something wasn't quite right. After George had thanked his dad for preparing him mentally for conflict, Isaac turned to his son and looked at him through misty eyes.

'We're proud of you, son, but it isn't over yet. I'm afraid I've got some terrible news for you. About Joe.'

CHAPTER TEN

September 1943 to May 1944
England and Scotland

Isaac told George that Joe had died in North Africa. He hadn't any details, only that he had been killed in action. George immediately felt the blood rush out of his face, and he felt first dizzy and then sick. He leant forward, put his chalk-white face in his hands, rested his elbows on his knees and stared at the floor.

'I'm so sorry, George,' Isaac began. 'There was no easy way I could tell you.'

George nodded, stood up and walked out of the room without a word. He lay down on his bed, closed his eyes and slept. It was teatime when he woke up, still in his uniform, and he made his way downstairs. His mother looked at him with concern and asked him what he would like to eat.

'Nothing, thanks, Mum.'

'Cup of tea?'

'Yes, please.'

George drank his tea and sat in silence while his parents listened to the radio with the volume turned low. Both his mother and father knew that it was pointless talking to him, so they left him to sit in silence until it was time for bed. One little thing that pleased them was that their son was beginning to regain his colour.

George did take his uniform off at bedtime, climbed into his pyjamas, and lay on the bed thinking about Joe and all of the adventures they'd shared. He wondered if Roger Martin, the Guv., knew. He and Joe went back even longer than the summer of 1939, when George had teamed up with the pair of them. Joe had loved Esther like a sister. He would have to make sure she knew what had happened to him. Long after midnight, George fell asleep, but he woke early, not long after six.

'I'm starved,' George said.

'I'm not surprised,' his mother replied. 'I'll make you a nice breakfast.'

George looked at his father.

'I'm due to report back for duty in ten days' time, Dad, but I don't want to go back.'

As his father began to respond, George continued.

'It's not that I'm scared. I'm just fed up with killing people like me and Joe who just happen to be German.'

Isaac reminded him of an earlier conversation they'd had when he had told him about the terrible rumours circulating about the Nazi treatment of Jews and other minorities.

'If I knew that I was killing people who were treating the Jews like that, I might feel different.'

Isaac looked at his son. 'I know how you feel, George, but you can't go absent without leave.'

'I promise I won't, Dad, but I've got to sort this out.'

'Perhaps Sir John or Roger can help,' Isaac suggested.

'Maybe. But I've no idea where the Guv is.'

'I'll ring Sir John and ask about Roger's whereabouts.'

'Thanks, Dad. Does he know about Joe, and what about Esther? Has anybody told her?'

'Yes, they both know. Now eat your breakfast and give me a hand with the van.'

Lifting heavy furniture into his father's van and then unloading at the other end was tough work, and it helped George to forget his misery for a while. After tea, George left his father to call Sir John, not forgetting to ask the diplomat to pass a message to Esther that he was okay, then went to call on Joe's parents. Although they would never recover from the loss of their son, it had been six months since his death and, though still sad, they had chosen to remember all the good things about Joe.

'He was decorated for gallantry, posthumously,' Charlie, Joe's father, said. 'Isaac says you're getting one too.'

'A medal, yes,' George said, thinking he'd rather have Joe than a bloody decoration.

George left after half an hour, promising to call on them again before he left for his next posting. At home, his father had kept his promise and called Sir John, who promised he would track down Roger as soon as he could. When they arrived home after work the next day, his mother told them both that Sir John had called, and that Roger would be round to see them after tea at about seven o'clock.

116

Roger arrived bang on time, smartly dressed in the uniform of a Major in the Special Operations Executive. He shook hands with the parents, then he and George approached each other and wrapped themselves in a powerful hug of sad remembrance for Joe.

'Look,' Isaac began. 'You two need to be left alone. We'll go into the kitchen and clear up and make tea.'

'Thank you,' said Roger. 'I'd love some tea, and I'm sure George would as well.'

George gave a weak smile and nodded, and he sat down facing the Guv. 'I should call you Major or sir,' George began. 'I'm only a Sergeant.'

'It's Guv., please, George, and you're a Sergeant with a Military Medal, one of the top gongs the Army can bestow on a man for bravery. Now tell me what's worrying you.'

George repeated to Roger what he'd said to his dad. 'You know, Guv., before the war, Joe and I helped you to stop the Irish blowing up Woolwich Arsenal. They would have killed loads of people if us three hadn't put a spanner in their works. Then we were part of getting Esther's parents out of Berlin and stopping the Gestapo from blackmailing her. I could look these people in the face, and I knew them. They were bad. It would be different if I could take on Germans that I know are bad.'

Roger was silent for a while. 'I do understand,' he said eventually. 'And I wouldn't be able to do this for most, but for you, well... I think I know something that would fit you like a glove, but I need to speak to my superior to see if we can arrange your transfer from the Infantry. But it will be extremely dangerous, far more than Sicily, and lots of people in my outfit have already lost their lives, mainly as a result of being dealt with by the Gestapo. And you'll have to undergo a long period of specialist training, even tougher than when they put you through it in the Infantry.'

'Where would I go to get at the Nazis, Guv?'

'France, at the moment, behind enemy lines. One thing we all know, including you if you've been listening to the chat, is that the Allies will be invading France in 1944. Where and when nobody knows yet, but one thing for certain is that the work of the French Resistance and the SOE will be crucial to the success of the invasion. I'll speak to my boss, Colonel Buckmaster, tomorrow, and if he agrees that you should join us, I'll arrange your transfer from the

Infantry. But before that, you need to know what you're letting yourself in for. When you've heard that, you can tell me whether or not you still want to join us.'

George nodded and listened attentively to what Roger told him for the next half an hour. At the end of it, he nodded again. 'Sign me up,' was all he said.

Roger telephoned the next day and told George that he needed to report to Orchard House in Baker Street the following morning. Colonel Buckmaster, Roger explained, wished to talk with him as part of the assessment to determine George's suitability to join the SOE.

In his uniform, displaying his Sergeant's stripes, George reported promptly at Orchard House and was shown into Buckmaster's office. The Colonel greeted him warmly, returned George's salute and asked him to take a seat. Sergeant Aaron took a quick look at the SOE officer, whom he guessed was in his forties, thinning on top but with a decent amount of greying hair at the sides and back. His brown eyes studied George for a moment, then a small smile broke out on his face.

'So you want to join the SOE, Sergeant?'

'I think so, sir, but I would like to know a little more about what would be expected of me.'

'Of course, that's one of the reasons why you're here. The other is for us to decide whether or not you're the right person for the job. Major Martin speaks very highly of you, so that's a good start.'

For the next hour, the Colonel got to know George. He delved into the East End boy's childhood, listened while George went through his anti-Fascist adventures before the war, including the work he'd done for the Guv in the summer of 1939. Buckmaster jotted down notes and then moved on to ask about George's family, his politics and his wartime activity.

'Well, I'm happy with what you've told me, Sergeant, and, at first glance, you seem the type of person we're looking for. I'll have another chat with Major Martin and if we're both happy, I'll arrange for your temporary transfer to the SOE, effective immediately.'

'Temporary, sir?' asked George.

'Perhaps I should explain. This little chat while I smoke my pipe is the first stage of our assessment of your suitability. The second will begin almost immediately at Winterfold House in Surrey. If you come through that, your transfer will become permanent, and you'll then begin a long period of preparation so that you can operate effectively in occupied France. That's always if you yourself still want to join us. Now, you need to go to the other office and speak to Vera Atkins. She runs this section and will give you all of the necessary instructions so that you can undertake the first part of your training in Surrey. It is so good to meet you, George. Good luck.'

George made his way to Vera Atkins' office, knocked and entered and was surprised to find a civilian busy writing behind a large desk. She looked up, left her seat and shook George's hand. To George, she appeared to be a tall, formidable woman dressed in a grey skirt and light green cardigan. Her brushed brown hair was parted on the right-hand side and he guessed she was in her late thirties or early forties. She welcomed him as Sergeant Aaron and asked him to take a seat while she pulled a sheaf of papers from her desk drawer. These were his orders which included a travel warrant to take him to Surrey by train on the following Monday. She asked him to sign the Official Secrets Act, shook his hand again, adding, 'It's very brave, what you're going to do,' gave him a brief smile and wished him good luck. George left, a mixture of excited, anxious and confused. Was this the right thing for him to do? Was anything the right thing to do in the face of war? He didn't know, only that he had to play a part he believed in.

That same evening, Roger called round and gave George a final briefing after first congratulating him for overcoming the first hurdle.

'It'll be quite a while before you go into the field, George,' Roger told him. 'There's much for you to learn. You'll be doing a lot of travelling in Britain over the next six months, if, that is, the people at Winterfold like you and you want to carry on. You'll get an idea about what we're really up to in the SOE before we meet again.'

'Where will you be, Guv.?' George asked.

'No idea, but probably not in England,' Roger replied with a wry grin. 'And one other thing, George. We're agents, not spies. We leave intelligence gathering overseas to the Special Intelligence Service. Our job will be to work with French resisters to make the life of the occupying Germans absolute hell.'

'Thanks for giving me this chance, Guv. I won't let you down.'

'I don't think you will. See you in the spring next year. I hope...'

Monday morning found George on his way to Surrey by train. The first thing that struck him as he left the sprawl of London behind was the huge number of trees he saw through the train window. As he watched the countryside flash by, he wondered whether he should say anything to Esther about what he was doing – but then, it was no more dangerous than being cannon fodder, was it? He decided against it – especially as he was sure the Guv would have advised him not to if he'd asked him. A Corporal collected him from Cranleigh Station and transported him to Winterfold House, the training base for new recruits to the SOE. Winterfold was a very large house which, to George's eyes, looked as if it had been there for donkey's years. Two tall chimneys were located at either end of the two-storey building, which had a number of small windows peeping out of the roof. A large glass-fronted balcony dominated the first floor and to the left he could see the rolling uplands of the Surrey Hills. Despite the pleasant outlook of the house and its surroundings, George felt nervous. He'd no idea what to expect, but his anxiety helped to reduce the sorrow he felt at Joe's death.

Colonel Buckmaster was there to welcome George.

'I shan't be staying long, but either Miss Atkins or I will call in from time to time to see how you are doing. Your training and assessment will start tomorrow morning. In the meantime, unpack your stuff, then have a stroll around the grounds, but don't step outside the surrounding fences. This is a top-secret establishment. Before Winterfold, Wanborough nearby was our base, and last year a man who turned out to be a Nazi spy was seen sniffing around.'

'What happened?' George asked.

Buckmaster smiled. 'Miss Atkins had him killed by one of her glamorous assistants. She stabbed him with a sharpened knitting needle in a churchyard. Then a couple of our men buried the body. We found a radio in his room at The King's Arms in Godalming,' the Colonel said, sounding satisfied.

George felt a chill run down his spine. These people don't mess about, he thought.

'Dinner is at seven. Dress is uniform. Good luck, Sergeant.'

'Thank you, sir.'

The following day, George was introduced to the world of codes by a studious-looking young man with fair hair and rimless spectacles.

'Wherever you go behind enemy lines, you will be accompanied by a fully trained radio operator but if anything should happen to that person, you may have to fill in.'

Next up was weapons training, and this was conducted by a tough-looking Scottish Corporal.

'I know you've seen action, unlike most of the bods we get here, but you probably used a Lee Enfield .303 rifle and a Bren. A revolver will be of more use to you in the field.'

George made a poor start with the Webley revolver. The recoil almost threw him off balance. He had used one before but had forgotten how tricky it could be.

'That last round would have clipped the top of the jerry's helmet or missed altogether,' the Corporal explained, giving him further instruction in stance and grip.

Things were happening so quickly that George didn't have time to feel nervous. He learned how to strip, clean and reassemble the Webley and experience silenced weapons, including the single-shot Welrod, which could be concealed in the sleeve of his tunic.

'You need plenty of practice, Sergeant,' the Corporal told him. 'The pistol is a close weapon. When you see cowboys in the flicks shooting Indians and villains from a distance with a Colt 45, it's a load of rubbish. You have to be right up close for a handgun to be effective.'

George spent most of the first week on weapons acclimatisation and learning about codes. Colonel Buckmaster called in to see how he was doing and to give him some background on working behind enemy lines.

'This work is extremely dangerous, Sergeant. Your chief enemies will be the Gestapo, the French Police and French collaborators. I know you've already had a run-in with the Gestapo before the war, but you were on home ground, as it were. On their own patch, they are far more threatening. They do have some weaknesses; they rely totally on violence to make captured agents talk, and when they fail to get anything useful, they've nowhere else to turn. That's because they're thick, and lastly, they're permanently at war with other Nazi intelligence organisations. The French police are either helpful, neutral or in league with the Gestapo. The worst of them is the Milice, a paramilitary police group, but they mostly operate in Vichy, where you're unlikely to go. Then there are the French collaborators, in my view the worst of the lot. Hardly any of them do it out of conviction. Usually, it's money that's their driving force or, in the case of younger women, either misguided love or nylons and cigarettes.'

Every day began with a run around the grounds. Usually, some sadistic NCO accompanied him, and George felt good when he was grudgingly told he was in good shape but was quickly brought down to earth when he reported for unarmed combat. A weedy-looking fellow with a toothy grin greeted him and invited him to try to throw him to the ground. Suspecting a trap, George circled the instructor before launching a lightning attack which ended with him flat on his back, with the weedy soldier smiling at him with his trademark toothy grin.

George persisted for several days to get the better of his adversary but only managed to achieve some kind of parity after five days of salutary sessions. Wine was served with dinner that night, but George didn't think much of it, thinking it tasted a bit like vinegar. There was humorous talk of what cover they'd each assume if they were ever sent into France, and George equally good-humouredly opted for one of his boyhood icons – an airman – even though he'd known he'd never make a pilot himself. 'Good one,' one of the instructors commented. 'And very apt – stick to it!' George agreed and after a tiring day, he went to bed early, fell into a deep sleep – and a disturbing dream. They came for him just after midnight. George was woken up from a deep sleep, feeling hands roughly grabbing him. He looked up to see two men in the black uniforms of the SS staring at him with a look of pure hatred in their eyes.

'Get up and come with us!' they shouted.

He was dragged down the stairs into what appeared to be a small cell with a filthy mattress on the floor and a bucket in the corner. Two other black, unarmed men carried a very large bowl of water into the cell.

'You're a British agent!' screamed one of the men.

'I'm an airman. I've been shot down,' gasped George.

'Pull his trousers down,' bawled one of his tormentors. He produced a thin bamboo cane and thrashed him six times across his bare buttocks.

'Where are the other members of your circuit?'

'I've no idea. I'm a Flight Sergeant in the RAF. I was shot down, and now I'm making my way towards our front line.'

The torturers punched him in the stomach several times but still got nothing from him.

'Kneel him in front of the bowl.'

They grabbed him round the neck and pushed his head under the water, and held it there. After a while, they pulled him out and asked him, 'Where are the other members of your circuit?'

George gave his name, rank and serial number.

The process was repeated several times before it became obvious that, if they didn't stop, he'd drown. Every time he was pushed under the water, he gave his name, rank and serial number when he surfaced.

He woke the next morning feeling really rough. As he got out of bed, he groaned at the muscular discomfort in his stomach and his sore bum. He dropped his pyjama bottoms and stood in front of the bathroom mirror and, to his horror, saw angry red stripes across his buttocks. 'What the?' he muttered under his breath and quickly pulled his pyjama bottoms back up. He went for his run, which was rather painful, and then had breakfast, quietly slipping a cushion on his chair before he sat down. He was too embarrassed to ask what was going on and was even more ill at ease when Colonel Buckmaster sent for him not long after breakfast.

'Well, that's the first bit over, Sergeant. How do you feel?'

'Err, alright, sir, but there is one thing I'm a bit worried about. What's the reason I've got a bruised stomach and a stinging bottom?'

'You've forgotten the nearly drowning too, then?' the Colonel asked, a twinkle in his eye. 'You were drugged last night and dragged from your bed by two men dressed in SS uniforms and interrogated to see how you would cope. You were very good, and the men got first frustrated, then frightened when you threatened to beat them to a pulp.' The Colonel laughed. 'We do this to all recruits, including women agents, so if you bump into other soldiers who are thinking about volunteering for the SOE, don't tell them about the mock interrogation, will you? You passed with flying colours, by the way – if you'd still like to carry on?'

'I won't, sir. And, yes, I would like to carry on with the training.'

'Good. You'll be off to Scotland now, Arisaig House in Scotland's Western Highlands. Miss Atkins will give you all the details. She'll be here after lunch. Rest up till then, and, by the way, your arse will heal in a day or two.'

Another long, dark, cold and uncomfortable journey by train up the West Coast deposited George in Fort William after midnight. Exhausted, he slumped into his very comfortable bed, slept like a log and was ready for a Scottish breakfast by 8 o'clock. The CO, Major Scott, sent for him shortly after he'd eaten and outlined what would happen.

'You'll be here about six weeks, Sergeant. During that time, you'll learn all there is to know about explosives, sabotage and other dirty tricks. You'll be taught how to navigate, on your own, through unfamiliar countryside and live off the land. When you leave, you'll be as fit as any Olympic athlete. Any questions?'

'No, sir.'

The young Major with a handsome face, black hair and an impressive moustache smiled at him. 'Good. Report to the basement at 0930 to start your explosives training. If you've time beforehand, have a stroll around outside. It's a very beautiful part of the world.'

The Major was right, George decided. It was a lovely scene, with the fine, three-storey, grey stone house perched on a plateau and surrounded by a thickly wooded area, through which could be glimpsed the foothill of the Western Highlands. George took a while to compare the surrounds of Arisaig, and earlier Winterfold, with the smoked-filled, crowded streets of East London. But George loved his hometown and would be relieved to return there after the war was over.

The time for sightseeing was over and for the next three days, George was in the hands of a studious young man from Glasgow who introduced him to the world of plastic explosives, or PE as he called it.

'It's useless and harmless without a detonator,' the young man explained. 'Slide in a detonator, and you can blow almost anything to kingdom come, depending on the size of the charge.' He showed George how to set a timer. 'Give yourself plenty of time to get away from the blast,' he warned.

George's head was spinning with all this new information after four days. He familiarised himself with PE, found out how to tear down telephone wires, derail trains by removing rails, blow up bridges, and block roads using trees. 'And another thing,' the Sergeant added, 'you can disable vehicles by putting Demerara treacle into fuel tanks or smearing sand on axle grease.'

All this learning new stuff wasn't a problem for George. He was highly motivated. He hated the war and wanted to do his tiny bit to help defeat the Germans and bring it to an end. Then there were his friends, Joe and Bert. He was desperate to take revenge on the Nazis for snatching them away so young. The instructors saw in him a man so driven as to be almost invincible, almost but not quite, because they knew the terrible dangers he would face behind enemy lines.

Before the start of instruction each day, George was taken for a run or a route march, sometimes in full kit. His final task was a twenty-four-hour TOD expedition where, armed only with a map, compass, torch, knife, sleeping bag and bivouac, he had to navigate around the toughest terrain he'd ever experienced. Epping Forest and even the Brecon Beacons were child's play compared with this. He ate off the land: insects, roots, skinned rabbits and small rodents, and drank from streams. He returned unscathed and on time and allowed himself a brief feeling of triumph.

Ringway Airfield, near Manchester, for parachute training, was his next destination. On the journey south, he reflected on where he was, and how far he had come in the past four months. Losing his closest friend had been the lowest point of his life. Did he imagine that the two of them would come through the war unscathed? On that train journey south, he accepted that he had believed that they both would. Now he understood the harsh realities of war. Nothing would ever be the same again, and he knew that, if he survived, he would have to adapt to the changed circumstances of his life, however difficult they might be. And he thought about Esther, wondering how she was coping. At that moment, he vowed that, if he lived, he would return to her and that they would love each other for the rest of their lives. If he lived...

One thing he was sure of, as he sat on his bed in a smart house on the outskirts of Manchester, was that the SOE had requisitioned the best houses to train their agents, and rationing was nowhere in evidence. The next day, he reported to the Headquarters of Number 1 Parachute Training School. Physically, he felt he was at his peak, and the SOE had challenged him daily, and he had come through everything they'd thrown at him with flying colours. Despite that, he was slightly nervous about jumping from a plane five hundred feet above the ground, with just a piece of cloth between him and extinction.

His instructors knew this, without saying so, and took George through a tried and tested and sensibly graduated programme. First, he had to land on a coconut mat after jumping from a ten-foot-high platform. Then, from a greater height, he jumped and landed wearing a chute that had been restrained by cords and pulleys. The third step was from higher still, from a gondola beneath a hot air balloon. This time, the parachute had to be opened by pulling the ripcord. The next day, George was being propelled through the air at five hundred feet after leaping from a Halifax bomber travelling at one hundred and forty miles an hour. To say he was nervous was an understatement, but he nailed his first jump safely. Four jumps later, and having found a new favourite hobby, George was again on his way south, this time to the Midlands, where he practised jumping on and off trains at various speeds, as well as being shown different ways of disabling trains, in addition to PE. Interfering with the transfer of German military personnel to the front was very important, and even destroying signal boxes could cause long delays.

En route to his final destination, Beaulieu in Hampshire, he noticed the huge build-up of men, materials and machines south of London. He knew this meant that the invasion was imminent. Logistically, it was so massive that it wasn't possible to keep something of this scale secret. Only a very select few knew when and where, though. On arrival in Beaulieu, he was surprised to discover that he'd been promoted to Second Lieutenant, and soldiers who had previously nodded at him now had to salute. It would take a bit of getting used to. Waiting for his orders, George honed his code and radio skills, learned how to hide and bury his chute and devoured everything he could about the French – their habits and culture, laws and emergency occupation laws. He even studied train timetables and familiarised himself with the area of Eastern France – where it was likely he would be going – by browsing Michelin Guides.

On June 4th, the Guv reappeared. 'Right, George. Your instructors say you're ready. Every test has been passed with flying colours. If the Nazis are half as frightened of you as the instructors seem to have been, those German bastards are in for a rough time. Great stuff. Well done.'

'Thanks, Guv.'

'So we're off tomorrow night.'

'Where are we going?'

'That I can't tell you right now, but rest assured, the training stops here. The next time you have to act, it will be behind enemy lines.'

CHAPTER ELEVEN

London
Autumn 1944 – March 1945

'I don't like the sound or look of these new bombs,' Esther said to Mary when she reached the Ambulance Station. 'There's going to be a lot of dead and injured if they're not stopped soon.'

Mary nodded in agreement and changed the subject. 'The Allies are doing well in Northern France.'

'Not too bad,' Esther said, 'but they're still stuck in Normandy. I wonder if George is there.'

'I was thinking the same thing,' Mary said, 'but we'll never find out, so we'll just have to keep our fingers crossed and hope he's safe.'

For a moment, Esther thought of George facing death over the Channel and, briefly, prayed silently that he survived. Then she deliberately and determinedly put him out of her head. She'd long ago decided it was the only way, or she'd be worrying all the time. But one day, she reminded herself. Because he'd promised he'd come back, so one day...

'Looks like that bomb in Mile End was a one-off, thank goodness,' their shift leader at Weymouth Mews said to the girls as midnight approached. Esther and Mary liked and respected their immediate boss, who had been the headmistress of a small school before retiring to raise a family. Known to Esther and Mary only as Williams, in the traditions of the LAAS, she demonstrated common sense, courage and determination, though none of those admirable qualities were needed that night. Nor the following night, though the girls weren't working, but on the Thursday, things changed much for the worse. Esther soon became familiar, through pictures in the newspapers, of the damage caused by the doodlebugs, as they now became known. Seventy-three of the wretched things landed in London. Scores were killed and hundreds lost their homes. Even more had been launched, but sharp shooting by the Anti-Aircraft gunners, coupled with interceptions from Spitfires and Hurricanes, had sent as many more crashing to earth or into the sea. Esther said to Mary, 'What makes these bombs worse is that you see and hear them up in the sky, then suddenly silence, as they head for the ground, followed by a giant explosion. Frightening.'

Only a very few made an appearance in the Weymouth Mews Station's area of responsibility, and Esther and Mary dealt mostly with civilians hit by flying debris. On the following day, the numbers increased, and it was clear that a major crisis was looming. Esther, Mary and some of their part-time colleagues were asked to switch to full-time work since there was no pattern of attacks; doodlebugs struck at any time, day or night. The girls found themselves working sometimes during the day, early evenings or night. Sir John instantly agreed that Esther should switch to full-time and hired a local schoolgirl to do the cleaning.

One Friday afternoon, the warnings went up in the Ambulance Station. 'That's us,' Esther shouted at Mary. 'Where to?' she called to Williams. They were told Praed Street, right up against Paddington Station.

The ambulance sped along Oxford Street, bells clanging, and turned right at Marble Arch into Edgware Road. Mary had become a most accomplished driver. Passing Sussex Gardens, they could see a huge pall of smoke ahead and headed for it. A policeman stopped them, and they parked up and raced towards the scene.

'Good lord,' exclaimed Esther, staring at the biggest pile of red bricks either of them had ever seen. Furniture, window frames, clothing, bedding and most of the contents of two terraced houses were blazing away. As they approached the devastation, the heat became almost unbearable. 'Casualties?' she asked an ARP man.

'Sorry, love,' he replied. 'Mostly dead, but we got three out, a mother and two young children. You'll need a couple of stretchers.'

'Bring the ambulance closer,' Esther said to Mary. 'I'll be with the casualties.' At this point, the girls were working automatically. The bomb had already exploded and as long as they kept clear of the flames, they didn't seem to be in any danger. Esther heard their vehicle approaching but, suddenly, the noise of the engine was drowned out by a far more sinister sound, the *phut phut phut* of another doodlebug. Esther was petrified. So far, neither she nor Mary had been present when a bomb had exploded, and Esther silently prayed that the bomb would carry on and land on the grass in Regent's Park or Hyde Park or anywhere but where she was, in a densely populated area and near to one of London's biggest railway stations. They had to ignore it and hope. She and Mary placed the two children on one stretcher and the woman on another. Just as they slammed the ambulance doors shut, the bomb's engine cut out and they watched it glide menacingly towards them and behind the line of houses opposite. Utter terror gripped them as they stared, waiting and frozen to the spot until a huge explosion ripped through the houses on an adjacent street. Mary was lifted off her feet and slammed into the side of the ambulance while Esther was thrown across the street, landing on the pavement.

'You two OK?' the ARP man asked.

'Not sure,' said Esther shakily, 'but I think so.' She examined herself closely, brushed the dirt off her uniform and then attempted a smile. 'Looks like I'm still in one piece, just a bit bruised.'

'Can you drive?' the ARP man asked Mary.

'It's not far to the hospital. I'm sure I can make it.'

'When you get there, get yourselves checked out too,' he advised. 'You might think you're OK, but you might have delayed shock.'

'What about the other bomb?' Esther asked. 'Where is it?'

'Sussex Gardens. There'll be plenty more ambulances on the way. You've done your bit for the day.'

The two girls were treated for cuts and bruises at the hospital and then told to return to the ambulance and go home. Both were suffering from mild shock, but they were back at work the next day.

The devastation increased, and it was a question of all hands to the pump, and ambulances were told to make emergency journeys outside of their own area. On the Friday evening in Hampstead, Sir John told Esther that the flying bombs had a limited range and could only be launched from sites located in countries occupied by the Nazis. 'As soon as the Allies kick the Germans out, the bombs will stop.' Esther and Mary refrained from mentioning to Sir John that the Allies were currently bogged down in Normandy and showed little sign of pushing the Germans out. 'Their top speed is only four hundred miles an hour. Spitfires and Hurricanes will blow them out of the sky, and we've moved our guns to the coast so we can stop them ever arriving on our land.' The girls didn't share Sir John's cheerful optimism but kept quiet. So many were landing that ambulances were having to come from all parts of London, not just their own areas. At the end of June, a bomb hit the railway embankment in York Road by Waterloo Station. By the time the girls got there, the rescuers had found three dead, but more than thirty were seriously injured. Several were taken by stretcher to nearby St Thomas' Hospital, but they were handicapped by lack of facilities, as it hadn't fully recovered from being hit during the Blitz, almost four years earlier. Esther and Mary helped to load four very badly injured into their vehicle. A teenage boy appeared to have a serious head injury, an old woman had clearly lost an arm and two men in railway uniforms were covered in blood from wounds on their torsos. Basic first aid had been applied, but the priority was to get them to hospital. Esther sat in the back, trying her best to help the patients, while Mary drove north towards the hospital as fast as she could. Totally focused on the urgency of her task, Mary crossed Waterloo Bridge, then sped up Kingsway and Southampton Row to University College Hospital, just behind Euston Square Station. Aided by hospital staff, they helped the patients out of the vehicle and then returned to Waterloo to see if more emergency transport was required. It wasn't, so they headed back to Weymouth Mews to await the next doodlebug.

'Strange, isn't it?' Mary said to Esther. 'The war is close to being won, but it's still going on. People are still dying, and buildings are still being destroyed.' The two girls were sitting in the sunshine outside the Weymouth Mews Ambulance station waiting for the next call. The Allies had broken the German lines in Normandy and were racing across Northern France. The Soviets were advancing on all fronts and were now in Romania, and Allied forces had landed in the south of France. 'All the Germans have left are these wretched rockets and loads of stubbornness,' Esther summed up the situation.

That month, August, there had been over seventy-five doodlebug attacks and around two hundred deaths, but there were hundreds homeless as Hitler's new weapons blew houses to smithereens. Towards the end of the month, the attacks became less frequent as the Germans rushed to find new launch sites as the Allies began to overrun their Northern France positions. The rockets started dropping again in earnest in September, with the deadliest appearing on the 8th and, for a short while, the ambulance service was close to being overwhelmed.

London was certainly not a smoking ruin as some Nazis were suggesting, but the emergency services in the capital were under severe pressure, caused first by the pilotless aircraft and then the V2 rockets. Already, as winter approached, more than ten thousand houses had been ruined beyond repair. Every day, as many as twenty thousand homes were suffering minor damage, creating an instant housing crisis. Esther and Mary were working, without complaint, up to eighty hours a week. The end of the war was in sight, although exactly when no one could say. Both were worn out and were worried about where the next bomb might drop and how many casualties there might be. Esther, in particular, had a lot on her mind. What would she do after the war? Whilst she loved working for Sir John, she didn't want to be a domestic servant for the rest of her days. He was a kind gentleman and treated her as an equal, unlike many other refugees who were little more than well-looked-after slaves. No, she wanted something more than that. She'd speak to Sir John about it. Neither could she get used to the odd hours, especially the but every time she woke up, whether it was morning, afternoon or evening, George was the first thing that entered her mind. Where was he? Was he still alive? Perish the thought, but she wondered how much danger he was in and when would he be home? Then, as she'd trained herself to do, she set him aside to focus on the day, and staying alive herself. With all this uncertainty and anxiety washing around her brain she sometimes wondered if she could continue without breaking down.

Many days were spent lounging around in the common room, just waiting for the next rocket to fall, and the tiredness was so great that they couldn't face the journey back to their homes without a half a pint of watered-down beer in the Dover Castle pub next to the ambulance station. The indiscriminate nature of the bombing meant that they could be called out at any time to anywhere. Train derailments were common, but usually, trains managed to limp into London termini stations where the ambulance crews were waiting to collect injured passengers and take them to hospital. Eight American servicemen, waiting for their postings, died when the Red Lion pub on Duke Street near Selfridges was hit. Eighteen died altogether and thirty-two were injured. The death toll rose again, and one hundred and sixty-eight died when Woolworth's in Lewisham took a direct hit, and more than a hundred died when a V2 struck Smithfield Market.

'Overpaid, overfed, oversexed and over here, that's what they're saying about the Americans,' Mary pointed out to her friend one evening after the end of their shift as they enjoyed a drink in the Dover Castle. The occasion was their promotion to Leading Hand, and they were now able to wear a single stripe on their uniforms.

'Let's hope the war doesn't go on long enough for us to get promoted again,' Esther said, although both were secretly pleased that their efforts had been rewarded with some kind of recognition.

Sir John was thrilled too and said so fulsomely. 'You should celebrate, you two,' he instructed. 'Have a night out on me if you can get the time off.'

Mary seemed keen, so Esther went along with it. 'Maybe just a coffee out then,' she said. 'Like we used to with George and Joe.'

Many of the tens of thousands of American troops who had crowded into Britain in the run up to the invasion of Normandy had gone now, but still, a large number remained, waiting either to cross the channel to serve as re-enforcements or be taken to another theatre of war. Esther and Mary were both attractive girls, and US troops frequently tried to chat them up in the streets or sometimes on buses, but this was mostly good-natured wisecracks. That evening in September, after their celebratory coffee, while Esther was making her way home along Portland Place towards Regents Park, she was approached in the blackout gloom by what she could make out to be a tall young man in what she recognised as a Yankee soldier's uniform.

'Hi'ya, honey. Going anywhere special?' he asked with a slurred voice, which suggested he'd been drinking. Esther was a bit frightened. It was pitch dark, there was nobody else about, and she was on her own. Mary had called in sick with a heavy cold.

'Yes, I'm going home.' Esther replied nervously, looking away from the soldier.

'What's the uniform?' he asked.

'I'm an ambulance driver. Now if you'll excuse me, I've had a long day, and I just want to get back to my home and have some supper before bed.' Panic began to grip her.

'I'm being shipped overseas in the morning,' he told her. 'Maybe I'll get shot and killed. I'm just looking for a bit of fun on my last night. Surely you won't deny a soldier helping to save your country that?'

'Please, I do have to go. I hope you find your fun somewhere else.' She knew what he was after and was desperate for someone, anyone, to appear and stop this nightmare.

'Come on. Just a little kiss,' and he moved towards her.

Esther was terrified. Men had approached her and Mary before but had never been at all threatening. Mostly, it was just harmless banter. This was different: a man determined to have his way with a girl before he left Britain's shores.

'Please just leave me alone,' Esther shouted as he grabbed her arm and dragged her into a deserted side street which was nothing much more than a number of skeletal buildings and mountains of rubble. She became hysterical and started screaming, then sobbing. She had to fight him off somehow. Petrified, she thrust her hands at his face and used her long nails to draw blood. She was completely at a loss as to what to do next. As every second passed, her sense of hopelessness grew, but she didn't give up as she tore at his uniform. He pushed her to the hard pavement, but she leapt back to her feet and kneed him in the groin. This crazed him even more.

'Fuck you, bitch.' There was no turning back now, Esther realised with horror. The soldier smacked Esther hard on her left cheek and then tore her tunic open and started feverishly groping her breasts. In desperation, Esther tried to knee him again between his legs, but this seemed to inflame his passion further, and he hoisted up her skirt and dragged her knickers down to her ankles. There was nothing she could do.

'Please, no!' screamed Esther. Where was everybody? She could hear traffic. It was pitch dark in the blackout. She began to think he might kill her, and her tears became a torrent.

Suddenly, she felt him enter her as pain ripped through her thighs, groin area and stomach. Then, as quickly as it had begun, it was all over. The soldier buttoned up and looked at her with pain on his face as she curled into a ball on the floor, trying to pull her clothes around her.

'Oh God, I'm so sorry,' he said, and then half-stumbled and half-ran away.

Esther pulled her clothes around her and screamed, 'Help me, help me!' as loud as she could. She could feel blood trickling down her legs but still felt so ashamed. She just wished she could just die there in that dark, wrecked London side street.

Before long, her distress attracted the attention of a policeman who could see immediately what had happened. He blew his whistle as loud as he could, and, within a minute or so a colleague came running.

'This woman's been raped. Get an ambulance!' Within minutes, Esther was on her way to hospital. Staff there recognised her torn and blood-stained uniform, and she was rushed onto a ward. A doctor examined her, confirmed that she'd been raped but said that she didn't have any life-threatening injuries and could go home when she was ready, probably tomorrow after they'd kept an eye on her overnight since she was so distressed. A kindly nurse helped Esther strip, wash and put on a fresh, clean hospital gowns. Someone had already checked her uniform and found Sir John's address on her identity card, and the diplomat soon arrived, a look of grave concern on his face. The policeman told him how he'd found Esther, but she wasn't yet in a fit state to answer any questions. Sir John took a seat at her bedside and stayed there till morning. Esther slept fitfully, sometimes waking up with cries of terror. Each time, Sir John took hold of her hand, gently squeezed it and coaxed her back to sleep.

In the morning, Sir John fetched a change of clothing but before Esther could leave, a plain-clothed policeman, who looked like an older version of the actor Jack Hawkins, arrived and asked her some questions. Esther was still in shock and finding talking difficult,having woken up and, to her horror, remembered it wasn't a nightmare that had disturbed her sleep but the dreadful, violent events of the previous evening. Nevertheless, she answered as best she could. She couldn't give much of a description of her assailant, hidden as he was by the blackout, but she remembered he'd seemed young, had an American accent and had been drinking. The policeman held up a large piece of brown cloth.

'The constable found this in your hand.'

'I tried to defend myself.' She spoke weakly as the whole nightmarish scenario began to play back in her fevered brain. 'I scratched his face and tore at his uniform. Oh, and he said he was being sent overseas today.'

'Thank you, miss. Can I ask you if he was black or white?'

'White,' she muttered.

'It'll not be easy tracking down an American soldier in the London blackout; but one who was being sent to fight today, had scratches on his face and a torn uniform should help us to narrow things down a bit, and we'll do all we can to get him,' the policeman promised.

Sir John gave the policeman his card. 'Esther works for me and lives in. Please keep us both informed of your investigation.'

'Certainly, Sir John. If we find him and prove conclusively that he did this horrible thing, we'll hand him over to the Americans. He'll face a court martial and if he's found guilty, he'll be executed. Good day, sir.'

Esther was shocked. If the soldier was caught, he'd be punished. But executed? She wasn't sure that's what she wanted.

Esther went home to Hampstead. Sir John and Cook looked after her. There was no sign of Roger or George, but Sir John told her they were both still alive. Esther healed quickly, physically, but her return to any kind of comfort in her own mind would take longer. She felt dirty, guilty, ravished and ruined and cried in bed almost every night. Constantly she wondered what people would think of her when they found out she'd been raped. But they wouldn't find out, of course. Sir John would never tell anyone. She imagined folk would suggest she had tempted him in some way, giving him the come-on. She knew that wasn't true, but would anyone believe her? Physically she was alright, but mentally she was a shambles. She decided not to tell her parents. What good would that do? Sir John knew and that was enough. She prayed the American would either never be caught or killed in action. That way, there wouldn't be a court case or identification parade. No, this would have to be locked in the deep recesses of her mind. Then she thought of George. What would he think of her? A filthy whore who'd had sex with the first man to approach her? A slut who was anybody's, no better than the prostitutes who paraded themselves around King's Cross? Slowly, she realised that George would not make those assumptions, that he would be sympathetic and not judge her; nevertheless, she found it hard to bring the dreadful episode to an end.

Esther recovered, but never fully. She returned to work with the Ambulance Service. There were less bomber raids but the V weapons kept dropping, creating havoc in the capital. However.

they became scarcer too over time as the launch sites were overrun by the advancing Allied troops. The war in Europe was winding down. Germany was beaten, destroyed and overwhelmed. The final surrender was only a matter of time, but Esther's world remained as torn apart as London had been by the V1s.

CHAPTER TWELVE

Behind Enemy Lines
June to October 1944

Roger had already established a circuit in the Vosges Mountains area of Eastern France. It was a small group: Roger, a wireless operator who had been recruited from the Post Office Research Station at Dollis Hill in North West London, and a French resister and his wife, Philippe and Catherine. A number of other cells in the area were also operational.

George was slightly disappointed that he would not be parachuting in, but instead being landed from a Lysander Aircraft of 161 Squadron, which would fly from RAF Tangmere near Chichester. This had been chosen because of the small amount of delicate items, like radio crystals, that were accompanying them. Ian, the wireless man, was already in France. Last to see them off was Vera Atkins, proudly wearing the uniform of a newly commissioned Squadron Officer in the RAF, who had travelled from Baker Street to carry out the vital last-minute check to ensure that nobody was carrying any telltale evidence, English cigarettes, London bus tickets or West End theatre tickets, or anything else that would blow their cover as French citizens rather than killer agents from the enemy. Vera had little to do this time. Everyone kept their fingers and toes crossed that these two brave young men would keep their nerve, use their skills and help to shorten the war.

George and Roger were at Beaulieu listening to a final briefing from Buckmaster, who had travelled down from Baker Street with Vera. It was June 1944, and there was an anxious excitement present both in this room and throughout England. The long-awaited second front was expected at any time, with a mass invasion of occupied Europe by a huge force of Allied troops, aeroplanes and ships.

'It's no secret that we're going to land in enemy territory very soon,' the Colonel began. 'The man selling the evening newspapers in Baker Street knows that as well as the rest of the population. What we don't know is where and when. Any time now, with decent weather and long hours of daylight, and the best guess is that it'll be somewhere on the coast of Northern France, though whether it'll be the Pas de Calais or somewhere else, we have no idea. The Secret Intelligence Service has been carrying out a huge deception operation, *Operation Fortitude*, which we hope will keep the Germans guessing until the very last minute. Rather like *Operation Mincemeat,* which helped you to a slightly easier passage in Sicily, Lieutenant, though you perhaps didn't realise it at the time. The invasion will not be successful unless we are able to mobilise hundreds of thousands of occupied French men and women to stab the Nazis in the back. As you know, the SOE has been doing that for three years with varying degrees of success. Most failures have been down to betrayal, predominantly by collaborating French people, but a tiny bit because our people have been operating as double agents. Most of these traitors are in the ground now, and we're ready for the big push. Hundreds of your colleagues are already in France organising new circuits who are preparing to throw spanners in the German works. Roger has already created a circuit in the East of France. A radio operator is in place. You'll be there to kill Germans and destroy their means of making war. One thing we do know for certain is that the invasion will be by sea, which means that those Nazis stationed where you'll be operating will be moving out of your area as soon as the Allied troops land to reinforce the defenders. Your first job will be to make life hell for them so that their rescue operation is seriously compromised. Major, you've been chosen to lead this team because you're fluent in both French and German, have had three years in Army Intelligence so you can spot a bad 'un a mile off, and because your pre-war activities with the Lieutenant here,' nodding towards George, 'suggest you're very accomplished in subterfuge. You're also politically astute. The French resisters are either Communists or Gaullists, and they are always falling out. I reckon you're the man to pull the two sides together and weld an effective fighting force. And the last thing I'm going to say for now is that the area in which you'll be operating, Alsace-Lorraine, is not occupied France but was annexed to Germany in 1940. So it's part of Germany, but our intelligence suggests that the inhabitants hope to be French again before too long.' The Colonel paused the briefing to sip some tea.

'The circuit is called *Cooper.* Don't ask me why. Perhaps in the dim and distant past, a member of one of your families made beer barrels. Further south, we have had a number of successful operations, the best of which was *Stockbroker,* run by an English schoolmaster, codenamed Henri. North of that, there is the *Chancellor* circuit. As the Major knows well, the Lieutenant, Philippe and Catherine are very familiar with the area. Their hometown is Molsheim, where there is a very threatening Gestapo office. Philippe and Catherine know everything there is to know about the district around Strasbourg and will have already started to recruit resisters, identify safe houses and so on. When you land on enemy soil later tonight, Philippe and Catherine will be organising the reception. God willing, the invasion will be successful, so your next job will be to interfere with the German retreat. The war will be over a lot quicker if we can prevent masses of German troops from reaching their homeland. Their soldiers are incredibly tough, and they'll fight like tigers to hang on to what they believe is theirs. The Rhine in Strasbourg was the pre-war border between France and Germany. Make it hell for them to escape across the river. Vera.'

Vera Atkins stood up and continued the briefing as she had done so many times in the past.

'Major, you will carry a French ID card showing you to be an engineer at the Strasbourg rail yards. You'd been transferred from a small town near Le Havre where their rail yards had been destroyed in an air raid. The Town Hall in that town was demolished in the same attack so all records will have gone up in smoke. You've already had your English tooth fillings replaced by French ones. You should look, even to suspicious eyes, French. You'll be flying tonight on a Lysander from Tangmere. One of the radio operators from the *Chancellor* circuit has already sent through the co-ordinates for the landing area. These arrangements will be confirmed by a cryptic message on the French Service of the BBC shortly. If you, Lieutenant, are questioned by the French police or the Gestapo, the game would be up immediately, and you'll probably be summarily executed. You'll be masquerading as a downed English airman. The only ID you will carry will be your RAF pay book. You will wear French clothes. If detained, you can claim you stole them, having buried your uniform in some obscure spot. You might just get away with it and be bundled off to a POW camp.

'Thank you, Vera,' Buckmaster said as he again took the floor. 'I think you should know what to expect in terms of security in enemy territory. The main German police are the Gestapo, and they are very dangerous. Alongside them is the SD, the SS internal security service. Then there's the Abwehr, their foreign intelligence service, rather like our SIS. On top of that, we have the Feldgendarmerie, a kind of military police. Last, but by no means least, we have the French police. Most of them are probably OK, but there are plenty who will hand you over to the Gestapo at the drop of a hat. It's in your favour that all these disparate organisations regularly fall out with one another, which makes them far less effective than they otherwise might be.'

Buckmaster let all that sink in and drew a deep breath.

Roger spoke up.

'One thing. When we've done all these jobs, how do we get out?'

'Good question,' Buckmaster replied. 'Three ways, one of which I can't tell you about just yet. The others are through a Lysander pickup or via Switzerland. Henri perfected this route. He really was a star.'

'Was?' asked Roger.

'Sorry, is. He got shot four times by a French policeman but managed to escape through rivers and woods to Switzerland. He's back here now, helping to train new agents. A couple of other things, finally. Anybody you find actively collaborating with the Germans, you must kill immediately and bury their bodies. And you'll each find a cork in your kit. Your suicide pill is concealed in there. If you're arrested, interrogated and tortured, use it only it as the absolute last resort. Godspeed, gentlemen.' Buckmaster stood up and left the room, his head bowed, knowing that perhaps for the hundredth time, he might be sending good men to their deaths.

George had hung onto the Colonel's every word. If he hadn't known it earlier, he was certainly aware now that, once he and Roger landed safely on French soil, he would be embarking on a very dangerous mission. He knew he might not survive, but then, neither would tens of thousands of Allied troops storming the beaches of Northern France. And, he felt, he would have more control over his destiny as an agent than he would have had as an infantryman jumping out of a landing craft under heavy fire from the German defenders. He and Roger were driven to a small cottage near RAF Tangmere where a hot supper was served and their pilot introduced to them.

George ate his food in silence. He was nervous, apprehensive, and even frightened. He'd faced death in Sicily, but this was somehow different. He felt he would be going into action for the last time. After this, he'd either be dead and never see Esther, his parents, and others close to him ever again; or he'd be so badly injured and never much use to anyone for the rest of his life. Or maybe he'd survive intact and live a long and happy life. But he recognised that the less he thought about this, the more likely he'd be alright. He'd responded well to the toughest training programme. He couldn't have been better prepared. Somehow, he finished his meal and looked at Roger, who stared back deep into his eyes.

'I bet you're thinking about the same things as me,' Roger said as he squeezed George's shoulder.

CHAPTER THIRTEEN

The skies over Eastern France.
June 1944.

George was crammed into his seat in the Lysander. Alongside him was his boss and friend, Roger Martin. There was a full moon, as there had to be for this type of flight, and George could easily make out the ground below, which was covered with trees. He was wondering how on earth they would find somewhere to land the plane when he spotted lights in the shape of an upside-down T below, which he guessed was a field. The pilot, Michael, had assured them that all would be safe and well. He'd done this trip many times, George remembered him saying; but still he prayed that the reception committee were members of the French Resistance, not the Gestapo. Roger had told him that there were a small number of Frenchmen prepared to betray their countrymen and their allies to the Boche. Several British agents had been arrested, tortured and then murdered by the Gestapo after a treacherous French whistleblower had fingered them. This had included a small number of very brave women too, so George was praying that it would be friendly French faces waiting to meet them when they landed. If the pair of them fell into the hands of the Germans, their vitally important mission, and probably their lives, would be over. He shifted nervously in his seat, glancing sideways at Roger, wondering if he felt the same way.

Michael gave an ample demonstration of both his skill and experience as he dropped the plane smoothly onto a field which was just long enough to guarantee a safe landing and take-off. George prepared to get out and then hesitated as he watched half a dozen figures dash from the gloom of the woods. He observed in silence as Roger, a fluent French speaker, stepped forward and introduced himself to the half a dozen men, who formed the nucleus of a circuit of French resisters and British agents in that part of France near the Vosges Mountains. There was no time for idle chatter, though and, after the initial introductions, the Frenchmen helped to turn the plane around. George had already unloaded the small amount of cargo, which consisted of some small arms, biscuit tin radios and spare crystals, as well as some dark clothing. Anything larger than that would either have been delivered by parachute already or be part of a later drop.

The small group waved the small airplane off as Michael sped along the field, and there was a collective sigh of relief as the Lysander lifted safely into the air and began its return trip to Tangmere. In less than a minute, the noise of the plane was replaced by the quiet of the night, with only the occasional bird, cattle or insect sound disturbing the silence. George heard one of the Frenchmen tell Roger that there were no Boche to threaten them and that they'd set off immediately to the safe house using bicycles hidden in the trees at the edge of the field.

The flight had been uneventful because most of the Luftwaffe were probably busy waiting for the invasion. Their journey had been straightforward, but George knew that now they were in occupied France, near the German border. *Straightforward* was a thing of the past. German troops based there would be racing to re-enforce their comrades defending the beaches of Northern France against the Allied invaders when they came. Later, when the Germans were hopefully on the run, Roger and George's job, together with the rest of the Special Operations Executive circuit, was to make life hell for the German Army as they first dashed west and, later, hopefully, as their defeated armies scrambled across the Rhine into their homeland, ready to defend it to the last man. And for this part, and at the time – despite his nerves - George couldn't wait.

The landing in a field next to a heavily wooded edge of the Vosges Mountains had passed without incident, and George and Roger dashed across the field to the waiting Philippe and his small band of resisters. Introductions were made, and they were hustled into a small clump of trees where a number of bicycles were waiting. Soon Roger and George were peddling their way behind Philippe's cycle with a hooded lamp towards the safe house, while the Lysander climbed into the sky to continue its return journey. George wondered why, with all the training he'd done, he hadn't been given the opportunity to improve his cycling skills as he wobbled all over the rough pathways. Still, it kept his mind off what lay ahead. He didn't want a humiliating fall in front of Roger and Philippe.

Catherine, Philippe's wife, a cheerful but worn-out looking thirty-something said hello to Roger and George when they reached the safe house, which was on the edge of a farm. She had soup and bread waiting for them, which they quickly ate and went immediately to bed.

'We're not here on any political mission. We're neither Communists nor supporters of General de Gaulle. When the huns have gone, you French must sort out your own future without any interference from us,' Roger said as he began the morning briefing.

'That's good news,' said Philippe, as he outlined what had been done so far. With the help of men and women from the *Chancellor* circuit, he had established four new cells in the new *Cooper* circuit. Molsheim, near their current location, was one. The others were in the localities of Dorlisheim, Rosheim and Obernai. Each of these cells had a number of safe houses associated with them. The weapons and explosives were spread out in various hiding places, and the custodians of these did not know of the whereabouts of the others in case they were tortured by the Gestapo and spilt the beans.

'You will need to be on the move all the time. You will have been told to keep your messages short, but the Boche have a fleet of radio detector vans. At the moment, there is little or no activity in this area, but once we start upsetting them, they'll be all over us.'

Ian, the radio operator who had recently joined them, nodded his understanding. George shook his hand and then turned back to Roger, who continued the briefing.

'Thank you, Philippe. You've made a great start. And thank you to Catherine for her hospitality. One thing that puzzles me is why so many buildings in this area are unoccupied?'

Philippe explained that when the Germans annexed Alsace-Lorraine in 1940, many of the inhabitants fled westwards, while others were forced out of their homes, and a lot of the young men were seized and taken to work as slave labourers in Germany. There were a great number of empty buildings and farms. Then he outlined the details of their first target.

'The French Service of your BBC have told us that the Boche have a huge stockpile of rubber tyres at a factory between here and Strasbourg. If we put a match to that, there'll be dozens of troop transport lorries running on steel rims.' Philippe laughed.

'Right,' said Roger, 'we'll join you tonight, and Ian will stay here and maintain radio silence.'

'You realise,' said Philippe, 'that once we do this, the Boche will know that there's resistance activity in this area and will do all they can to stop it.'

'Yes, I realise that,' Roger replied.

'I've had a look at the tyre store,' Philippe continued. 'It's about thirteen kilometres from here. It's not heavily guarded, but there seem to be four Boche soldiers patrolling outside. I think we can get in without being seen. It's going to cause a lot of trouble when it goes up in smoke, but the backlash will be greater if we kill any of their men. They often arrest and shoot innocent local people in retaliation when they lose one or more of their own. We'll return here afterwards, then tomorrow move somewhere else.'

George, who'd been silent but attentive throughout, remembered the stink of burning rubber during the Blitz and wasn't looking forward to smelling it again, although circumstances would give it a less offensive stink than in the autumn of 1940.

Roger asked how they were going to burn the tyres.

'I've bought some plastique, detonators and petrol to do the job.'

'Petrol?' asked Roger. 'Where did you get that? I thought it was rationed.'

'It is, but we have what you call a black market.'

Roger grinned, knowing that there was plenty of that type of thing going on back home.

'We'll go by bike. If we're stopped, we'll say we're on the early shift at the Strasbourg rail yards, but we'll keep off the roads as much as possible and stick to fields and woodland paths.'

That evening they ate a late supper and set off. Unlike the previous night, the sky had an inky blackness; yet, despite the absence of any moonlight, they made good progress and soon found themselves in a small wooded area. In the blackness, they could just make out a large barn with a double-doored entrance about twenty metres from where they were concealed. Two German soldiers were stationed there, lighting cigarettes, and then they set off in different directions to complete a lap of the building. George guessed the Germans probably reckoned that two was enough to cover a low-key target, not the four that Philippe had suggested earlier. George had sneaked up unobserved on German guards in Sicily. Although this was a much less threatening situation, he was still extremely nervous.

'How long for once round?' Roger whispered to Philippe.

Philippe glanced at his watch and timed their strolling; it took five minutes to amble back to the front. Stopping for a chat, the soldiers shared a joke, laughing briefly, then set off again. When both soldiers were out of sight, Philippe signalled to Roger and George, and the three of them scrambled over the grass to the doors, which were locked, but the Frenchman made short work of the chain and padlock with a sturdy pair of cutters. As soon as they were indoors, Philippe switched on his torch and identified pile upon pile of large tyres. The place stank of rubber. Having neither the time nor the resources to burn every tyre, they concentrated on the stacks near the walls, doused them in petrol, attached plastique to each, and Roger and George slid in pencil detonators. Philippe had warned them that he'd once put some in the wrong way and the plastique hadn't ignited. Philippe moved to the door while the two Englishmen made the explosives live. Joining the Frenchman at the doors, George whispered that they'd set the charges to go off in fifteen minutes. The guards returned from their five-minute patrol, exchanged a few words then set off again. Gesturing to his English comrades, Philippe silently opened the doors, let Roger and George out and equally quietly closed them behind the escaping saboteurs. Moving quickly and quietly back to their bikes, they mounted them and set off pedalling as fast as they could. Signalling them to stop, Philippe glanced at his watch, and as it ticked round to fifteen minutes, a series of explosions rocked the night sky.

Soon the petrol began to do its job, and the whole building was ablaze with jet-black smoke belching into the night sky. Murmuring his satisfaction, Philippe turned to his companions.

'A result, my friends. Well done.'

When they reached the farmhouse, George let out a huge sigh of relief. It was as if he'd been holding his breath since the start of the operation. He sat down with his elbows on his knees and the palms of his hands on the side of his face. Slowly, a mood of exhilaration overcame him. He felt he'd done a little something quite useful. A smile spread over his face.

Two days later came the news that most Frenchmen and women had been waiting for. A huge Allied force had landed on the beaches of Normandy, supported by an armada of ships and thousands of aircraft. The three of them focussed their efforts on preparing for the next stage of their mission, which was to harass the German forces as they moved westwards to reinforce their troops in Normandy. Ian's radio contact with England was kept to an absolute minimum, and most of the messages came the other way, via the BBC French Service.

All over occupied France, German communications and transport links were attacked. The *Cooper* circuit was already slowing down traffic on the roads and lorry loads of German troops rushing west, after June 7th. When the German High Command finally decided that the site of the invasion was actually Normandy and not the Pas de Calais, as they'd been led to believe by those responsible for *Operation Fortitude*, the travelling re-enforcements were hindered by large potholes in the road surface, big trees lying across the highways, and direction signs pointing in the wrong direction. Another tried and tested form of transport was the canal network of Eastern France; the blocking and disabling of lock gates caused no end of disruption. Exercises such as these were sometimes carried out in conjunction with destroying essential supplies, which were being transported by water. All kinds of important goods were delayed or even destroyed on their way to the front, including tanks and other forms of war transport, cement and other raw materials, food and fuel. Canal bridges were blown up.

Attacks on German communications grew. Pylons were pulled down and transformers blown up, blacking out electricity supplies and killing telephone lines. In the factories, men worked slowly, or not at all, and when they did, they often threw spanners in the works to slow down production. There were even one or two strikes, and there was nothing the Germans could do. They could neither kill them nor sack them, because there were hardly any replacement workers, many of the men having been rounded up and sent to forced labour camps in Germany, while the rest were living rough in camps for resisters in the forests. As George took in all this information as it came in via Ian, he began to grow excited that it was possible that the Germans would be defeated and this bloody war would be over.

The juiciest targets for Roger's circuit were the trains. These were primarily used for transporting troops and armour to the front, and many incidents slowed this down to a trickle. Signal boxes were put out of action or staffed by resisters who sent trains off on the wrong lines or, on one occasion, caused a train to stop at a red light. Shortly afterwards, a following train, not warned of the stationary train up ahead, ploughed into the back of it, killing scores of German soldiers and blocking the lines for days.

One evening in a Rosheim farmhouse, Ian decoded a message from England telling them that intelligence had identified a very long train which was due to leave Strasbourg carrying troops to Normandy with several flatbed trailers accommodating tanks and field guns. It was to head for Paris and then make tracks rapidly to the front. Philippe cleared the table and spread out two large maps. One looked like an official French railway map and the other was hand drawn.

'Where on earth did you get that?' Roger asked.

'We have many friends in the railways,' Philippe replied. 'The line to Paris passes through here,' pointing to a collection of small villages clustered together. 'This is the best place to attack the train. If we mounted an assault with our people, we'd be massacred. There will be far too many well-armed Boche for us to cope. We must choose the right spot and blow it off the rails.'

'Belt and braces, as you English say. We'll take up some rails, but before that, we'll cover a part of the track with some of your dirty tricks – I thought some rats stuffed with explosive might do the job. Even then, the train will be travelling slowly, and these things might be spotted. Both the engine driver and fireman are our men, but there will be at least two soldiers in the locomotive looking out for this type of thing. Someone will have to board the train and set the plastique to make sure the job is done.'

'No doubt that someone will be me,' George said with a grimace.

'Of course. I believe you have had training in this.'

'I have,' George admitted.

Philippe pointed to the large-scale sketch map, which had been copied and enlarged from the official one.

'This is not an easy route for trains. There are numerous bends and plenty of hilly stretches. When the train reaches here,' he said, pointing to the drawing, 'the train will slow down. You should jump on towards the front, scramble up to the roof of the first carriage then make your way towards the rear. There will be ten coaches, with a hundred soldiers in each. Fix a lump of plastique in every other one where the carriages separate. When you get to the end, you'll need to dispose of the guards,then put plastique on the flat trailers and jump off at the rear. Set the timers for twenty-five minutes. The driver and fireman have been told to drive as slowly as they dare. Two of my men will jump on the locomotive and kill the German guards. Our four men will jump off and head for the woods with the train still running. See here, as the bend ends, the track is hard up against the bank at the side with a big drop at the other side. With any luck, the train will roll sideways with the impact of the explosion and fall down the slope, killing most of the soldiers and destroying the tanks and field guns. Simple.'

'Hmm, sounds it,' said George sarcastically. 'What happens if the plastique doesn't explode?'

'Then either the exploding rats or the missing rail will stop the train, but not as effectively. You are our best chance.'

'When do we go?' asked George.

'Tomorrow. The railwaymen in Strasbourg say the train is scheduled to leave at five a.m. so we'll need to travel overnight by bicycle.'

They all needed rest before their ordeal, but sleep didn't come easily for George. He had complete confidence in Philippe and his men, and he thought the plan was sound, but still he tossed, turned, dozed and woke up wondering whether or not he was up to the job. Jumping on and off a moving train in the heart of enemy territory was a good deal different from performing the task on trains in the English Midlands. But, he constantly reminded himself, the German troop train would be travelling a good deal slower than at those practice runs, and there was the added advantage that there were so many tunnels in that mountainous area the Germans would not place guards on the carriage roof as they sometimes did. By the time he was ready to go, he'd persuaded himself that he was up to the task.

He was dressed in a black woollen hat, pulled down over his ears, dark brown jacket and trousers and sturdy rubber-soled boots to ensure as much silence in landing on the train and creeping along the roof. George had blacked his face. He loaded his haversack with plastique and detonators and filled his pockets with the tools of killing: a silenced pistol, a Webley revolver, the wicked-looking commando knife, a deadly garrotte and three hand grenades. Nervously, he climbed on his bike and set off behind Philippe and

Roger. He was anxious, not so much for himself, but rather because of the responsibility he was bearing to carry out the sabotage successfully. George knew that hundreds of such attacks were being carried out all over France, and each had a small part to play in the success of the invasion.

Black night, no moon and the likelihood of heavy cloud throughout the morning increased the chances of George getting on board the train unseen. The three of them reached the chosen spot and hid their bicycles in a wooded area.

'When you're safely on the train,' Philippe began, 'we're going to push all three bicycles through the woods. When you've completed your business, walk back through the woods close to the embankment and I'll meet you. The train will come slowly around that bend. As you can see, there's a long upward slope; you'll have to work quickly. It's only three kilometres to where the line is next to the steep drop.'

George nodded.

'My men are already in position. They'll be spreading the exploding rats and dismantling the track and the two who are to rescue the railwaymen are in place. We'll set off. You'll hear the train coming and see it belching out black smoke. Good luck, my friend.'

Fifteen minutes later, an alert but nervous George heard the engine and saw the tell-tale black smoke. He was lying on the ground between the rail and the embankment. His moment had arrived. As promised, the train was crawling. Getting on board would be easy, but doing it unseen was a lot more difficult. He was not a heavy person. He was in peak shape and, as the locomotive ambled towards his prone figure, he lifted his head and saw his opportunity. He moved from lying to standing in a fraction of a second, then leapt like a cat and got a firm footing on the attachment between the coal tender and the first coach. He didn't bother to congratulate himself on the success of the manoeuvre but scrambled onto the roof, lay flat and listened.

Hearing no commotion or increase in the volume of conversation below, he assumed he'd arrived unnoticed and began his journey along the roof on his stomach. Only a very small gap existed between the coaches, but there was plenty of room to attach a lump of plastique. He was concentrating like mad, making certain the detonator was thrust in the correct way. George completed the task and resumed his front-lying, prone position and made his way to the gap between the third and fourth carriage with swift caution. The train was very noisy, which helped to mask the sounds of his movements as it rattled along the tracks, but the smoke was thick and acrid, and he had to struggle at times to suppress a fit of coughing. Reaching the end of the last coach, having set the charges on five pieces of plastique, George glanced at his watch and saw that only ten minutes had elapsed since he had set the first charge. He had a quarter of an hour to complete the job, but he knew that this would be the most dangerous part of the whole exercise. Those minutes would determine whether he would live or die and whether or not these vital reinforcements would reach the enemy. He examined the two large flatbeds attached to the end of the train. On the first was the huge and threatening sight of two Tiger tanks and, on the second, three of the menacing eighty-eight mm field guns. As Philippe had predicted, there were four guards, one just below George, one each side of the tank trolley, and the final guard stood at the end of the whole train. All were armed with rifles and were looking either to the sides or rear, and none at him. So, commando knife in hand, he noiselessly dropped behind the first guard, grabbed the collar of the German's tunic and cut his throat. What did he feel at that moment? Nothing. Although this was not his first person-to-person kill, George did what was necessary and moved on to tackle the first of the two soldiers in the centre of the trailers. Using the enormous Tiger tanks as cover, George wielded his garrotte to despatch the first, and he was so determined to make sure that his enemy was dead that he almost decapitated him. At the other side of the flatbed trailer, he crept up on the third guard, whose back was turned to him. He was within touching distance without being detected, so he tapped his enemy lightly on the shoulder, stepped back and shot him in the forehead with his silenced pistol as the German turned around to face him. With three down and one to go, George should have been feeling confident. He was, in fact, but not complacent, and still that edge of fear kept him totally focused.

Although the job was almost complete, he knew that one lapse in concentration would result in his death and would give the guard time to raise the alarm and have the explosives made safe. His luck almost ran out. For no particular reason, the German turned round

154

and saw George approaching him. He quickly pulled his rifle into position but couldn't get a shot off before George came charging at him and collided with his midriff. George had used his single-shot Welrod pistol to kill the third guard, so was effectively without a weapon in his hand when his final struggle began. The two of them collided with the rail at the back of the trailer and tumbled over, falling onto the rails. Again, luck was on George's side as he landed on top of the German, cushioning his fall. He rolled away and glanced at the soldier, who was struggling to unbutton his hip holster and pull out his pistol. George was kneeling, but the urgency of the situation galvanised him into action, and he leapt to his feet, grabbed the German from behind and broke his neck with one brutal twist.

Scrambling up the bank on his hands and knees, he took one last glance at the receding train and then lay down. He was shaking and ice cold, and within seconds, he was violently sick too. He'd just killed four men in cold blood and would soon be responsible for the deaths of hundreds of other young men. Weeping silent tears, he slowly came to terms with what he'd done. Realisation dawned that he had played a tiny part in speeding up an Allied victory if the next part of the operation went to plan and the plastique exploded. Thinking back to his training, he muttered his thanks to those who had taught him to perform automatically. Exhausted by his efforts, he wearily made his way back towards Philippe, Roger and the bicycles.

Long before the two met, there was a series of huge explosions in the distance, and George knew that he'd done his job. He just hoped the two railwaymen had managed to escape. Philippe and Roger appeared, wheeling the three bicycles. The Frenchman took one look at George and then reached into his own haversack and pulled out a bottle of brandy, offering it to his comrade, who took a grateful slug.

The return journey to the safe house was long and extremely tiring. No one spoke much. They stopped several times to rest and eat some of the bread and cheese each had brought with them. Eventually, they reached the farmhouse where Catherine and Ian were waiting for them. Food was on the table, but all George wanted was to sleep and after giving the others a brief report on the day's events, he went to bed, where he slept soundly throughout the night. He woke up wondering where the hell he was. Then he remembered.

What was he doing there? He asked himself. Then it all came back to him – the train, the killings, the fear and, eventually, the excitement.

The sun was peeking through the curtains. He quickly washed and dressed and joined the others who were already having breakfast. He was ravenous and needed no second invitation to join them. They ate in silence, but at the end of the meal, Philippe looked at George and smiled.

'Thank you, my friend. You are a true Frenchman.'

George grinned and then replied, 'That's very kind, Philippe. Thank you. I'd much rather have you as an ally than an enemy.'

Philippe chuckled.

'When you two have finished throwing compliments at one another,' Ian interrupted, 'I have some news from the BBC. A big parachute drop is scheduled for the next moon in three days' time. It's weapons and ammunition. No agents. We have to arrange reception. I also learned that the Germans are almost beaten in Normandy, and they're expected to be on the run soon.'

'Then we must prepare for the next phase, the destruction of their escape routes,' Roger said.

Ian was incredibly excited. He switched off the radio. He'd been listening to the BBC French Service and hastily scribbling down notes as the announcements were read out. He looked at the other three.

'There's been a second invasion. This time it's the Mediterranean coast. Mostly Americans but some other Allies as well. Plenty of ships and planes as well as troops.'

'Where have they landed?' asked Philippe.

'As far as I know, lots of places between Toulon and Nice.'

'Good,' said Philippe. 'That means they'll be coming our way soon. What about Normandy?'

'Looking good. The Germans are besieged in a place called Falaise. The Canadians are trying to finish them off.'

Roger looked at the others with a thin smile of satisfaction on his face. 'So now they have to defend themselves on three fronts, one in Eastern Europe and two in France. They can't win this war.'

'You're right, but don't think it'll end quickly,' Philippe said with a shrug. 'I hate to say anything good about the Boche, but they know how to fight. I've been living under them for four years now, and they're the most ruthless, cruel, determined and stubborn warmongers on this earth. Sure, we'll win, but at what cost?'

The five of them moved to another safe house and lay low for several days. Ian kept them up to date. The Germans had been crushed in the Falaise pocket though many thousands were fleeing east towards the Belgian and German borders. The Germans had sped out of Paris without offering any resistance.

'So we've got Allied forces not far from where we are now. Their objective is to cross the border into Germany,' Roger began. 'The Nazis will fight like hell to prevent that from happening. The next few months will be very tough. Eventually, there'll be a big battle in and around Strasbourg. Apart from being a German city, according to them the Rhine runs through it and forms the proper border, according to international law, between France and Germany. What we do in the next few weeks will determine how easily our troops will overcome the Nazis.'

Then Roger spread a large map across the kitchen table. 'This is Strasbourg. You'll see that Philippe and I have made marks on the map. These are our targets. We'll start with the railways, which we'll put out of action tonight. That spot,' Roger said, pointing to the map, 'is the location of the railway yards. I'm intending that we destroy every workshop and shed, all the locomotives and other rolling stock, as well as the lines approaching the yards. I don't think they're expecting us, but the area will be heavily guarded. We'll have to take out some Germans. That doesn't mean banging them on the head and tying them up – it means killing them silently. George and I will set off the firework display. Philippe will keep a lookout for any problems and let us know if we're in danger. He does a wonderful pigeon impersonation,' Roger said, turning to George. 'We'll leave here at 2300. We're taking the van so no cycle training tonight. Strasbourg is about seventeen miles away – sorry, Philippe, twenty-seven kilometres. We need to set the charges by 0100 to go off at 0300. We'll have to work very quickly. We'll use pencil timers. Each of us will carry a revolver and a torch, and George and I will each have a knife and a garrotte. By the time we've set all the charges, we'll have an hour or so to get out of Strasbourg and be well on the way to getting back here. Any questions?'

'How safe are we here?' asked George, who was expecting the Gestapo to burst in at any minute.

'Hard to say,' replied Philippe. 'We use a number of safe houses, none of which have been blown so far. You'll know about the precautions we're taking with the radio. For a while, the Boche didn't have enough soldiers to keep an eye on us, but now they're on the back foot that's changed. Still, I think the only way for us to be uncovered is through betrayal.'

As quietly as possible, Philippe drove his truck towards Strasbourg. The headlights were hooded to permit just enough light to escape to allow the Frenchman to drive safely through the gloom. Apart from a plentiful supply of explosives, all five of them carried a Bren gun, pistol, knife and spring-loaded cosh, as well as hand grenades, flammable material to turn the bombs into incendiaries if they needed to. Roger and George each carried a silenced gun concealed in one sleeve and a deadly dagger hidden in the other. A shooting match was to be avoided at all costs, but they'd fight their way out of tight situations if needs be. German patrols and road blocks were a constant threat, so Philippe stuck to minor roads, which were little more than cart paths most of the time.

Handily, there was a wooded area with a clearing about four hundred metres from the railway yards which, despite the blackout, was easy to spot. The workforce, entirely French, were working round the clock on twelve-hour shifts. The sheds were lit up like a Christmas tree and presented a formidable challenge. Guards wandering aimlessly around the edge of the railway property confirmed that the Germans weren't expecting an attack. Most sabotage from resistance and SOE groups had, up to now, taken place away from urban areas in the countryside where a quick getaway and easy concealment could be accomplished. Trying to do the same in a busy, well-garrisoned city was like entering the lions' den.

As they waited for the attack to begin, George switched on his fear mode because he knew that he would be at his best, as he knew he needed to be. He looked at the others and nodded. All the agents wore dark clothing, soft-soled boots and had faces blacked as they crawled to the yards, each with a bag full of explosives on their backs. Men were working industriously in the sheds, ensuring that the occupiers had plenty of locomotives at their disposal. They'd agreed previously not to kill any railwaymen who were predominantly French and, in any case, would be as keen as anyone to see the Nazis suffer. Any railway worker who caused trouble would be put to sleep with the cosh for a few hours. How to prevent what might be called friendly fire, killing a lot of innocent railwaymen was a big issue. A fierce debate raged between the leader and the Frenchman, which was hopefully resolved when it was agreed to place one device in a harmless place and set it to explode a short while before the others to give warning to everyone that the premises should be evacuated. As they got closer, they found that the numbers busily carrying out maintenance were relatively small, which was a relief.

Roger took command. Operating by a crude form of sign language, he gave the other two their orders, and they proceeded to set their charges, quietly and efficiently. Breathing heavily, George crawled towards the first of eight locomotives in the huge shed. A huge lump of plastique was slapped on to a rear wheel, and George took great care in setting and attaching the detonator. Then he quickly scarpered on all fours to the next train and repeated the process before finishing that part of the job. The turntable, which helped manoeuvre engines into the arrival and exit positions, was next on his list, and he quickly did the necessary work to disable it. Leaving the building, he joined the others in setting charges to blow up lines, though they knew this was probably a waste of time since they could quickly be re-established. Rolling stock escaped. How could carriages, freight cars and wagons function without locomotives?

Philippe led the way to the concealed truck. They aimed to be as far away as possible when the balloon went up. If they couldn't see anything, too bad. Philippe would get the full report from his resistance friends the next day. Such was the enormity of the series of explosions that they could be seen and heard well over the German border, probably halfway to Stuttgart. The warning shot, a small detonation that had ripped a pair of large entry doors off their hinges, went unseen by the agents, but hopefully, it had happened less than an hour after they'd left the yards to cause the evacuation. Within half an hour, enormous flashes, deafening bangs and dense smoke filled the night sky, destroying both German escape routes and supply lines. Back at the farm, Philippe drove the van to its hiding place. The weary agents ate a brief meal and then, exhausted, went to bed.

The following morning they reviewed their next steps.

'What's next?' George asked.

'Roads and bridges,' Roger replied.

'If we're going to stop them escaping to Germany or having access to supplies to help them to defend Alsace,' Philippe added, 'we need to finish off what we started.'

'Of course,' said Roger. 'If we disable the bridges over the Rhine, we'll stop them getting in and out.'

'How about other communications, Roger?' asked Philippe. 'Radio station, telephone exchange and so on?'

'Dead right,' Roger replied. 'We'll lay low in our new hideout Philippe's taking us to for a couple of days, let the heat die down and then do bridges and roads. Start with the rail bridge that links the city with Kehl on the German side. After that, we'll make a mess of the road bridges. A third trip should see us finish the job with the radio and telephone systems.'

'What about the German barracks?' asked George. 'That would be the icing on the cake. A few hundred less German soldiers able to resist would help, wouldn't it?'

'It would,' Roger replied, 'but we don't want to take more risks than we have to. The war is nearly over. If we disable the river crossings, it'll probably take a month at least to repair them, by which time the Allies will be here. Anyway, we need to leave something for our troops to cross the Rhine when the time comes. The Allies will have the resources to make quicker repairs than the Germans.'

'How about a big air raid on Strasbourg?' Ian asked.

'I'd thought of that,' Roger replied. 'The danger is that one or more of us could get killed while we're setting our charges, or if the raid precedes our arrival, it'll warn them that something's up. And, of course, innocent citizens will die, and we need to avoid that at all costs. We don't want a repeat of the attack on the Peugeot factory when innocent citizens were killed, and the factory was hardly touched. We'll just have to stay out of sight and be bored for a day or two, and then we'll get our stuff ready for the next trip.'

Two nights later, the team of three left their new refuge by truck, entering Strasbourg just after midnight. Philippe parked the van, and the trio set off on foot. Strasbourg is a big city, but the most important buildings were closely bunched together so it didn't take too long to set charges at the telephone exchange and the radio station. On their way back, they did the same at three electricity transformers so, less than an hour later, eruptions started that would deprive the Germans of radio and telephone communications and power for the foreseeable future. Twenty-four hours later, they returned to inflict serious damage on the railway bridge over the Rhine but decided that to blow up any of the road bridges and the barracks was pushing their luck and planned yet another move the following night.

As they settled into their new base, Philippe sat the others down, including Catherine. He had a serious look on his face. 'I've heard from our man in the police station. The Head of the Gestapo, Braun, is furious about the damage we've caused, but he thinks he will soon know where we are. He's been having an affair with a teenage girl in the town, and she's become very worried what will happen to her when this area is liberated, so he's promised to take her to Germany with him if she finds out where we're hiding. We could be in trouble.'

George looked at Roger. 'Time we made ourselves scarce, isn't it, Guv.?'

'You're right. Ian has made contact with Baker Street and arranged for us to get out. What about you and Catherine, Philippe?'

'We'll be alright. There are still plenty of safe houses we haven't used. We've finished all we set out to do. Time to go.'

Forty-eight hours passed, and the small group nervously sat in the safe house, waiting for a reply from Baker Street. On the third evening, Ian told them a Lysander would pick them up the following night and asked for the coordinates for the landing. Philippe immediately set off in the evening darkness to organise the pick-up point, arriving back a little before midnight, and gave the details to Ian.

Philippe had hidden the van in woods. He'd concealed weapons and explosives in the vehicle half a mile away from the farmhouse. As they were trying to relax after the good news had been decoded, the door swung open, and four armed German soldiers burst in, followed by Braun.

'Put your hands up and drop your weapons!' the Gestapo man said.

George shot the first soldier in the throat, and an eruption of gunfire followed. Ian went down quickly, having taken a round in the temple, and Roger, Catherine and Phillipe grabbed hold of George,pulling him towards the back door. The young lieutenant was last out, and just as he reached the door a bullet hit him in the left shoulder. Catherine turned back to help him.

'Stop firing,' screamed Braun. 'We need them alive.'

One of the soldiers hit George on the head with the butt of his rifle, and he slumped to the ground but still conscious. He watched as Roger seized hold of Philippe and dragged him towards the door.

'Catherine, my wife!' screamed Philippe.

'They won't kill her,' Roger shouted. 'You heard what the Nazi said. He wants them alive.' George watched, helpless, as the two of them sprinted across the farmyard, firing indiscriminately at the farmhouse. By the time the German soldiers dared to leave, George reckoned that Philippe and Roger would be in the woods and safely in the van riding away from the scene of the tragedy.

George and Catherine were dragged roughly into the police station in Molsheim. George was now fully conscious. During the journey, he had felt wretched as he thought of Ian, the brave radio operator, lying dead in the farmhouse. His mind was filled with misery. He prayed that Philippe and Roger had escaped, and he knew that, if they had, the two men would come to try and rescue Catherine and him. He sat on a bed in the cell, his head pounding where he'd been hit. Braun came in.

'Stand up,' said the Gestapo man.

George, his shoulder aching and still leaking some blood, did as he was told.

'Who are you?' Braun asked.

In a well-rehearsed reply, George told the German that he was an RAF navigator whose plane had crashed, and he was now trying to make his way back to the Allied lines. Braun asked him where his uniform was, and the agent told him that he had buried it after he had stolen the clothes he was wearing from a French house. George gave his false rank, name and serial number and then shut up.

The German didn't believe him and repeated the questions. George gave his name, rank and serial number again, and Braun struck him across the face with a whip he was carrying. Asked again, George gave the same reply and was again hit. Braun angrily strode out to an adjacent cell, and a few minutes later, George heard further blows being struck. He assumed they were being directed at Catherine.

The German told the Police Chief in English, and loud enough for the prisoners to hear, that he would have the prisoners taken to Natzweiler, where there were facilities and specialists to make them talk and be quietly disposed of when they'd given up their secrets. The Police Chief agreed that this was the best course of action and then flattered Braun by asking how he had managed such a coup. The Gestapo man had great belief in his own ability as a secret policeman and smiled.

'Quite simple, really. I have been using my charms on a local girl and, so desperate was she to get into my bed, she said she would do anything to help me. So I persuaded her to use her obvious skills to get some information about the terrorists. And she did. Brigitte is her name.'

'Ah, yes. Many men in Molsheim know Brigitte. She is what you call a tease.'

George's shoulder had been bleeding profusely when they left the farmyard in the German truck, but Catherine knew her first aid and tore some material from her petticoat and bound it up during the journey as the guards looked on in silence. By the time they had reached the police station, the bleeding had almost stopped, and the blood was clotting, but it still looked like a nasty wound. George and Catherine were forcibly marched out of the police station after the initial interrogation and dumped into a truck that promptly set off southwards. When they reached their destination, they were taken from the truck down the side of the huts to a building standing at an angle to the rest, which they soon discovered housed cells. They were thrown into adjacent rooms and the doors slammed shut. George took stock. The floor was of cold grey stone, and the walls looked as if they had been covered in whitewash. A large light blazed down from the centre of the ceiling. Glancing around, he couldn't see any sign of an on/off switch. The room was about two metres by two and a half. A bucket stood in one corner and a rusty-looking bed with a thin mattress and a filthy cream-coloured blanket took up the space along one wall. Lying on the bed, he waited in fear.

'What is your name?' Braun began an hour later, speaking in English in a nearby punishment cell. It was a large room with all kinds of paraphernalia, including a bath. In reply, George gave his name, rank and serial number as before.

'And who were the others at the farm with you?'

'What others?'

Braun stood up and punched George with a strong blow to the side of his head. 'Answer the question. What others?'

'Oh, them. They were my fellow aircrew. They've already set off towards the Allied lines.'

'Who is the woman brought here with you?'

'No idea. She must live in the farmhouse. We forced our way in and demanded food.'

'Rubbish!' Braun shouted and hit George again. 'I can see we're going to have to give you some of our special treatment. Then you'll give us what we want. Everyone talks in the end.'

George was sitting upright in his chair. His head was ringing from the blows Braun had administered, but he was determined not to give the others away. Besides, he hadn't a clue where they were. What he did know was that they wouldn't be far away. What he didn't know was whether or not they'd get to him before he died because he was absolutely certain that he wouldn't talk and would persist in silence.

'You are part of a resistance cell. Apart from yourself, there were three other men and a woman. She is in our custody. I believe that it is you and your friends who were responsible for the sabotage in Strasbourg. Well?'

'Where's Strasbourg? I've never heard of it. Never been there in my life.'

Exasperated, Braun stood up, strode across his office, opened the door and shouted for a guard. 'Take him back to his cell. Make sure the light stays on. He may have water but no food.'

George lay on his bed and turned towards the wall, hoping to block out some of the light. It was no good. He was scared. His head ached terribly, and his shoulder had a sharp, throbbing pain. How many blows to the head could he take? What else were they planning for him? Warned during his training that it might come to this, he resolved not to give the Germans a single snippet of information.

It was approaching lunchtime when George was again frogmarched into the punishment cell. Waiting for him there were Braun and a young, black-suited SS man with short fair hair. The furnishings included a bath, a table on which there were some electrical gadgets and another table on which there were bamboo canes, whips, a long wooden pole, matches, cigarettes, some pliers and a variety of knives. There was also a couch of the sort used by doctors to examine patients.

'Take his clothes off and sit him on the bed,' ordered Dieter, the SS officer.

Stepping forward, Braun disdainfully examined George's naked body, stopping when his gaze reached George's groin.

'Ugh! A filthy Jew. You should get extra pleasure from this one, Dieter. I will ask the questions. Every time you fail to answer, Dieter here will play one of his little games with you. He loves inflicting pain. Where are the remaining members of your resistance cell?'

'What resistance cell?' replied George, shakily.

Braun nodded at Dieter, who walked over to one of the tables and picked up a bamboo cane. The guards forced George to lie on his front. Dieter took aim, then hit him very hard ten times on his naked buttocks. Angry red stripes began to form, and one or two began to bleed. He could feel his skin tingling at first, but that soon turned into a sensation of his buttocks being consumed by an uncontrollable fire.

'Where are the remaining members of your resistance cell?' Braun asked, his voice rising.

'What resistance cell?' from a slightly weakened George.

Dieter ordered the guards to hold him down on his stomach, and he then proceeded to rain blows with the cane on George's bare feet. Twenty times George felt the terrible pain spreading over his feet, but soon, first his toes, then the rest of his feet became totally numb. Not once did he cry out, though, not even when the guards stood him up.

'Where are the remaining members of your resistance cell?' an increasingly frustrated Braun shouted.

'What resistance cell?' George answered, his voice barely above a whisper.

'Lie him on his back,' Dieter ordered the guards. 'You know what's next, don't you, Jew? I think I'll have a cigarette. Do you smoke, Jew?'

'No, thank you,' croaked George.

The German lit up, took a long drag then touched George's left nipple with the bright red tip.

George screamed.

'Didn't you like that, Jew? Try some more,' and he pressed the tip against George's right nipple.

George screamed again, but he was growing weaker. Dieter pressed the cigarette into George's navel, and George groaned and almost passed out, but he just about picked up the sadist's voice.

'He's gone for the time being,' Dieter reported to Braun.

'Very well. Take him to his cell,' Braun ordered the guards, 'and return him here at fourteen hundred hours.'

George was totally shattered. He came round slowly, every inch of him screaming with pain. His buttocks and feet were still bleeding, and the burns on his torso were dreadfully painful. He didn't even bother to think about what they planned for him in the afternoon. All he knew was that he had to say nothing and wait for Roger and Philippe to come for Catherine and him, which, against all logic, he knew would happen, possibly that night. Thinking briefly of Catherine, he decided she was probably okay since he hadn't heard any other screams. On the other hand, she might be dead. He'd changed his philosophy of killing. Those Germans who had tortured him and killed Ian had to die and would. It was as simple as that. It would prevent the Nazis from carrying out the unspeakable acts that he had suffered on anybody else. Knowing that he would never betray his friends and that they would soon come for him helped him prepare for the likely horrors of the afternoon. How they would get into the camp, let alone his and Catherine's cells, he'd no idea. He just knew they would. He glanced at his wounded shoulder. It was beginning to sting, most likely turning septic. He'd have to get out soon and get it looked at, otherwise he might even lose part of his arm.

The cell door swung open, and two guards dragged him off his bed and into the punishment cell. Braun was waiting alongside Dieter, who had a smile of anticipation on his cruel face. Despite his resolve, George was nervous and very scared, but he reminded himself it was only pain and only temporary.

'Did you have a nice lunch, Jew? Ours was very tasty, wasn't it, Dieter? German sausage and sauerkraut? Delicious. What did you have, Jew?' George looked at him in such a dispassionate way that the German began to realise that this might end badly for Dieter and him. Brushing off these concerns, albeit briefly, the Gestapo man pulled a handkerchief from his pocket and pinched his nostrils together. 'Oh, dear. I think I smell dirty, unwashed Jew. I think he needs a bath, Dieter.' The black-uniformed SS man nodded to the guards who grabbed George, ripped his clothes off and forced him onto his knees at the end of a full bath of water.

'Where are the remaining members of your resistance cell?' Braun asked again.

'What resistance cell?' George replied. One of the guards seized his neck and plunged him head-first into the water. They pulled him out a minute later, then repeated the process several times more. As the volume of Braun's question rose, George's reply became much quieter.

'He's nearly out,' Dieter said to Braun.' You won't get much out of him this way.'

Frustrated, Braun instructed the guards to lift him onto the couch. George slowly recovered a small degree of consciousness and heard Braun instructing the guards to hook him up to the camp's electricity supply with electrodes attached to his balls.

'Where are the remaining members of your resistance cell?' Braun asked yet again, only to receive the same reply from his prisoner. On the table, Dieter pulled a lever slowly towards him. Excruciating pain shot through George's testicles, his penis and up his rectum into his lower back. Even when the power was switched off after what was, in reality, a very short space of time, but felt to George like a lifetime, pain was coursing through his lower and middle body. The same question and reply. George could barely hear what was being said, but Braun was ordering the sadistic Dieter to give the prisoner another dose. Best bet, George thought, was to feign a lapse into unconsciousness. The torture ceased, and when he opened his eyes, he saw a short man wearing a white lab coat, whose dark brown eyes, which seemed almost black, and matching hair, swept back and greased, gradually took shape through George's blurred vision

'Check this prisoner,' Braun ordered, 'and tell me when we can resume treatment, please, doctor.' The doctor went about his work. Twenty minutes later, he gave his report. 'He's in a very bad way. You'll get nothing out of him today. You've probably gone too far. Hopefully, he'll have improved enough in the morning to give you a short time to question him. But he won't last long if you carry on torturing him. Then there's his shoulder. It's turning septic. Gangrene is a real possibility.'

The Gestapo man thought for a moment. 'Put his clothes on, take him back to his cell, give him some food and water. If he's still alive in the morning, I'll question him then and, if he doesn't respond, we'll throw him in the oven.'

'Sedated?' asked the doctor.

'What, waste good phenol on a fucking Jew? No, sling him in as he is.'

The doctor waited for a minute before asking Braun: 'I have a special request to make. You know that I'm carrying out research into Jewish anatomy and physiology?'

'Well, what of it?'

'Before he's killed, I'd like to insert a wooden pole up his anus and collect the resulting sperm to compare with samples I've taken from our other Jewish guests. Then, when you kill him, could I ask that he's hanged? I'd like his skeleton to add to the other Jewish skeletons I've accumulated in my research.'

'Right,' replied Braun. 'Glad to be of help, doctor.'

It was several hours before George became aware of where he was. A table beside his bed had a bowl of disgusting-looking cold soup and a flask of water on it. He couldn't face the soup but drank the water greedily; it helped to revive him a little, and he remembered the horrors of earlier that day – or was it yesterday? He had no idea. He felt absolutely drained but remembered he'd given nothing away despite the sadistic treatment meted out to him. Would he survive the next dose? He was sure he would. Suddenly, his spirits were lifted by a short coughing noise, followed immediately by another. He'd recognise that sound anywhere. Silenced shots. But whose? The Nazis or his rescuers? Seconds later, he got his answer as the rattle of keys was quickly followed by the sound of the cell door swinging open, and Roger rushed in and, without a word, lifted him up and carried him into the passage outside the cells. They met Philippe, who was carrying Catherine. They stepped over the bodies of the two guards and found two others lying prone on the ground outside the cell block.

'I can walk, Guv,' George protested, even though his legs felt like broken sticks. 'Put me down. It'll be quicker.'

Catherine also asked to be put on her feet, and the four of them silently made their way along the perimeter fence. As they passed the guardhouse, George spoke in a whisper.

'There's that bastard who tortured me. Dieter someone or the other.'

'He won't be there much longer. Come on, get a move on.'

Within a minute, three loud explosions filled the air. Two guard towers and their inhabitants toppled to the ground, and the guard room went up in a fireball, suggesting that the charge had been spiced up with incendiaries.

The four of them continued their cautious journey along the edge of the fence.

'Give me a gun, Guv,' George said quietly.

Roger passed him his Webley. 'There are six rounds in it. Hopefully, we'll be through the hole in the fence, and you won't have to use it.'

But the Major was wrong as three figures came running through the gloom towards them, two black-uniformed SS men and Braun. Before the Germans could do a thing, two shots rang out, and the two SS men dropped to the ground, Roger and Philippe having despatched one apiece. An enraged Braun continued towards them. He took aim at Roger but before he could squeeze the trigger, the left side of his head was blown away by George, who was standing with his right arm pointed at Braun and his left gripping the wrist of his gun arm with every ounce of strength he could muster.

They reached the comparative safety of the trees, but the ground was very hilly, and George and Catherine struggled up the slope. Philippe collected a reel of wire and continued upwards. George glanced backwards and saw about fifty soldiers racing through the main gates, accompanied by loudly barking Alsatian dogs. Sirens were blaring, and the whole area was illuminated by four huge floodlights. George had gone quiet but was mercifully still breathing. Further up the hill, they stopped for a moment, while Philippe told Catherine to lift her feet, and Roger took extra precautions helping George over the wire. Then they made their way to the van. When they reached it, Roger took out his night glasses and watched what was happening in the camp.

Roger wrapped his arm around, George's shoulders. 'Thanks. You saved my life.'

'You too, Guv. Let's get going,' George said, hardly above a whisper.

'We'd agreed beforehand that making a dash for immediate safety was out of the question,' Roger explained to George. 'We'll need a head start if we're going to get away successfully.' George watched as his Guv went to the back of the van, where he found a small metal box to which he fixed the wires that they'd fetched up the hill. Minutes later, three transport vehicles were seen heading towards the camp gates, laden with troops. There were also several dozens of soldiers on foot,who raced up the hill in pursuit, accompanied by loudly barking dogs. They passed the first wire, which was lying harmlessly and unseen on the ground, and nobody spotted the second either as a soldier's boot tripped a volcanic explosion which immediately turned into a raging furnace ahead of them. The terrified dogs dragged themselves free and raced down the hill back towards the camp. Just as the Alsatians cleared the danger area, Roger pressed the handle on the metal box and a second eruption took place, followed immediately by an inferno sweeping through the trees. The pursuers were now trapped, and their horrible screams echoed through the troubled night air, which was immediately filled with the stench of burning flesh. George watched open-mouthed and saw three troop-filled lorries set off after their enemies through the main gates.

'We'd better be off,' said Philippe. Carefully, George was laid against the back of the van, where Catherine squatted alongside him, cradling him in her arms. Roger sat in the front seat next to Philippe, the driver. George, though in terrible condition, had his spirits lifted momentarily when Philippe announced: 'The Allies are some thirty kilometres south of Colmar.'

'We'll head there.' Behind them, the first of three pursuit trucks was making good progress until it ran over an innocent-looking cow pat and was blown high into the air. The second truck took evasive

170

action and swerved to the side, where the local cattle had left another surprise which cleared the road of a second group of pursuing Germans. The third truck turned back to the concentration camp.

Dawn was breaking. George was drifting in and out of sleep. He heard Philippe's voice:

'It's unlikely we'll be attacked by the Allies, but just in case, we'd better find something white as a flag of truce.'

'Philippe,' George began quietly, 'I know who betrayed us. It was a girl called Brigitte. I heard that Gestapo guy bragging about it.'

'Thank you, my friend. She'll be in the ground before the end of the day. Catherine, my dear. Please make us a flag of truce.'

'Seems like what's left of my petticoat will be needed again,' said Catherine. It was mid-morning when two American soldiers stepped in front of the van, which was flying a white ladies' petticoat. Roger quickly explained the situation. One of the soldiers looked in the back, glanced at a flagging George, and then spoke into his radio. 'Our perimeter is a mile up the road, sir. Medics will be waiting for you.'

'Thank you.'

At the main gate of the Allied camp, the medics were indeed waiting. Before anyone could blink, George felt himself being lifted and secured onto a stretcher and loaded into an ambulance.

'We're taking him to our field hospital, sir,' George heard one of them say. He felt the ambulance set off then lapsed into unconsciousness.

George eventually awoke in the American military hospital in Paris, where the doctors had done a wonderful job on him in his period of unconsciousness. Saving his arm had been a priority, and later he was told that they'd worked day and night for almost a week to prevent gangrene from taking its inexorable hold, and thanks to their persistence and the new wonder drug penicillin, they eventually succeeded. Attention then turned to his horribly scarred body, the results of electric shock treatment and cigarette burns administered by a sadistic SS officer. George had assumed that this man had died in a fireball when the room in which he was working at the time was blown to bits by plastic explosive. The man who had ordered the torture, Molsheim Gestapo Chief Heinz Braun, had also died when George had used every ounce of his rapidly diminishing strength to shoot him, thereby saving the life of his boss and great friend, Roger Martin.

Recognising the wonderful efforts that the doctors were making, George worked as hard as he could to rehabilitate – at least physically. Eventually, the chief surgeon told him that his life was not in danger and almost all of his wounds had healed well. But, the American told him, there was little more that they could do about his testicles, although some revolutionary new skin treatment might help. Unfortunately, this was not available in Paris, and so he found himself returning to England by plane three months after landing in that moonlit French field to begin his mission. Physically he was healing – or most of him was – but mentally, he was still an open wound.

In London, he came under the supervision of a young plastic surgeon called Mark Sinclair, a Scotsman who'd been a pupil of the legendary Archibald McIndoe, who had pioneered plastic surgery on pilots badly burned in their cockpits when their planes had caught fire during the *Battle of Britain*. Sinclair was quite a small man with a round, friendly face dotted with freckles matching his ginger hair. He explained to George that he intended to take some undamaged skin from another part of his body and graft it onto his testicles. He would be assisted by George's old friend, penicillin, because the risk of infection was always present during these risky procedures. More painstaking surgery seemed to do the trick and, by the time spring made its first cautious appearance, George was able to leave the hospital. His body was, it seemed, healed, but his mind remained broken. Nightmares persisted, and in his waking hours, he hardly spoke a word and was frequently observed silently staring into space, his face blank. In Paris, it was impossible, of course, for his friends and family to come and see him, and visitors were not welcome at all in the London hospital, where strict quarantine conditions prevailed. Letters, flowers and other gifts arrived almost daily but most remained unopened on his bedside table, although nurses did take the trouble to put the flowers in water and open and display the cards he'd received. A tough time lay ahead for George, and he wasn't at all sure if he would ever cope with the dreadful memories of the past two years – until one day, an unassuming young man approached him.

'Lieutenant Aaron? I'm Colin Walters, one of the staff here…'

CHAPTER FOURTEEN

London
Spring 1945

As if she hadn't suffered enough, Esther now began to feel sick in the mornings. She'd missed her period, and her breasts were beginning to feel tender. Cook, the mother of two grown-up children, knew exactly what was happening and asked Sir John to send for his doctor, who quickly confirmed that Esther was pregnant. The news threw Esther into a further state of total panic. What would she do? Abortion was out of the question. There had been enough deaths already. Could she adopt the child or perhaps even keep it? What would those close to her think, especially those like George and Roger, who were unaware of what had happened to her?

Sir John showed great concern about her mental state and made sure she had the very best medical supervision. Sir John told her that the police had tracked down the soldier who had raped her. He had been killed in France.

Towards the end of winter, Esther and Mary were called to a huge explosion near Edgware Road Station. It was daylight when they arrived, and there were already several ambulances in attendance. At least a dozen three-storey buildings had collapsed, and a number of adjoining structures were looking as if they wouldn't last much longer. Debris was strewn everywhere, and there was the usual cacophony of screams, cries, shouts and moans, to which those attending these disasters had become accustomed. Judging by the amount of damage, it was clearly the work of a V2. Everybody got to work, shifting rubble to release the trapped, alive or dead, administering first aid to the walking wounded and taking the badly injured by stretcher to the waiting ambulances. Esther and Mary worked furiously alongside their colleagues and were just about to transfer a badly injured young boy to an ambulance when there was a roar of falling slates, tiles and bricks as one of the tottering houses collapsed on top of the two girls. Helpers rushed into action. The child, miraculously, had escaped further mishap but was screaming. Esther and Mary were both buried, and the rescuers tore the rubble away, causing many hands to bleed. Both of the girls were unconscious and were rushed to hospital.

Three days later, Esther awoke in a hospital bed to find her father and brother sitting alongside her. She opened her eyes and saw smiles of relief spread across their faces. A doctor was summoned who described her injuries.

'You've suffered a severe concussion, but that will clear up shortly. Both of your collarbones were broken. They, along with your broken left arm and right ankle, will heal in due course.' He looked sideways at her father and brother and coughed awkwardly. 'But I'm terribly sorry to tell you that the child you were carrying did not survive, but your reproductive organs weren't damaged in any way, and you'll be able to have further children in the years to come.'

Simon Abrahams looked stricken, but he reached across and took her hand in a comforting grip. Esther squeezed it back, thankful for the people she loved supporting her without question.

'What about my friend, Mary?' Esther asked in a quiet voice.

'I'm so sorry,' the doctor said, 'but she died at the scene. Death would have been instantaneous. She won't have suffered at all.'

'Thank you, doctor,' Simon Abrahams said. Neither he nor Peter had known about Esther's baby, but they said nothing.

The doctor smiled, nodded and left.

'Baby?' her father queried gently. 'George's?'

'Oh no, no,' Esther cried then as she'd never cried before, and in halting words told them what had happened.

'Oh, my poor, brave girl,' Simon said at the end of her tale. 'But now you can pick up where you left off and start again.'

Esther was trussed up like a chicken with plaster of Paris pots and her right leg up in the air on some kind of pulley. Her head ached. She thought of poor Mary, and her heart sank. Then she thought sadly of the fate of the poor child she had carried, another victim of this bloody war.

'We're leaving now,' Simon said to his daughter. 'There are two others outside who wish to have a quick word with you, then you must sleep. We'll be back tomorrow. Good bye, Esther. We both love you very much.' Simon and even Peter kissed her on her cheek.

After they had left, Sir John came in with Roger Martin's fiancée, Jane.

'We won't stay long,' Sir John said. 'You must get as much rest as you can so you can get back to serving my breakfast as soon as possible.'

Both managed a weak smile.

Jane said how dreadfully sorry she was about all the awful things that had happened to her since they had last met in September 1939. Sir John had told her that she should come clean about the rape with those closest to her, but Esther had resisted telling her father, whom she felt had suffered enough. He now knew but not the full details. However, Jane knew both about the assault and the loss of the baby. When Roger came back from overseas Jane would tell him, with Esther's permission.

'That would help me a lot, Jane, but what about George?'

'I think you should tell him yourself, Esther. I don't think you need be worried. He'll be shocked, but he'll understand – and you haven't done anything wrong, have you? George loves you, Esther, even if he hasn't told you.'

Esther sat in silence for a short while, then asked about Roger.

'I don't know where he is, Esther, but he's got George with him. Roger's a Major now, and George is a First Lieutenant. You'll have to start calling him sir.'

The three of them laughed gently, and then Sir John and Jane left. Esther thought back on what Jane had said. She knew she had to tell George about everything, including the lost baby, but Jane had re-assured her that it would be the right thing to do. Knowing and doing, however, were two different things. She also thought about what her father had said after they'd gone. Could she? He supposed she had to, somehow. But alone – no Mary, no Joe and possibly no George now, yet her father was right. She was brave, and she *would* start again.

EPILOGUE

England
October to December 1945

Colin had been working with George for more than three months. Progress had at first been quick, and Colin had cleverly built on George's enthusiasm for the result of the General Election. Then things got tricky when Colin took George back through his experiences at Natzweiler.

'I just can't believe that one man could treat a fellow human being in that way. I know now that I wasn't the only one to be on the receiving end of such barbaric behaviour. Not by a long way. The bastards were murdering everybody they could lay their hands on - Prisoners of War, resisters, Jews, agents, hostages, anybody they could string up or throw in the ovens. And they bloody enjoyed it.'

'What about when you were on the battlefield? How was that?'

'I did have some problems with that on the way out to Egypt. I was scared of dying and worried about killing other people, the Sixth Commandment you know, but I came to terms with that, and I saw that if I didn't kill the enemy, he'd kill me.'

'What about fear?' Colin asked.

'I soon realised that everyone was frightened. Even those soldiers who'd seen action before. That helped a lot and kept you on your toes. I didn't want to die. Up to that point, I'd had a good life with friends, a girlfriend, and parents who loved me. I'd been happy growing up. I wanted more.'

Later that week, they talked about Esther. Colin kicked off.

'You mentioned a girlfriend?' Colin asked.

'Esther. I got involved with her before the war.'

'What was she like?'

George sat back in his chair, and a smile spread over his face.

'Beautiful, funny, brave, loving. Everything I wanted in a girlfriend.'

'Did you love her?'

'I hadn't had much experience of girlfriends, but I think I did.'

'Did you see her during the war?'

George sighed. 'At first, everything carried on as usual, the *Phoney War*. Then it all started getting really serious. Esther and her family were locked up on the Isle of Man, and her mother became very ill and died there. When she got back, the Blitz was in full swing. She got a job on the WVS stand outside Liverpool Street Station. She's got guts, you know, Colin. A bomb could have hit her at any time. My friend Joe and I used to chat with her when she was working on the stand with her friend, Mary. Things between us were sort of on hold. The war was going badly, and I knew that it would last long enough for me to get called up. I didn't want her sad because I'd been killed in battle, so I kept her at arm's length. A casual relationship.'

Days passed. Colin knew he was making progress and was beginning to feel George could be mended.

'I suppose you were terribly upset when you heard your friend, Joe, had been killed.'

A shadow passed over George's face. 'I was devastated. I loved him like a brother. We'd been close friends since we were nippers. We did everything together. Our parents got on well with each other. I'll never forget him, Colin. Sometimes I think back to the things we got up to, and I find myself smiling.'

'How often do you think back to the war, George?'

'All the time. I'm glad we didn't turn the other cheek. The Nazis were terrible shits. They deserved all that came to them. When I remember all those awful things that happened, I just say to myself, it was just the bloody war. There must never be another one, Colin.'

The rapport between the two grew. One morning as autumn turned to winter, Colin asked George:

'Do you feel ready to leave here, George?'

'Thanks to you, Colin, I'm thinking seriously about it. You know, before the war and the early years of it, I could identify the bad people and, if necessary, dish out some punishment like with the Gestapo man at Harwich or the looters in Bateman's Row. Then I started wondering what it would be like in battle, shooting enemy soldiers who were really just like me. Of course, I did know that if I showed signs of weakness or dread, I'd be sent home to look after barrage balloons. Germans who behaved like that would be shot.

178

Understanding that, because of that, their motivation was greater than mine made me vulnerable, I suspected. So, I had to pull myself together and trust my training and my fellow soldiers.'

'Lots of others had to face that reality,' Colin reminded him, 'but it wasn't really just that, was it?'

George looked Colin in the eye. 'I can't believe that human beings could do to another human being like me the torture I suffered at Natzweiler. My father was right. The Nazis at the top were evil and only stayed in power because ordinary soldiers defended them. And the film from Belsen, Buchenwald and camps in Austria and Poland somehow justified the war. I had to fight, Joe had to fight, my friends in Sicily, Steven and Bert - they had to fight too, and, sadly, some died. I'll probably miss Joe every day for the rest of my life, but I'll remember the good times. Thank you, Colin. You've helped me to come alive again.'

'Good. I'm delighted for you. There's a queue of visitors a mile long, all anxious to come and see you. Are you ready for them?'

'I think so. My parents first, please.'

They came to see their son the next afternoon. Both showed looks of concern, but these vanished as a big smile spread across George's face as he greeted them.

'Good to see you smiling, George,' his father said. 'How are things?'

'Nearly there, I think, thanks to Colin. Have you met him?'

'Yes. A lovely man,' Sarah said. 'He spoke very highly of you.'

'He's a great guy. Taught me to look ahead but warned me that I'll never completely wipe the memory of what happened. Told me that was a part of my life, but it happened in the past.'

'What are you going to do, George?' his father asked.

'Haven't really thought about that, but I will now that I know I'll soon be home. We can talk about it when I get home. First, I've got to get demobbed. I'll do that as soon as I get out of here.'

'And don't forget you've a Military Medal to be presented with. We're so proud of you, George.'

They talked for another half an hour, and then Isaac told him that Joe's parents had travelled with them and were waiting outside. They asked George if he would see them.

'Of course,' said George. 'Please ask them to come in.'

Joe's parents followed Isaac and Sarah in to see George. They said how pleased they were to see him recovered and thanked him for being such a wonderful friend to Joe. They couldn't wait, they said, to see him causing mayhem on the streets of East London again.'

The visitors kept coming. The next day, it was Roger and Jane. They embraced him like the brother he'd been to them both.

'One thing, Guv.,' George began. 'Thank you for rescuing me from that dreadful camp. You saved my life, and Catherine's as well. How tough was it?'

'It was not easy, but not quite as it hard might have been. The Nazis had begun to evacuate the camp, so there were less guards than there probably would have been earlier in the year. And, by the way, thank you for saving my life. You've made quite a habit of getting the better of the Gestapo. They certainly taught you how to shoot straight in the infantry and SOE. Congratulations on your medal. There'll be another in 1946. The French are going to decorate us in the New Year and Philippe and Catherine as well. Bit of a drag, but we'll have to go to Paris to get the gong.'

'Paris, that sounds good, and no Nazis to spoil the fun.'

They laughed together.

'Before he forgets to tell you, George,' Jane began, 'Roger has been awarded the same decoration as you. Rather appropriate, don't you think?' Jane asked.

'It sure is. Congratulations, Guv.'

'Thanks. By the way, I thought you'd like to know that Jane and I are going to get married before Christmas, and I'd like you to be my best man.'

George's mouth sprang open. 'Best man! Thank you, Guv. What an honour but what will the church say, a Jew best man to a Christian?'

'They can like it or lump it,' Jane said. 'If they don't like it, we'll get married in the Registry Office. Anyway, my Maid of Honour is Jewish.'

'Oh,' exclaimed George. 'Who's that?'

'Esther,' replied Jane.

George looked down for a second. 'I haven't seen her or been in touch with her for ages.'

'Of course, you haven't. You've had other things on your mind,' Roger said. 'But terrible things have happened to her as well. I'm sure she'll tell you about it when she's ready, but I warn you, she's very nervous.'

'I am too, Guv.'

'The wedding's only a couple of weeks away. After the church service, we're all going to the restaurant in my father's store for the reception. Why don't the two of you find a quiet corner and tell each other about what's happened over the past five years?'

George thought for a moment. 'You're right. It's time we both drew a line under the past and tried to move on. What did happen to her, Guv?'

'She has to tell you that, George.'

Others visited George before he was discharged, including Steven Morgan, who'd stayed in Italy until the bitter end. He'd ended up a Sergeant and was now studying at Cambridge University. He'd been told that Captain Pearse had been killed at Monte Casino. Both had liked Pearse and were sad that he'd gone. They enthusiastically agreed to stay in touch. Simon and Peter Abrahams arrived and thanked George for all that he, Joe and Roger had done for them, and Sir John turned up, thrilled to see George had overcome his desperate unhappiness.

On Tuesday of the following week, George went home after thanking the staff, especially Colin Walters. The next day he was demobbed.

It was a bright but cold December Saturday. Christ Church in New Malden was full for the wedding of Roger and Jane. The guests wore a mixture of uniforms and civilian clothes. The congregation was supposed to be silent in church, but there was an excited murmur as they waited for the arrival of Jane and her father. Roger and George were in the front pew, close to the altar, both resplendent in the uniform of the Special Operations Executive and each with the Military Medal, one of the highest awards for bravery, pinned to their tunics. George was worried about carrying out his duties correctly. The organ struck up *Here Comes the Bride,* and many of the guests turned to see Jane's father in a grey worsted suit walk down the aisle with Jane, in a spectacular white wedding dress, on his arm. Behind her, holding the train of the bride's dress, was Esther, also beautiful in white. As they reached the front of the aisle,

Roger and George took their positions in the centre alongside Jane and her father. George glanced across at Esther, who was shyly smiling at him. His heart nearly stopped. She looked absolutely stunning. He returned the smile and then began to worry that he'd lost the wedding ring.

Of course, the ceremony went off without a hitch, and shortly afterwards, the guests gathered outside the church to throw confetti. Two taxis arrived to transport the main players into Kingston, while those who had cars went to collect them, returning to offer those without lifts a ride to the reception.

The meal was all chatter, tasty food and good humour. Various speeches were made, including one from George who read out telegrams from those unable to attend and then proposed a toast to the bridesmaids. He'd been worrying about this, but he carried it all off with flying colours before he sat down with relief. When the formal proceedings were over, people either stayed at their tables or broke up into groups to chat and await the arrival of the wedding cake. George knew his time had come, and he looked at Esther and smiled at her as he got to his feet. She, too, was aware that her moment of truth was on her, and she took his outstretched hand, and they walked to a corner of the restaurant and sat facing one another. Any passer-by would have noted that both were nervous, thought Esther.

'You know I've not been well, Esther, and I'm sorry to have been distant over the past few years. You should know what happened to me, and then I'd like you to tell me about your troubles.' She looked at him. Her eyes began to well up, but she was determined not to cry.

'I've hated this bloody war,' he began. 'Many close to both of us have died because of it. I was captured by the Gestapo and horribly tortured but never gave even a whisper of information. Roger and a brave Frenchman rescued both me, and the Frenchman's wife, who was also a prisoner of the Nazis . It took a lot of courage for them to do that, and I'll never forget it. Before that, I fought in Sicily with the infantry. One day I'll tell you the whole story, but that's not important now. I was dreadfully injured by the Nazis, but thanks to some brilliant doctors, I made a full recovery.' Awkwardly, he told her more and more of the details as he watched her reaction and saw that she didn't flinch or look disgusted, only sympathetic and concerned. 'But my broken mind took a bit longer,' he ended with, 'and I've only recently been sent back into the world, totally restored to my old self. A brilliant guy called Colin Walters made that happen. And that's it. Well, not quite totally; there's still one thing missing.'

'What's that?'

'You. Please tell me all those awful things that happened to you.'

Esther hesitated for a moment, and then it all poured out: internment, her mother's death, Joe getting killed in North Africa, the V bombs, Mary dying and finally the rape, her injuries and the miscarriage. By the time she'd finished, tears were cascading down her face. George took hold of her hand and gently lifted her onto her feet and threw his arms around her, hugging her ferociously. 'How awful for you.'

'I feel so ashamed.'

'You've nothing to be ashamed of. There was nothing you could do to stop any of those terrible things happening.'

'He was killed in battle, you know, the man who raped me.'

'Another victim of that bloody war, along with your mother, Joe, my friend Bert, Captain Pearse, Mary, Ian in France. He would most likely never have behaved like that at home in America, but he was terrified of going into battle, of being killed. The list never ends; they're saying fifty million lost their lives, but it's over now, and there must never be another one.'

'Thank you, George,' Esther said.

'For what?' George looked bewildered.

'For not rejecting me. You mean everything to me.'

'And you to me. What are you doing tomorrow?'

'Nothing.'

'Fancy a night up west?' George asked with a grin on his face. 'Maybe a film or some grub?'

'Sounds good to me,' Esther replied. 'Six o'clock at Kings Cross?'

'It's a date,' said George, and he joyfully hugged her again.

Roger and Jane appeared then, carrying a small plate in each hand with a slice of wedding cake on it.

All four sat down and discussed what they were going to do next. Jane was going back to her accountancy office, Esther was starting teacher training, and Roger was going back into the newspaper business.

'My old paper's taking me back – well, not actually the same paper but the morning edition. I'm to deal with special projects. What about you, George?'

'Not sure yet. I need to discuss it with my dad. Maybe Esther will have some suggestions when we go out together tomorrow night.' Roger and Jane looked at each other and smiled knowingly.

'Glad to hear about that. My new job means I'll be doing things like tracking down bent politicians, MPs and so on.'

'That sounds interesting, Guv,' George said.

'I'll need an assistant. Someone to do the leg work and research. Fancy it? You'll get paid.'

The four of them sat in silence while George absorbed what he'd been offered. Then he looked at Roger, a grin on his face.

'When do I start?'

AUTHOR'S NOTES

ACKNOWLEDGEMENTS AND THANKS

The Oxford Editors for untiring professional help and advice.

Debrah Martin, my editor, who was unrelenting in her drive to make me produce a story worth telling and reading.

People who read and helped me to correct early and later drafts. Brian Cooper, Alan Barker.

The Godalming Writers' Circle, who sat through many Monday night readings of parts of the novel and made numerous useful comments.

Friends and relatives who sat back, listened, and later commented while I read extracts from *Ordinary Heroes* to them, including the Godalming Writers' Circle, Roger and Di Sheffield, Liz and Neil Young.

Martyn Adams, who made the text of the manuscript look good and who taught me to put a memory stick in the side of my laptop.

Staff at the Tangmere Military and Aviation Museum near Chichester, who taught me all about the Lysander aircraft and the importance of the airfield in SOE history.

Staff at The D-Day Story at Southsea, Portsmouth, who taught me all I needed to know about landing craft.

READING

I read widely in researching the events described in this novel, but there were so many books I'll just list a small sample here.

The Secret War	Max Hastings
A Schoolmaster's War	Jonathan Ree
They Fought Alone	Maurice Buckmaster
SOE Manual	SOE
Sicily '43	James Holland
Wartime Britain	Juliet Gardiner
The Second World War through Soldiers' Eyes	James Goulty
Battle Scars	Jason Fox

CHARACTERS

Most of the characters in the novel are, of course, fictional, but one or two did exist and played an important role in the secret war.

Maurice Buckmaster OBE (1902-1992)
Head of the French Section of SOE. Awarded a Croix de Guerre by the French.

Vera Atkins CBE (1908-2000)
Assistant to Buckmaster. A Romanian-born Jew who continued her SOE work even after it was disbanded in 1946 by searching for agents who disappeared during the war. She was awarded the Croix de Guerre and is one of the subjects of several films, including *Odette* and *Carve Her Name with Pride*. Her remarkable story is told in her biography *A Life in Secrets,* by Sarah Helm.

Joanna Cruikshank (1875-1958)
Nurse, Nursing Administrator, founder and later Matron-in-Chief of the Princess Mary's Royal Air Force Nursing Service. She was made a Dame in 1931. During the Second World War acted for a time as Commandant of the Women internees' camp on the Isle of Man.

Natzweiler-Struthof Concentration Camp
The only camp of this type built on present-day French soil. It housed about fifty-two thousand prisoners during its three-year existence. Of these, twenty-two thousand died, some of malnutrition and others of disease. Many were murdered, including members of the French Resistance and SOE agents.

Fritz Hartjenstein, the Commandant at the time of events in the novel, was preceded as Commandant by Josef Kramer, who moved to Bergen-Belsen and was later hanged by the British for war crimes. Hartjenstein himself was found guilty of war crimes but died of a heart attack while awaiting execution.

The site of the camp, which includes a museum and The European Centre for Deported Resistance Members, is open to the public.

Note:
The killing of a German agent in Godalming in Chapter Eleven is part of a short story titled *Graveyard* in Godalming Tales Vol. 3

THE PRINCIPAL FICTIONAL CHARACTERS

George Aaron — Soldier Eighth Army, later Special Operations Executive

Esther Abrahams — London Ambulance Service

Roger Martin — Soldier Army Intelligence, later Special Operations Executive

Joe Richards — Soldier Eighth Army

Sir John Blum — Diplomat Foreign Office

Colin Walters — Army Psychologist

Isaac Aaron — Father of George

Sarah Aaron — Mother of George

Charlie Richards — Father of Joe

Margaret Richards — Mother of Joe

Mary Rabenstein — London Ambulance Service

Bert Davis — Soldier Eighth Army

Steven Morgan — Soldier Eighth Army

Richard Pearse — Soldier Eighth Army

Philippe Dupont — French Resister

Catherine Dupont — French Resister

Simon Abrahams — Father of Esther

Deborah Abrahams — Mother of Esther

Peter Abrahams — Brother of Esther

Ian Evans — Soldier Special Operations Executive

Heinz Braun — Kriminal Kommissar Gestapo

ABOUT THE AUTHOR

David Lowther was born in Surrey but brought up from the age of three in South Wales. After qualifying as a teacher in 1966, David taught in schools in Leeds before working in sports management in the Midlands, retiring in 2008. He was awarded an M.Ed. at Manchester University in 1981 and later earned a distinction in the Institution of Leisure and Amenity Management's professional qualification scheme.

While teaching in Leeds, David taught A level history for his final three years in the profession. He became fascinated by the period he taught, British Social and Economic History up to the outbreak of the Second World War, and when he retired, he began writing and used that period to complete his first novel *The Blue Pencil* in 2012. Three further novels followed, and one non-fiction title.

David Lowther is now back in Surrey, living close to his family but remains a life-long supporter of Cardiff Rugby, has a new-found enthusiasm for Brentford FC and follows track and field athletics closely. His wife Anne died in 2020 after fifty-one years of marriage, and his son now lives close to him with his wife and dog.

BY THE SAME AUTHOR

THE BLUE PENCIL

1936. The UK government is doing all it can to prevent another war, but many, including young journalist Roger Martin, believe that conflict is inevitable and post warnings about Nazism and the perils to come. Appeasers will go to any length to silence Roger and his colleagues including framing them for crimes they didn't commit, blackmail and physical violence.

THE LIBERATION OF BELSEN

The story of how the Durham Light Infantry working alongside the Royal Army Medical Corps laboured ferociously to save the lives of the survivors the notorious Belsen Concentration Camp. Many of the horrors of the liberation are recalled by the soldiers who left tape-recorded testimonies of their harrowing experiences.

TWO FAMILIES AT WAR

An adolescent boy and his parents, Jewish refugees from Berlin, run up against a vicious crime family during the London Blitz. As the bombs rain down in the winter of 1940, the two families clash with violent and tragic results.

THE SUMMER OF '39

Journalist Roger Martin returns, hunting for IRA terrorists who are causing havoc with a series of bombings on the UK mainland in the months before the Second World War. Recruiting two teenage East End boys, the three discover a dangerous link between the IRA and the German Secret Service which leads to a dramatic confrontation on the eve of Prime Minister Chamberlain's declaration of war on Germany.

All of the above books were published by Sacristy Press.

Printed in Great Britain
by Amazon

30796273R00112